THE
REFINER

KRISTY MARIE

First Line Editor: Fairest Reviews Editing Services
Proofing: All Encompassing Books
Cover Design: RBA Designs
Cover Photography: Wander Aguiar Photography

Copyright © 2022 by Kristy Marie
Published by Kristy Marie Books, LLC

For my sister, Lebron.
May I never know a world in which you don't exist.

But Ruth replied, "Don't urge me to leave you or to turn back from you.
Where you go I will go, and where you stay I will stay. Your people will
be my people and your God my God. Where you die I will die, and there
I will be buried. May the Lord deal with me, be it ever so severely, if even
death separates you and me."

Ruth: 1:16-17 New International Version Bible (NIV)

THE
REFINER

PROLOGUE

Keagan
Two years ago

"Come on, Keagan, it'll be fun!"

I lower my voice and narrow my gaze at the grinning liar in front of me. "Fact check, my dear, sweet sister: fun is watching you have a meltdown when forced to use a porta-potty. This—" I wave my hand around the fancy room with chandeliers and balloon bouquets, "—'party' as you call it, is nothing but a hoard of rich people eloquently bragging to the person sitting beside them." I punch Piper's arm hard. "You tricked me. I thought we were getting shitfaced with the possibility of twerking."

Piper chokes on the expensive champagne, coughing like an eighty-year-old smoker.

"Great, now you're drawing more attention to us," I complain.

"Stop." Piper laughs, trying to scold me between gasps of air.

"You stop. You're the one looking foolish. I'm merely standing here, trying to have a grown-up conversation with my manipulative big sister."

I'm being dramatic. I know that. But I did not drive three hours to visit my sister for the weekend, only to share her attention with a room full of stuffy doctors.

"I didn't manipulate you." Like a proper doctor, Piper seems to have recovered her composure amongst her peers. "I told you I needed to show my face, and then we could leave."

I glance around the room, scanning the dresses that likely cost more than my car. Even my sister, who wore thrift store dresses during my teenage years, fits in with her baby pink, sequined gown more than I do. My flowy white skirt, mocha crop top, and dozens of boho bracelets stand out in a sea of extravagant beauty queens. Not one part of me screams formal. Though, in my defense, Piper mentioned attending no such party when I was packing. And while we're the same height, we are not the same size. Somehow my sister has crossed over to the dark side with her devotion to starvation. She says it's the stress of the hours she keeps, but it's more like she forgets to eat when she's working a twenty-four-hour shift.

"And now that you have—shown your face, I mean—can we go?" I'm not above whining.

My sister knows I'm allergic to formal parties.

Piper sighs. She knows this party sucks a salty nut too. "Fine. Let me speak to Rebekah, and then we can go."

"Hallelujah." I grab the glass of champagne from her hand and toss it back. "Go do air kisses and swoon over blood diamonds. I'll be over here holding back my gag reflex."

Piper flashes me a stern look that would make our mother proud. "Please behave. These are my colleagues."

"Unfortunately."

Why she didn't become a vet, so I could love on all the dogs, is beyond me. Humans aren't all that impressive.

"I mean it, Keys. Keep your snarky comments to yourself."

I wave away her concern. "What am I? Twelve? I know how to

handle myself in front of assholes. Trust me. Go, do your thing so we can leave."

Piper isn't a fool. She knows that my track record with keeping my mouth shut is pretty spotty. Unlike my sister, I take no shit from people who deserve a pop to the mouth. I hate entitled assholes who think the sun shines just for their pretty faces. If the world is big enough for their egos, it's big enough for my opinion.

"I'll be right back," Piper says, as if it's some kind of warning rather than reassurance.

I bow. "I'll be right here, madame, waiting for your scraps of time."

Piper's face falls. "Keys…"

"I'm just kidding. Gah, you're such a mom. Go, I'm fine." Goodness, she's such a worrier. "I'm just going to grab another glass of this shitty champagne."

Alcohol is alcohol when you're desperate.

And I am the definition of desperate at this party that's supposed to be a baby shower for this woman my sister "sort of" knows—which is insane. Why would you come to a boring party and suffer for someone you only 'kind of' know? Piper claims she isn't here for the soon-to-be mom but here to support a friend. We've simply been loitering in a sea of plastic sharks.

Fine, they're doctors with their wives, or maybe their mistresses, I can't tell. All I know is I was ready to go when someone gave me the first air kiss on the cheek. I draw the line at air kisses and squeals about a sonogram that looks like fat tissue.

Don't get me wrong, I have nothing against children. I just don't find the fascination with grainy photos and stories of poop and vomit. I'd rather subject myself to my sister's operating room dictations about her urology surgeries. At least with those stories, I learn new words to refer to a penis. My sister can't bring herself to talk about a dong in my presence, so I find it beyond amusing to say as many uncomfortable penis words to make her squirm.

"Freaking finally!" Spotting a server, I locate the last glass of bitter champagne atop his tray. "Oh my gosh, you've saved a life, good sir."

The server lets his chuckle slip, and my faith is renewed that non-stuffy people still exist in this artificial world.

"I'm serious; I was about to smother—" A figure steps out of the corner, a lit cigar in his hand, causing the air to grow thick with his scent of spice and chicory. He snags the glass from the tray—the same glass I was just about to down. "Uh, excuse you. That was my drink."

The man lifts his head, and I take an immediate step back. His mouth is set in a grim line, his piercing blue eyes nearly swallowing the pupils as he blinks slowly. "I'm sure this gentleman will be happy to bring you another." His words sound like a sweet threat.

And that's where I get a little silly. "Of course," I scoff. "How dare I take a drink meant for the weirdo lurking in the corner like a wraith. Wait, let me guess, not a wraith, but a pompous ass doctor." I point at his fancy suit. "A surgeon, to be exact."

The guy smirks, utterly unfazed by my outburst, and sets his cigar down on the server tray. "Cute. Who are you here with? I don't recognize you."

He pulls a flask from his inner pocket and chugs it while holding the glass of champagne captive in his free hand. What in the total hell? That's it! I'm so done with men like this. "If you had a flask all along, why did you need the last glass of shitty alcohol?"

The man pockets his flask and directs his attention to the champagne, swirling the liquid around in the glass like it's a fine wine. I would be mesmerized by the motion if he didn't then put the glass to his lips and tip it back until he drained the contents.

"You're unbelievable. You could have saved the crappy alcohol for the people who needed it."

He hisses through his teeth like downing all the liquid at once burned. I hope it did. Dick.

"How do you know I didn't need it?" He picks up his cigar off the tray, putting it to his lips and inhaling.

Gah, he's an idiot too.

I put a hand on my hip, noting his eyes tracking the bracelets jingling at my wrist. "Uh, because. You. Have. A. Flask."

I've always wondered how some people became doctors. This one confirms that a pretty face can score you an A, just like a night of studying can.

"I'm almost out," he argues, like that justifies him taking *my* glass.

"*Almost* is not empty... yet." Just like my hand *almost* reached out and choked him with his fancy tie. "There is a difference."

The server turns to the pain in my ass. "I'll get you another, Dr. Potter."

"Astor," he corrects him with a tip of his chin.

"Yes, sir. I'll get you another, Dr. Astor."

"Cute." I roll my eyes, watching the server scamper away without his pride. "I bet that makes you feel all warm and fuzzy, scaring the wait staff like that."

He cocks a brow. "Was he scared? Scared would mean he feared me. I believe Matt, 'the wait staff' as you call him, is dedicated to his profession. He's making sure the guests aren't without a drink. Even rude guests such as yourself."

Oh no, he didn't. "Just like a man! You're making me the asshole in this situation." I scoff. "I should have known better than to think—"

"Astor." My sister's voice stops me. "I've been looking everywhere for you."

Oh. My. Goodness.

I turn and watch my sister make a b-line to this dick. Immediately, a smile pops on his face, and he drops his cigar into the empty champagne flute and shoves it at me, opening his arms wide to welcome my sister, who makes this silly squeal before burying her face in his neck. The asshole has the nerve to pull in a deep breath like my sister's mere presence calms him.

"I'm so glad you decided to come," she tells him, rubbing his back like he's some kid. "It's very admirable and shows a lot of strength."

Admirable? All he did was walk from the valet to the door. And how much strength can that really take from a man who looks like he spends eight days a week in the gym?

But then it hits me, holding this man's flute with his discarded cigar. My sister doesn't just coo and coddle everyone like they are delicate flowers. "Wait a minute?" I direct my question to Piper. "This is the chick we came to hug?"

Piper turns in Astor's arms and shoots me a scathing look. "I never said we were coming to hug a woman."

"You said your friend needed your support during this difficult time."

I eye Astor's swollen arms shoved into his suit, his gaze hardening.

"Why would Mr. Fancy Pants need support? It's a baby shower." I mean, is this not insane? Am I the only one confused about why my sister needed to console a grown-ass man at a baby shower? "The hardest decision is guessing whether or not the baby is a boy or a girl." I chuckle at the craziness of this party. "Unless she's an ex that got tired of waiting for the proposal. Or something cliché like that."

Piper's mouth falls open, and Astor tenses.

Oops. Did my love of storytelling hit its mark? "I'm sorry," I try to explain. "I didn't mean—" I might not like this man, but I never want to press my finger in someone's wound if that's what this is.

Astor steps back from Piper, leaning down and kissing her cheek. "Thank you for coming."

"Anything for you," Piper responds, shooting me a glare. "Let us drive you home."

I want to argue that he's fine. That's why we have cabs and Uber. No need to make things more uncomfortable.

Astor flashes me a wink, seemingly recovered from my outburst, which I really regret, if I'm being honest. I was mad, and rude things sometimes bypass my proverbial filter when I'm angry.

It's not something I'm proud of.

I track Astor moving in closer. "It was nice to meet you, Piper's sister."

Ugh. Now, I feel like a *real* asshole. "I'm sorry."

He waves me off, takes his discarded glass from my hand, and brings me in for a hug, his breath skating over my ear with his words.

"I bet upsetting betrayed surgeons makes you feel all warm and fuzzy inside."

I try wrenching from his hold as he throws the exact words I said to him earlier back in my face. His grip only tightens. I try faking a smile at Piper, who is glaring hard.

"Is that what you are?" I grate out between clenched teeth. "Betrayed?" Who would be crazy enough to betray this man with his oozing power and sex appeal?

Well, likely someone stupid like me who can't seem to stop poking the bear.

Dr. Potter's voice is hypnotic when he nuzzles my hair, the smell of bourbon on his breath even more intoxicating than when he whispers, "Goodbye, Keys. It was a pleasure playing with you."

It takes a solid five minutes after he disappears back to the black hole he crawled out of before the chills recede on my arms.

Dr. Potter knew who I was all along.

And Piper is to blame.

CHAPTER ONE

Keagan
Present Day

"Ding dongs are so overrated."

I'm three margaritas over my limit—which, my limit, if I'm being completely transparent, is pretty generous to begin with. I can drink most men under the table without so much as slurring.

But tonight, I'm celebrating—and plan on drinking until my teeth go numb. (Yes, I know teeth do not go numb. This should tell you how drunk I plan on getting.)

"Like, why do men think they are so fucking awesome with this muscle pendulum swinging between their legs? It's not like it gives them a superpower."

I toss back the last of my drink and slam the glass down on the wooden bar. "But they think it does. And do you know why they think a muscle has a superpower, Kenny?"

"No, but I'm sure you're gonna tell me, sugar."

Kenny might have one of those supercharged penises, but he knows it's all bullshit.

Because Kenny is cool.

And my total bro-ho.

We go way back to when I needed somewhere to drown my sorrows after my sister moved three hours away to South Texas. Kenny may not have wanted to become my friend, but like everything in my life, I plowed right through his wants and took what I needed.

A friend.

And a bomb-ass bartender.

"You're damn right. I'm going to tell you, boo." I'm pretty sure it sounded like I just called him poo. "Men think their penis is powerful because society tells them it is."

I lean over the wooden-topped bar and motion for Kenny to come closer. Instead, he pours me another drink.

It's fine. What I have to say isn't a secret. "But you know what, Ken Kardashi-wan?" I raise my fist in the air victoriously. "Today, I stopped that pretentious entitlement of the dong."

Clearly, it's Kenny's fault I'm this drunk, but as a good friend, he knows days like today are rare and should be cherished with no less than four drinks.

Kenny grins, and it's invitingly hot. I would totally ask him out if he weren't my wingman on Thursday nights (and liked vaginas). But instead, I keep slandering his fellow men and their appendages. He's okay with it, though. He thinks men suck six days out of the week too.

"Dong be gone! Keagan McKellan is no longer under your reign!" I chant, raising my glass against Kenny's, clinking them together.

"May she continue to bruise egos and break hearts forever," he adds with a grin.

"Damn straight." We chug our drinks and set them back down, and my tone turns serious. "This is my Susan Lucci moment, Ken Doll." I hold up five fingers, and Kenny holds up one of his, already knowing what I'm about to say. "Six times, I applied."

"And six times, you were rejected," he adds, dropping his hand and brushing a lock of hair from my face. "But not anymore. You—Keys, darling—have always known you were the best game writer out there. You didn't need a promotion to solidify that fact."

"True, but my bank account did. I was doing twice the job of Ass Face McGee, yet he was paid an obscene salary to go along with his arrogant attitude."

The gaming industry is a man's world.

And I busted the balls that held it together.

Ass Face McGee and his cubical of terror will never be a threat to me again. The CEO of Pretentiousville will never have to look me dead in the eyes and lie straight to my face that my male colleagues beat my storytelling pitch ever again.

A twenty-million-dollar project. And it's all mine.

Kenny tops off our drinks and flashes a grin that insists I will regret this night in a few hours. "Where's Piper?" He looks at his watch. "I thought she was coming up this weekend?"

I make this weird scoff-like noise that sounds a little like I'm being a petty turd. "She got called into work."

"Another penis emergency?"

Didn't I say Kenny was my man? We both know that urologists do more than look at penises all day, but we still like to poke fun at Piper for choosing such an exciting career for us to laugh at. "Apparently, there've been peen emergencies for the past six months." My words carry heavy sarcasm as I repeat Piper's most common excuse.

Kenny settles against the counter. "You think she's lying to you?" He arches a brow. "Maybe she's seeing someone?"

"Piper Prudence?" I wave away his craziness. "She wouldn't know what to do with a man outside the exam room. I can't even remember the last time she had a date."

"Who knows, your big sister might be naughtier than you think."

My lip curls in disgust. "Just for being nasty, you get to buy me another drink." How dare Kenny insinuate that my sister, who studied during summers and went to science camps for fun, is being naughty. Uh, no. Piper wouldn't know naughty if it bit her in the ass.

Kenny tops off my drink, not even bothering to give me a new glass. "Whatever happened to that hot doctor she was friends with? What was his name, As—"

"Asshole. That's the one you're talking about? From the baby shower?"

"Yeah." Kenny slides me a bowl of cherries. "Yeah, the guy you got mad at for drinking your booze."

"Don't be a hopeless romantic, Kenny." He's always had a thing for happily ever afters. "Piper and Dr. Dick are still *just friends.*"

Kenny raises his brow. "I don't know about you, but a man like that wouldn't *just* be my friend."

Kenny and I might have done a Google search after I told him about the betrayed Dr. Potter. The online stalking was just to ensure my sister was safe and not hugging a hot, doctor psycho.

"Well, K-Love, we're not talking about you. We're talking about Piper, and Piper would totally be his friend because she's sensitive like that. Who else would dole out hugs to dick bags on the regular?"

"Maybe he isn't a dick bag to her?" He waggles his brows ridiculously. "Maybe he asks her to call him Dr. Daddy in the evenings."

I gag. "Stop. You've crossed the line with that comment. Under no circumstances would my sister ever call someone Daddy, especially Dr. Prick."

Kenny must be going through a dry spell. Freaking *Dr. Daddy.* I can't even with that nonsense.

"I'm just saying, Piper has been really quiet these past few months. I wouldn't be surprised if she were keeping a slutty little secret with icy blue eyes and an ass that makes your mouth water on the side."

I changed my mind. Kenny can no longer be my bro-ho. "If you keep talking sweet about your fellow dong squad, you can't celebrate with me." I swing my arm around, encircling the front of my body. "This is a dong-free zone, remember?"

Kenny chuckles. "Fine. My dong appreciation is silenced until you give the word, my lady."

Now, see? Why can't the men at my office react the same way when I request a little penis detox? "Thank you. Now that gentleman over there seems to need a drink." I point down the bar, where I've felt a stare beaming into the side of my head for the past fifteen minutes.

Granted, this is a bar, and Kenny is tending said bar until close, but we needed a few uninterrupted minutes to celebrate. "Thanks for your patience," I tell the guy just as my phone buzzes on the bartop. "The service here is always super slack."

I grin at the hand gesture Kenny flips me behind his back and answer my phone. I already know who it is by the sound of the machines beeping in the background.

"Keys? Can you hear me? It's Piper."

I can't tell if the bar is too loud or if she thinks the hospital is too loud. Either way, it doesn't deter me from messing with her.

"I'm sorry, who is this? Because if this is Patricia from the mailroom, I said I was sorry for stealing your yogurt. I'm poor, and the Lunchable I packed just wasn't enough."

My sister, Piper, sighs. "Don't do this. I already apologized. I can't help that I got called into work."

No, she couldn't, and I love her for it. Doesn't mean I have to be happy about not seeing her on my big day.

"Do what? Remind you that I haven't seen you in months?" Nothing like a few drinks to bring out the petty among sisters. "I'm starting to think you're avoiding me because you let that one chin hair of yours grow into a full beard. It's okay if you have. I told you, I won't judge you. But men will. They like to say they want their women natural, but they only mean wearing organic makeup. As awesome as it sounds, No-shave November is not for us girls."

A very, and highly unladylike snort comes across the line. "How drunk are you?"

"Not enough, but Kenny is working on it."

Her laughter fades. "Promise me you'll catch a ride home?"

I roll my eyes. There's my responsible sister. "I plan to commandeer Kenny's full-size bed." However, he doesn't know it yet.

"Good. Just don't drive or go home with a stranger."

"Or snort a line off Kenny's eyebrow," I tease.

She laughs. "Yes, that too."

"Gotcha, no fun then." Not that I would ever do drugs, but it makes my sister squirm just talking about it. Deep down, the girl has a heart of a mother. She might not have any children, but she has me, and she says that is enough for her.

"So, I thought I could still come up tomorrow when you get off work, since I couldn't leave tonight."

Something feels off. Piper has missed weekends and celebrations due to work, and sure, she tries making up for it, but not with an urgency in her voice. "What's wrong? Do you need a kidney? Because you can totally have one, but just know they aren't of the best quality anymore. You might be better posting an ad on social media."

"Haha. Fortunately, I don't need your haggard kidney, but thank you for the sweet offer."

Sarcasm runs thick in the McKellan bloodline.

"Seriously, though, I still want to see you, and I have news!"

Her tone softens at the end, and I'm instantly alert.

"What kind of news?" Kenny's secret lover theory pops into my head. I'll kill Dr. Annoying if he proposed without my permission. No one takes my sister away from me, ice blue eyes or not.

"The kind you tell someone over dinner. Tomorrow, Keys. I'll meet you at your apartment. Don't be late."

"I'm never late."

"Sure you aren't. Bye, Key-money! Love you bunches!"

My sister is up to something. "I know your game, Pippy Short Stockings, but I'll let this secrecy slide until tomorrow when I can bribe it out of you."

The girl loves Ring Pops. She might sneak and suck on one in private like a respectable adult now, but she never goes a birthday without her plastic crown, a candy necklace, and a Ring Pop. The McKellan sisters will always be queens of our imaginary castles.

"Muah!" She ignores my comment and makes a kissing noise on the phone. "Congrats, kiddo. I'm so proud of you! Don't rub it in Asshole McGee's face too bad tomorrow. Remember, subtlety always packs more of a punch."

She's crazy. "*Ass Face* McGee—not asshole—will choke on my success like he's in the final two seconds of a hot dog eating contest. No exceptions."

Who does she think I am? Her sweet little sister?

Several voices mask Piper's sigh, and I know duty is calling her away. "Be mean, Pipe. Remember, guys like it."

Not really, but my sister is too sweet for her own good.

She chuckles, but unlike earlier, I can hear the exhaustion in her voice. "Love you, Keys."

"Love you, too."

I stare at the phone several minutes after we hang up. Surely, she's okay…

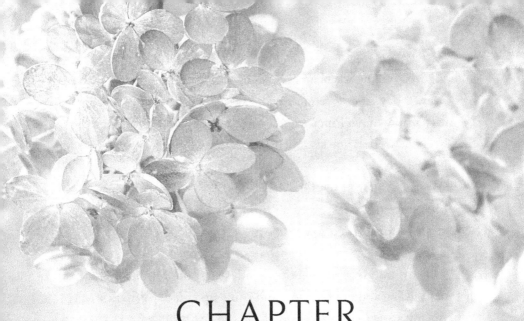

CHAPTER TWO

Keagan

It's not the phone that wakes me at seven a.m. but the pounding in my head.

Punishment is what this pain is.

I knew I shouldn't have had that last drink on the hood of Kenny's Honda. But he had gummy bears, and well, I can never turn down those cute little bites of squishy goodness—especially with an apple martini. Ultimately, those two things pushed me over the edge and led to this raging headache.

I snatch my phone from the charger, pushing through a wave of nausea as I half groan, half yell into the speaker. "What? What could be so damn important that you're calling me before the sun is up?"

The line goes quiet for a second. "Ms. McKellan?"

"Yeah."

"This is Lyla from Bloomfield General Hospital."

I groan, recognizing the name of the hospital where my sister works and roll over, pulling the blankets over my head. "Tell Piper it's an abuse of power to have you give me a wake-up call." Doctors... am I right? No matter how much Piper tries to be like an average person, she can't. She's still my overbearing sister who has someone give me wake-up calls when she's too busy.

"Umm...You're sister, Dr. McKellan..."

Her voice trembles, and I sit up in the bed, headache forgotten. "My sister didn't ask you to give me a message, did she?"

"No, ma'am. I'm calling on behalf of Dr. Cox."

I roll around the name in my head, searching for any memories of Piper talking about a Dr. Cox, and come up empty. "What's wrong? Where's my sister? She's *not* dead." I say the last bit like I can will it to be true. I can't relive this again. Not without my sister here to console me, like when our parents died.

"No, ma'am. Your sister is alive."

I blow out a breath. "Good. That means I'm gonna kick her ass as soon as I get off the phone with you." How dare Piper have this woman call and upset me for nothing.

"Ms. McKellan, we need you to come down to the hospital."

"Oh, I'm coming down to the hospital, don't you worry. This kind of phone call deserves a swift kick to the pootnanny."

The line goes quiet again.

"The vagina," I clarify, in case the slang term is a little confusing. "Piper is getting a running shoe in the vag for scaring the hell out of me. What did she do anyway? Take another case with Dr. Cox and needs to cancel tonight too?"

I'm already putting this woman on speaker so that I can text just those words to Dr. McKellan. She's gotten too big for her doctor britches if she thinks she can have her nurse buddy call me to grovel. She's sadly mis—

"Your sister had an accident. She's slipped into a coma."

I don't think either of us breathes after she says the words. Not even one little gasp of air escapes us.

"What do you mean Piper is in a coma?" I recover enough to ask. "I just talked to her last night. She was fine."

The woman on the other end of the phone clears her throat. "I think it would be best if you could come to the hospital. The doctor can explain better than I can."

I sure the hell hope so because she's giving me nothing but panic. "It'll be three hours before I can get there, but I'm on my way." Every moment I spend on this phone with this woman is another minute I'm not by my sister's side.

The nurse tells me where I can find Piper and where to park. Honestly, I don't remember a word of it. All I know is my beautiful sister is lying in a bed, and no one can tell me why until I get there.

Tossing a bag in the back seat of my car, I call the only person I know—the one who I ended up leaving last night, opting to sleep in my own bed instead of his. "Kenny," I leave on his voicemail. Unlike me, he doesn't need to be back at work until tonight. "Piper is hurt. I'm on the way to the hospital. Call me, okay? I know you don't do tears, but I might need a friend later." *Might* is a loose guess. I will most definitely need a friend, and unfortunately, the only other friend I have is the one I'm going to see. "Okay." I fight off the tears as I pull out onto the road. "Bye, Ken-sue."

Pressure mounts behind my eyes.

Suck it up, Keys. Piper will be fine. She's like a cockroach; an atomic bomb couldn't kill her. She's too stubborn.

And human.

As much as I joke, my sister is just as human as everyone else. Her bones break. Her body gives out. She isn't made of superhuman parts. She's just my sister, the human hero.

"No!" I scream, banging my fist on the steering wheel. "You will not pull this shit on me, Piper! You will not leave me, too! I won't allow it."

I don't care that I'm not making any sense. For all I know, Piper is in a medically-induced coma. Maybe she annoyed Dr. Cox, and he knocked her ass out for a few hours. Piper can drive you to do crazy shit.

Deep down, though, I know this isn't a simple matter. If it were, the nurse would have told me on the phone. I know the protocols. Piper has told many stories of families being brought in to make final decisions for their loved ones.

My heart beats faster.

No, this isn't the case with Piper. They just need me to come and sign the paperwork to give her CPR or something. She's gonna pull through whatever this is. I'll make sure of it.

But first, I need to call my boss. They will expect me to be there and lead the team on the new project.

My stomach clenches as I think about Ass Face. He won't hesitate to step up and take over my new position.

Don't worry about things you can't control, Keys. Get to Piper, get her better, then you can deal with Ass Face and the project.

Dialing the office, someone picks up on the second ring. "Yeah."

Ass Face. The last person I wanted to deal with this morning. "I need to speak to Archer. Get him on the phone." I don't have time for pleasantries.

"Hey, Keys, I hear we owe you a thank you."

Don't respond. You seriously don't have time to go to jail today.

"Who knew anyone could blow the boss so well that he would start blubbering out promises of promotions."

Do you see why he's called Ass Face?

Only his mama would think he should be named anything less than Fucker.

"I hope it holds up, kid." The asshole has the audacity to laugh. Belittling my promotion was a given. I knew McGee and his Dong Squad wouldn't handle me being their equal for long. I knew they would be jealous—hate me even more.

But guess what?

I do not give one single, solitary damn.

I achieved this promotion, fair and square. I didn't fondle the boss's balls or give him the dong-wash of his dreams. I worked hard, and no one, not even Ass Face, will take that away. "Get Archer on the phone now!" I have far more significant issues than Ass Face or my promotion.

"Aww. Don't go gettin' all emotional. I'm sure Archer will let you keep the title if you're a good little girl."

A tear slips down my cheek as my voice lowers to a deadly tone. I may not have time to turn around and slaughter McGee, but that doesn't mean I won't put it on my to-do list. "McGee, if you don't transfer me to Archer right now, I will post all of the dick pics you sent me when I first started at the company. Trust me when I say, we'll both be traumatized reliving that glitch of time when you thought me being nice to you equated to me wanting to see your junk." I am so done with today. So freaking done.

McGee clears his throat; all the laughter is gone from his voice instantly. "You always gotta go too far, Keys. I was just having a little fun. You women never know how to take a joke."

If I weren't so mad, I would laugh. "We women" know how to take a joke just fine. If we didn't, every time men like McGee pulled their dick out, we'd sob instead of laugh.

"Get Archer." I have nothing left for this man. Not today.

"Sure."

There are two things I like about Archer. One, he gave me a chance to work at *Game Tales* as a game writer fresh out of college. That chance means a lot when you're twenty-two years old with no real work experience. And two, he gave me a promotion.

But that's where my fondness of Archer ends.

"Keys, you better be calling to tell me the reason you're late is that you stopped to get me a coffee."

Did I mention I worked with a bunch of assholes? "No, sir. I'm calling to tell you that my sister in South Texas slipped into a coma last night, and I'm on my way to the hospital."

I owe this man gratitude for a job, not my soul. I'm not asking for permission to be with my sister. I'm giving him a heads-up that I'll only be reachable by phone. "I don't know how much time off I'll need, but I will work remotely on the Skyward project if possible."

Archer doesn't speak for a moment, and I imagine him choosing his next words carefully. Finally, he sighs. "Take a week with your sister."

A week? That sounds like she's going through a mid-life crisis and needs a girl's trip to clear her head.

"We'll touch base next week and go from there."

If my heart weren't already on the verge of shattering, his tone— the one he uses when letting me know I didn't get the other six promotions—would have broken me. But I can't afford to break right now. I can't be the younger sister and act recklessly. Piper needs me, and I need this job, especially if I need to take care of her long-term.

"I understand, sir. But just know, no matter what, I can handle the Skyward account and run the team from my sister's house." Because there is no way she isn't waking up from this coma. If I need to guilt her into opening her eyes, I will. No behavior is beneath me when it comes to Piper McKellan.

"I know you can, kid." He says the words more resigned than encouraging.

He's already planning to remove me from the account and possibly withdraw my promotion; I can feel it. I've played right into the stereotype—an emotional female who will put her family before her job.

You know what? Fuck him. Fuck *GameTales*. I won't let him take this promotion away from me. I am not a stereotype. I am a woman who will put her family first and still crush the shit out of her job. I don't need a man's approval to feel valued, but I won't mind shoving my success down his throat and watching him choke on his apologies when I earn it.

My sister is all I have.

She's everything that matters to me.

And nothing, not even a vague underlying threat, will scare me into not getting to her. "We'll talk soon, sir."

There's no way he's taking away that promotion.

And there's no way Piper won't be okay.

CHAPTER THREE

Keagan

I'm about to rush Dr. Cox like a linebacker.

I did not break several traffic laws and get here in two and half hours, only to be stopped in the hallway, mere feet from my sister's room.

"I know you want to see your sister, but we need to discuss her condition…." He looks at the nurse next to him as if he's looking for support. "…and her wishes."

That term has me whipping my head around. "What do you mean, *her wishes?*"

Dr. Cox extends his hand. "Let's go to one of the conference rooms where we can discuss this in private."

Every muscle in my body locks up. Doctors usher you into conference rooms because they want you to have privacy when you break down from the news. "No. Tell me here in the hallway."

In the back of my mind, I know that not going to a conference room won't change the outcome of this news, but I can take control of this one small thing. I can decide where I hear this news. And I decide that this hallway, a few feet from my sister, is where I want my life to change irrevocably. Dr. Cox might not let me be next to my sister when he destroys my life, but I can stay close. Just knowing my sister waits for me a few feet away is enough.

"Are you sure, Ms. McKellan? The conference room will be more comfortable."

Straightening my spine, I lift my chin and take a deep breath. "I won't cry. I won't disturb the other patients." I've loitered in hospitals waiting on Piper more times than I can count. I know the concerns. "Please, just tell me what's wrong with my sister."

I must applaud Dr. Cox. I thought he would try to shuffle me into the conference room one more time. Instead, he sighs and rubs his forehead like I'm already bringing on a migraine. "Last night, Piper stopped breathing in one of the sleep rooms."

Deep breath, Keys, you promised this man you wouldn't cry.

"Her heart stopped, and she was in distress until a resident physician came in and found her on the floor."

I already don't want to hear the rest of the story. "But Piper's okay, right? She's alive?"

Dr. Cox offers me a grim nod. "We were able to save the baby, but Piper—"

The what?

I shake my head and chuckle. "I'm sorry, Dr. Cox. I think this all has been a huge misunderstanding. My sister wasn't pregnant. She doesn't even have a man." Or a side piece. "I think you have her confused with someone else." Maybe someone stole her hospital badge, and Piper is laid out on her sofa, napping like a queen?

"I'm sorry to give you this news, Ms. McKellan, but Piper was thirty-six weeks pregnant before delivering the baby in an emergency C-section."

No, no, no. Piper would have told me if she was pregnant.

Piper's phone call last night comes back to haunt me.

"I have news!"

"What kind of news?"

"The kind of news you share in person."

With the ice-blue eyes, Dr. Hottie pops into my head, right next to Piper's cryptic call.

Was Kenny right? Was my sister sleeping with her doctor friend? Did he knock her up, and she was too ashamed to tell me? Is that why she's been avoiding me and canceling our dinners for months—because she was showing?

I'm going to kill him.

And if it's not Dr. Hottie that knocked her up, I'll kill that man too.

Ultimately choosing to put this shocking revelation behind me—for now—I level Dr. Cox with a pointed stare. "You said you were able to save the baby, but Piper…" I wave my hand for him to finish since I cut him off earlier.

"Piper was without oxygen too long." His head drops to his chest, and he pulls in a breath. "Dr. McKellan is brain dead."

Who knew two words could destroy your life?

Brain. Dead.

"You said on the phone that she's in a coma." My brain searches for anything to hold on to instead of the word death.

"She's in a vegetative state after suffering from heart failure," Dr. Cox clarifies. "The pregnancy caused peripartum cardiomyopathy. The condition occurs in one out of every four thousand pregnancies. Only 25 to 50 percent of women survive it. In Piper's case, we didn't catch it in time."

"So you're saying she's not in that lucky 25-50 percent of women who make it?" My chin quivers and I fight back the tears. I promised I wouldn't cry. "That even though she's lying in that bed down the hall, there's no hope? My sister won't pull through this?"

The slight dip of Dr. Cox's chin is answer enough. "I'm sorry, Keagan. We did everything we could."

Obviously not. "Can I see her now?" I can't stand one more second without my sister.

"There's one more thing."

I let out a ball of frustration that sounds more like a sob and less like an unimpressed laugh. "Sure, hit me. What could be worse than hearing my sister is brain dead?" The very words tear through my chest like razors. My sister, my beautiful sister, who I will never talk to again, is brain dead.

"Your sister has an advanced directive."

I wipe under my eyes and breathe through my mouth harshly. "What is that? Is it like a will?"

"Sort of. It's her wishes in case she's ever in this type of medical situation."

Now I really do laugh. "Now that sounds like my responsible sister—always prepared for anything." I shake my head. "Do I need to sign it so you can do what she wants?"

Dr. Cox doesn't look all that happy with my guess. "Yes, when you're ready."

I don't have time for niceties. I just want to be with my sister. "Give it to me. I'll sign it now."

I look at Dr. Cox's empty hands, but he clarifies the situation with one sentence. "Dr. McKellan does not wish to be on life support."

I can't breathe. All I can do is choke back the tears I promised not to cry. "Are you saying you want me to let you kill her now so we can all go home?" My words are untrue and bitter. I know they aren't killing Piper. If she's brain dead, only the machines are keeping her body alive. But I just got here. I haven't even seen her yet. They can't expect me to just let her go *right now*.

"No, Ms. McKellan, that's not what I'm suggesting. Piper wishes to remain on life support until her next of kin—you—can make the final decision." Dr. Cox swallows. "It's an unusual request, but not one we haven't encountered before."

The tears I promised not to shed roll down my face in waves, dropping onto my shirt like heavy boulders of agony. "Our parents died instantly in a car crash," I tell Dr. Cox through the tears, swiping angrily under my eyes. "I was young at the time."

I remember screaming at Piper that it would have been easier if we had been able to say goodbye. If our parents had just made it to the hospital and lived a moment, we would have been able to make better peace with their deaths. Piper argued that it was better this way—quick. They felt no pain. But I didn't care. They could have taken a moment of the pain for the agony we felt losing them for a lifetime. It was only fair.

And selfish.

I see that now.

But my damn, too-sweet-for-her-own-good sister is giving me what I wanted back then. She's giving me the chance to decide. "She's giving me peace," I admit to Dr. Cox with a sniffle, "and control of the situation. She's giving me closure on my terms." Gah, I want to wring her fucking neck and then hug her until she opens her eyes and tells me to get off her.

"It's a heavy burden to bear, but she wanted you to make the final decision when she could leave this world."

I nod at Dr. Cox. "Is she in pain?" I want time with my sister, but not at the expense of her suffering.

"We have her comfortable, but her body is tired."

It's an answer within an answer. Piper's holding on, but it would be selfish of me to keep her here for any longer than necessary. "Okay," I whisper. "I understand. I'd like to see her now."

"Of course." Dr. Cox finally steps to the side, clearing the way to my sister.

I brush past him and the nurse, and keep my gaze locked on room 456, the room that holds my very soul and my last goodbye.

I can feel Dr. Cox and the nurse at my back, following, waiting for me to have a meltdown in the hallway. But I won't. I won't break because my sister expects me to be strong. For her. For me. And for the new baby.

Pushing open the door, I pause, inhaling, and willing the tears away as I lift my gaze to the lifeless body. The gown hangs off Piper's shoulder, her face pale, her lips dry. It looks like she's simply asleep. If it wasn't for the dozens of wires covering her chest, the machines beeping with the sound of her heartbeat, I could pretend that she's only resting.

In the morning, things will be better. Piper will wake up, and we'll all have this big laugh about how she pranked us good.

But what keeps me from retreating to that alternate reality is not those wires or machines but her belly. The flat stomach I remember is no longer smooth against her hips but rounded where she kept her deepest secret from me—her baby.

This simple change in her appearance is what keeps my feet rooted in reality.

My sister had a baby.

And ultimately, she died for this baby.

Why? Why didn't she tell me? I wouldn't have given her hell about it. Okay, I would have. But I wouldn't have meant it. I would only tease her because she gave me so much shit as a teenager about not getting pregnant before I was ready.

Piper's circumstances are different than mine, though. I will never be ready for a baby. I can barely take care of myself, but my sister? She could definitely raise a child and be a well-respected surgeon all at the same time.

She's badass like that. Or was badass like that...

My chest clenches, and I want so much for this to be a nightmare— one where I wake up next to Kenny and curse him for letting me have way too much to drink. How can one person be forced to endure so much tragedy in one lifetime?

Haven't Piper and I suffered enough? Was losing our parents when Piper was a teenager not payment enough? Was it not enough that she dropped out of high school two months before graduation to work full-time in order to take care of me? Was it not enough that she jumped through hoops for social services to prove she was fit to take care of her little sister? Did Piper not pay enough to the world by giving up everything to raise me?

I don't bother drying the tears when I say to Dr. Cox and his nurse, "Piper loved being a doctor. It was the only thing she did for herself. The rest of her life, she sacrificed for everyone else."

Just like she did for her baby.

Piper would have been the best mother. She's long proved herself with me.

"Is the baby okay?" I finally ask.

"She is. She's in the Neonatal ICU. She's a little premature, but she's doing well. You can see her if you'd like."

I shake my head. "I can't right now." I don't want to leave my sister's side. If my time with her is finite, I want to spend every second with her until her final breath. She gave up her life for me; I won't let her leave hers without knowing I'm here.

"Of course, we planned to notify the father after speaking with you."

So they know who he is. Well, there's a light in this pit of doom. Someone I can take out all this pain on. "I'll take care of it. Do you have his number?" I make it sound like Piper would want me to be the one to do it.

The nurse nods and tears off a slip of paper, handing it over. "All we have is the office number."

I nod, staring at the numbers. "That's all I need."

CHAPTER
FOUR

Astor

A ll I taste is copper—blood.

"What the fuck? Are you trying to kill yourself?" My brother Vance hauls me to my feet, pushing me against the ropes of the boxing ring where I've been letting him beat my ass for the past half hour. "Put your fucking hands up and hit back, or I'm going home. I'm in no mood to take your dumbass to the hospital."

I chuckle. "Don't act so scandalized." I spit out a mouthful of blood. "I told you I needed you to hit, not talk. Besides, you owe me."

My younger brother stares at me, likely trying to figure out my change in behavior from hours ago when we saw each other at the office. "You couldn't sleep or something?"

"Or something," I agree.

I didn't ask my brother here for a heart-to-heart. I asked him here for the numbness. Vance is ruthless in the boxing ring; he doesn't care if you're having a bad day. He'll fight with you as if it were your best day.

Luckily for him, I was counting on it.

But rather than bask in his win, he's pissed. "So, you couldn't sleep and decided to come here and just let me beat you into a blackout?"

Something like that.

He scoffs. "Jeez, Astor. What the fuck is wrong with you? I could have killed you."

Doubtful. Just because Vance is aggressive in the boxing ring doesn't mean he's the better fighter. He's slow and acts on emotions. Something I don't do.

Emotions were a liability I could no longer afford.

Except now, ever since I met with Piper, I can't manage to keep them in check because she asked me a question. One, I still can't answer. "How far are you willing to go to get what you want, Astor?"

An unexpected blow stings my cheek. "Answer me, brother. Should I be concerned?"

I lick the blood from my lip.

How far was I willing to go? Could I put my pride aside and admit defeat?

I think of the excuses Rebekah voiced while she packed her bags, never looking back when she set her wedding ring on the table and said goodbye. I couldn't be who she needed me to be.

I could only be what I am: a brilliant surgeon who lived for his patients and not his wife.

I would never be the husband Rebekah wanted. I would never make her father proud or her siblings jealous. Ultimately, I was just a man who couldn't give her the lifestyle she desired.

I'm jarred awake by Travis's voice. "The first thing I'm gonna do when I get home is bend my wife over the kitchen table and spank her ass for sending me nudes these past six months."

I open my eyes wide enough and see Travis, my roommate, glaring at the computer screen before slamming it shut. "My wife never sent me nudes until I agreed to come on this mission trip." He blows out a breath and tries to get comfortable on the narrow bed next to mine. "When I was home, she always had a freaking headache and wasn't in the mood. But now!" His voice rises. "But now she misses me all the time and can't wait until I'm home to put a baby inside her."

He throws himself back onto the pillows, staring at the piping running along the ceiling. "Like what the fuck is that? Why couldn't she miss me when I was home seven days a week? Why send me nudes and hot emails when I'm thousands of miles away? I can't do shit about her needs here. I can only attempt to avoid getting hard during surgery."

Travis, like me, is a surgeon. We were paired together after both joining the Grace of Mercy Mission Ship, which travels to poverty-stricken countries, providing healthcare to the needy. Travis and I are two of the handful of surgeons aboard who specialize in children's surgery.

"I'm gonna have to lie and tell her the reason my hands are blistered is from all the surgeries I've performed."

I grin. "I'm sure she'll believe that."

"Here," he tosses me the laptop, "check in with your family. They probably think you've fallen overboard."

I run my fingers along the edge of the computer. Opening it breaks the blissful bubble of solitude I've acquired these past six months. I might have signed on for this mission trip to help children with malformations obtain the surgery they need for a better quality of life, but I also joined this trip because I knew I would be so busy—so consumed—that I wouldn't have time to dwell on the past or the solution Piper proposed before I left.

I just wanted an escape.

An escape from my brothers.

From my practice.

From my thoughts.

I wanted to come back to a place that made sense. Medicine. Scientific, evidence-based practice made sense. Helping children made sense. I couldn't help my ex-wife; I couldn't even help myself. But I could help these children. I could make a difference in their lives.

"Come on, man. You're not gonna call your family? What about tomorrow when we go home? You gotta ride?"

I'm sure my assistant Halle arranged a ride for me from the airport, but given I didn't bring my phone and I haven't even called to check in with her once during my stint on the Grace of Mercy, Halle likely arranged for an unpleasant ride home.

Just thinking about facing the wrath of my assistant brings on a headache. "Nah," I tell Travis, sliding the computer away, "I'm good. My assistant will have a car waiting for me at the airport."

"Your assistant. That's your brother's girl? He's the burn surgeon, right?"

Travis and I have discussed a lot of things during our time together. He likes to overshare personal information, and I want to keep our conversations steered toward our professional lives. He knows I have two brothers, both plastic surgeons, with Vance being the burn surgeon and Duke being the cosmetic surgeon at Potter's Plastics, the practice we share. "Yeah, Vance. My assistant, Halle, is the only one who can tolerate him longer than eight hours a day."

"You're not scared she'll be working for your brother when you get back? Six months is a long time to be away. Things change."

"Not Halle. She's as loyal as they come." My brother is a fortunate bastard—at least where Halle is concerned. Like me, Vance has his demons, but at least he's had Halle as a buffer, so he doesn't make everyone around him miserable.

"So, you don't think you'll get back to the office and be without an assistant?"

"Not at all." On the other hand, Vance is likely to have run off his assistant. Duke too; he's notorious for dating the staff at Potter's Plastics. I could be walking into an office with a completely new team, apart from Halle, for all I know. I'm sure she's the only thing holding the practice together.

"What about your girlfriend?" He tips his chin to the business card on the small bedside table. "Do you think she's moved on?"

I chuckle, snagging the card off the table and dropping it into the drawer where it will stay until I leave. "Dr. McKellan is not my girlfriend."

"Could have fooled me with how you stare at that card for hours."

He's being dramatic. We only have time to stare at the bodies on the operating room table. "Dr. McKellan and I are friends and colleagues."

Travis laughs. "So, you're saying you'll keep my business card on your bedside table too?"

Why couldn't his wife have entertained him for a little longer? "Why don't you get some sleep?" I try to redirect this line of questioning. "What's it been, twenty-four hours since you've had a nap?"

"Thereabout." Travis cocks a brow. "How long has it been for you?"

While it's been fulfilling helping all the children in need, it hasn't been easy or restful. There are more patients than doctors. "Going on thirty-six hours now, I think." It could be forty. I think I lost count after twenty-four.

"You should rest."

I chuckle. I should remind him I was trying to do just that when he had the meltdown about the nudes. "I plan to when I get home. Probably around the same time you're spanking your wife."

Travis belts out a laugh. "You should try it."

"Spanking your wife?" Now it's my turn to arch a brow.

"Hell no. You know what I mean. Spanking your girl."

It's been fun fucking with Travis. Being on a ship in international waters hasn't been the most entertaining way to spend half a year, but Travis has kept it interesting with his non-stop chatter. "Afraid I'm forever a bachelor." I can see the wheels turning behind Travis's curious stare. He's seen me flip Piper's card through my fingers in thought, but he's never seen me call a woman or mail a single letter since being on the ship. He's confused, and rightfully so.

"Bullshit. You must have a girl. At least one for those lonely nights." He waves his hand in my direction. "A top-notch surgeon doesn't sleep alone."

"I don't sleep alone." I don't sleep, period—at least not for long.

"Thank goodness." Travis whistles. "I was getting worried about you there for a minute. You've been out on this ship performing surgery after surgery, barely sleeping and eating as it is. Should I be your accountability partner for when you get home?"

"I'm not suicidal or depressed," I clarify, just in case he's serious.

"Then why did you come on this trip? You don't need it for your resumé. You writing a piece for a medical journal?"

I laugh. "Can I not just want to help the kids?"

"Sure. Sure." He waves me off. "But not for six months. Physicians of your stature don't agree to such a long stint away from their practice unless...."

He leaves his words hanging between us.

And I get it.

He's not wrong. Most surgeons, like myself, wouldn't dare take six months off from their patients unless they were doing rehab or running from something. In my case, I'm avoiding. I'm distracting myself from thinking about my last conversation with Piper and the date we set.

She thinks I'm ready.

I think she's insanely optimistic and more patient than a pre-k teacher.

"Fine, tell me one thing then."

I close my eyes, hoping he'll let all this go. "What's that?"

"If you have nothing going on with business card lady, why did you rip up the letter she sent?"

The letter he's referencing flashes in my mind.

Dear Astor,

I know you need solitude on the trip, so I'll only send you this one letter, then we'll finish this conversation in my office as planned.

I stumbled across some new data. I think you'll be pleased with the results. However, it doesn't change my recommendation, even with this new data. We'll hold with our previous plan.

I'll see you in my office the day after you return.

Be safe, my friend.

And please take care of yourself.

xx Piper

My jaw clenches, thinking about the one sentence that mattered: *We'll hold with our previous plan.*

Our previous plan took months for me to agree to. Months. I would have never agreed to such a deal if it didn't come from one of my closest friends. Piper is the only one who's ever been able to convince me to try. To achieve what I always wanted.

But with every achievement comes a price.

A price that I was still unable to pay.

I glance over at Travis. His eyes are drifting closed when I answer, "I tore up her letter because our deal is off."

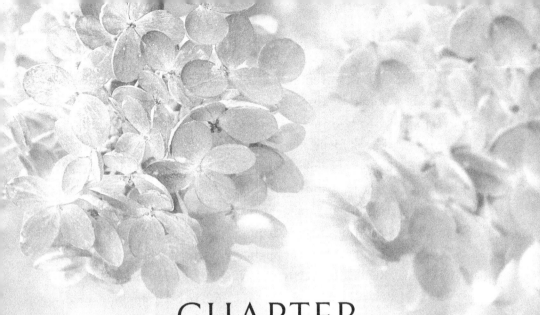

CHAPTER
FIVE

Astor

Vance's assistant is a tacky bastard.

I couldn't be prouder.

"Dr. Crotch, huh?" I shove the teenager waiting for me at the airport and snatch the sign held at his chest. "You're so fired."

"Thank fuck. I've been trying to get away from your brother since you left for your *cruise*."

He huffs like he's annoyed I've been gone for the last six months and left him to deal with Vance on his own.

"Somehow, I find that doubtful."

Remington, Vance's adopted son/assistant, shrugs a shoulder, fighting off a grin. "True. The pussy is too good to let your brother's shitty moods drive me away."

Part of his statement is true.

My brother can be temperamental.

But that's not why Remington continues to work at our plastic surgery office, Potter's Plastics.

"Pussy *and* my favorite assistant," I add, shoving him forward toward the exit. "How's Halle anyway?"

At the mention of Halle, Remington's face softens. "Halle's sane and seems happy with that demon brother of yours."

I eye his crisp suit and bulkier chest since the last time I saw him. "Seems like she isn't the only one happy."

Remington and my brother might seem like they hate each other, but it's obvious Remington has thrived living with my brother and Halle.

Turning slowly, he narrows his eyes. "You've been smoking weed, haven't you?" He moves his hand up his chest, lowering all the fingers but the one in the middle. "If you're gonna get fucked-up during office hours, the least you can do is share." His tone is flat and sarcastic as he turns around and walks ahead, leaving me laughing—hard until I catch up to him.

Maybe I have missed my family. Some.

"So what's with the haggard look? Too much ass on your cruise?" Remington doesn't bother turning around when he speaks. He keeps pace like he doesn't have time to breathe public air.

"My 'cruise,' as you call it, wasn't filled with martinis and bikinis. I spent twenty hours most days in the operating room." I'm dehydrated and likely suffering from a mild case of exhaustion. But instead of going home and sleeping, I'll end up at the office, checking on my brothers and staff, because that's all I know how to do—stay busy so I don't think about calling Piper and canceling our meeting.

"Of course, you did. What a waste." Remington scoffs sarcastically and shakes his head. "So, Hal said I'm supposed to take you home, but you look like you need a few beers and a smoke first."

"I'll pass on the smoke, but a beer sounds good," I answer as Remington unlocks the car. I've never been a smoker, but Remington never misses an opportunity for a smoke break—cigarettes, not weed. However, he won't turn that down either.

"What's wrong with you?" He eyes me over the hood of the car. "You get food poisoning from the lobster?"

Food poisoning would have been a blessing, considering the hell I've been through. Being part of the Grace of Mercy was as rewarding as it was brutal. It was an excellent way to strip me of the stressors that have plagued me the last few years and reminded me of the man I am at my core.

A craniomaxillofacial surgeon.

The most sought-after plastic surgeon for children in Texas.

A career I've managed to neglect for the past few years.

Unlike Vance, nothing catastrophic happened that excused my late arrivals to the office or the lack of leadership required as the oldest brother. No, all that fell to Vance, my middle brother.

He was the one who stepped up and made our father proud by continuing his legacy, rebranding Potter's Plastics with the intent of being the most distinguished practice in all of Texas.

And he succeeded.

All on his own and without the help of his big brother.

While I was exploring other countries, Vance was making me money.

And then he collapsed last year.

Nothing makes you wake up and realize you've been pissing your life away than death.

My brother lost his best friend.

And I nearly lost my brother.

If Halle hadn't come along, I don't know that I would be going home, back to a conscious brother who has always been one of my closest friends.

"Earth to Astor." Remington lets out a bird whistle that grabs my attention. "Should I offer you my bottled water?" He tilts his chin, his gaze turning serious. "Or should I go by the office and let Vance-hole check you out?"

I make a noise in my throat. "While your... *concern* is appreciated, there will never come a day when Vance will 'check me out.'" This kid has killed too many brain cells. "Take me home. I'll get water there."

"Whatever you say, but just know if Halle asks me how you seemed, I'll tell her you looked two seconds from crying into my cupholder."

Vance is right; Remington really should be fired.

"I'll dock your pay."

He shrugs. "I don't work for you."

Halle has worn off on him.

I get into the car without another word. Really, there's nothing left to say. I don't have the energy to keep lying.

My house is cold and empty like I left it, with one noticeable difference.

Remington eyes the paper taped to my front door. "Who'd you piss off?"

Ignoring him, I snag one of the dozen notes and read it.

I hope you're enjoying your vacation on a yacht, DICK BAG! At this point, I wouldn't be mad if you wandered too close to the edge and fell. The world could use fewer men like you.

Why does everyone think I've been on vacation?

I turn the note over in my hand. It's not signed, nor does it have a return address. "I haven't been here to piss anyone off," I say, especially for someone to be this mad. It's been a long time since I've been called a dick bag.

Despite his smile, Remington's posture tenses. "Well, you must have upset her pretty bad."

I turn around and face him. "First, your input isn't needed or wanted. Second, how do you know the person who left these letters is a woman?"

It's likely a woman, but again, I haven't been here for six months.

I haven't even spoken to a woman since I left on the Grace of Mercy Mission Ship.

Remington ducks his head, lighting up the cigarette I wouldn't let him smoke in the car. "Now is not the time to act like you don't have a medical degree. We all know you're smart enough to know that only women go this crazy." With a quick inhale, he blows the smoke out to his right. "They are the only ones who think writing letters is somehow more romantic than sending a text."

While he's not wrong about the whole letter writing thing, this—the twenty or so slips of paper—seems a bit excessive, even for romance. "Maybe this person has the wrong house?" I muse, but even I know it's doubtful.

No one I know would be desperate enough to contact me by leaving half a spiral-bound notebook worth of pages taped to my front door.

Remington arches a brow. "In this neighborhood? Where you need two forms of ID and a reference to get through the security gate?" He barks out an amused laugh. "Hate to break it to you, Pops, but whoever this crazy is, she is looking for *you* and *only you*."

He's right. This neighborhood is upscale. Therefore, killing him for the unwanted commentary on the front lawn would likely upset the homeowner's association. But still, he's right. Whoever this is would have to live in this neighborhood or be on my (or someone in the community) acceptable entry listing. Security would have checked identification before allowing them through.

"But you never know, women are crazy. This could be one of your neighbor's wives getting all pissed off that you went on vacay without her."

I don't bother responding to Remington's insane theory. I didn't sleep with another man's wife, and I haven't dated anyone in my neighborhood. Not since Rebekah, anyway.

Ripping another note off the door, I open it and read it.

You're a piece of shit.
But I need you to call me anyway. 555-259-6347

Okay, so not such a mystery now. I at least have a number. I pluck another note from the door.

Astor,

I hope this message finds you dealing with a violent case of crabs, but I need you to call me. Piper is in the hospital. 555-259-6347

Ps. Delete this number after you call. I will never want to speak to you again.

Fucker.

Hate you much,
Keys

My stomach sinks. Piper is in the hospital. I pull out my phone and dial her office number from memory. Travis was wrong. I wasn't fantasizing while I was staring at her business card. I was memorizing her number for when I called her and canceled our agreement. I wasn't a man in love. I was a prideful man who refused to admit defeat.

The phone rings as I pace the front yard, watching as Remington jimmies the lock on my front door, letting himself in.

"Dr. McKellan's office, this is Stephanie. How may I direct your call?"

I barely give her time to finish the spiel. "This is Dr. Astor Potter. I need to speak to Dr. McKellan. Now." Piper is fine. This is all simply a huge misunderstanding.

The line goes silent as the woman on the other end of the line takes a breath and clears her throat. "I'm sorry, Dr. Potter. Dr. McKellan was admitted to the hospital several days ago."

"What?" I'm already running to Remington's car. "What's wrong with her?"

"I'm sorry, Dr. Potter. I think it'd be best if you spoke with the doctor. I'll let him know to expect you."

I don't have time to argue with her. I just need to know what's wrong with Piper. "What hospital?" I'm already in the car, backing out of the driveway when she rattles off the address, and Remington rushes out the door, his face redder than the ink Keys used to write me all those hate letters.

This will be a good lesson for Remington. All the time he's spent with us has made him soft. He would have never left his keys in the car before meeting Halle and my brother. The posh lifestyle has made him too trusting, which I'm sure he will adjust after today. But it was an emergency. I didn't have time to go inside and get the keys to my car. I need to get to Piper quickly.

If she…

I can't even finish the thought. She's fine. Being a doctor has conditioned me to expect the worst. But this is Piper we're talking about. She's one of the strongest women I know. She won't go down without a fight.

Whatever this is, it's fixable.

We're surgeons, for fuck's sake.

We can fix anything.

CHAPTER
SIX

Keagan

"Piper, don't be such a prude! Take your shirt off."

For the past three minutes, all Piper has been able to do is make excuses and wring out her hands. I get it, she's nervous, but this was her idea.

"This isn't a date, P-Titty. Your insides aren't going to turn into a puddle of goo, and the only tingling your skin is going to feel is the zapping of V's tattoo gun."

I shove my sister into the vinyl table. "Do not act shy about this. I've seen you do the running man in a bikini atop a rickety coffee table. Do not act all modest now. Venom doesn't give a shit about your padded bra, do ya, V?"

Piper steadies herself and stands, cutting me a nasty look. "I can't believe I agreed to this."

The deep rumble of laughter from the man who calls himself Venom, our tattoo artist, makes me smile. So does the large chip in the wall that looks like a make-shift glory hole, complete with a white substance that dried as it dripped down the wall once upon a nasty time.

"This place is disgusting, Keys. Couldn't you have picked somewhere a little less HIV positive?"

I could have, but where would have been the fun in that? Piper said we could get matching tattoos for my eighteenth birthday. I wasn't about to give her time to change her mind. I also wasn't allowing her to ruin this moment with a sterile setting and a boring guy named Josh doing our tattoos. I wanted a birthday to remember, and Venom, with his orange and pink mohawk, looked to fit the part.

"Piper, getting a matching tattoo for my birthday is a once-in-a-lifetime occasion. We can't get it somewhere nice."

I shrug and take a step back. Piper looks like she's about to grab me and sprint for the car.

"Okay," I try to explain, "I'll admit, Ink Stainz is probably a low-key cesspool of diseases that the CDC has yet to classify, but you only live once, am I right?"

A tear drips onto Piper's hand. She didn't remove her shirt that day. She couldn't bear for Venom to put the matching tattoo on her ribs like I did. Instead, she chose her inner wrist where her watch would cover it.

But her watch doesn't cover it today.

Today, that sweet Bible verse we tattooed on ourselves years ago stares back at me, mocking our stupidity.

Ruth: 1:16-17

How dare we think we would always be together—that we would never be separated? That even death couldn't keep us apart.

But it will.

Because death took my parents. Death taught me what it felt like to truly feel alone. To fear an unknown future without a family to support you—to be there for you when you fucked everything up. Death taught me to work hard, to make sure I didn't fail because failing was the end.

There are no do-overs when you're broke and have nothing to fall back on. All you can do is climb and hope you find something to hold onto.

Death is a dream killer.

For Piper, her dream of hearing her daughter call her mama is gone. So is the dream of seeing her take her first steps and get married. The career she worked so hard for is gone, snatched right out of her grip. All those years she spent taking care of me, using her downtime from school to work, so I had school supplies and lunch. It was all time she could never get back. Time she can never fill for *her*—for her daughter.

My sister sacrificed everything for others to have a better life.

And when she finally started doing things for herself, death took all her possibilities.

Piper got the shit end of the stick, and she didn't deserve it. She was a better human than most people. She deserved more than this world took from her.

She deserved better than me.

Better than that piece of shit man who knocked—

"Keys?"

I would know that voice from anywhere. I've only spent days cursing his name as I've sat by my sister's bedside, waiting for him to return my call.

"Oh, look," I mumble to Piper, dropping her hand and wiping the tears from my face, "it's Dr. Douche. He's finally come home from his cruise to see you." I tuck Piper's hands under the blanket. I don't want Astor to see her tattoo. My sister went to great lengths to keep her image as a doctor boring. I don't want Astor to see she was full of life and fun when she wasn't wearing a lab coat. Granted, he's probably seen her tattoo and knows she's fun seeing how he knocked her up, but still. The tattoo was mine and Piper's secret. I won't allow him to steal anything else from me.

"I'm sorry, I've been overseas. I just heard about Piper."

You know, if I hadn't seen the book full of letters and pictures in Piper's den, I would have thought he sounded sincere. But what man leaves his pregnant girlfriend-one-nighter, whatever they called it, and goes on vacation for six months? I'll tell you. One that wasn't ready to be a father. Oh, I've seen dick bags like him before at work. Those guys are so excited for any work trip to get away from their wives and kids, living it up like bachelors, wining and banging total strangers on the company's dime.

Yeah, sell that sincerity somewhere else, sweetheart, because I'm not buying.

"I heard. I hope it wasn't too much of a hassle to cut your trip short. I know how needy Piper can get."

"What?"

I don't bother looking up or making eye contact with him because tears start falling. Big, raindrop-sized tears start pouring from my eyes for the stupidest reason.

"She's really gone." I lie my head against Piper's hand, seeking comfort that never comes. "If she were still here with me, she would have hit me for being mean to you. She hated when I was ugly—especially to you. And now—" I feel the weight of his presence before I have the courage to turn my head and open my eyes, taking in his simple jeans and gray t-shirt. "And now…" I blink back the tears, noticing his skin's paleness, tired eyes, and firm mouth. "And now you just look a hot mess, and I can't even tease my sister that she was catfished."

Really, him looking like an average Joe and not Dr. Dreamy is perking me up. In Keagan's mental health reservoir, distractions are always welcome, especially at someone else's expense.

"I'm glad I can amuse you."

His deep baritone voice snaps my joy. "Well, at least you're good for something. Clearly, being a decent man isn't one of those traits."

I'll admit, the jerk of his body and the confused look almost has me doubting myself. But the evidence in Piper's house was clear. This man avoided her like I avoid McGee.

"I'm sorry, Keagan, I didn't know. Otherwise, I would have—"

"What? Cut your trip short to watch her die?"

Wake up, Piper. Wake up and tell me to stop being mean to him. Plead his case and tell me he isn't the man I think he is. Tell me I have this all wrong, and he loves you and plans to marry you. Tell me that he wanted this baby more than you did, and y'all were just waiting on the right time to tell me that you were moving in together. Just. Wake. Up.

I watch Piper's chest move up and down, the machine forcing air into her lungs, keeping her here with me until I can be brave enough to let her go. I want to, I do. Seeing Piper lying there with tubes all over and machines forcing her body to do what it doesn't want, it breaks my heart.

"Do you think she's suffering?"

I don't know why I ask him. Maybe I want him to tell me that she's fine and Dr. Cox is senile and doesn't know what he's talking about. Perhaps I just want someone to talk to me. Sitting here for days without anyone has been brutal. The only enjoyment I got was writing Astor nasty notes and using Piper's ID to get into his neighborhood. I would have keyed his car if it hadn't been in the garage.

Astor sighs and rakes his hands through his hair. "I don't know."

"Did you talk to Dr. Cox?"

He nods his head.

"Did he tell you she's brain dead?"

Everything inside me clenches.

Say he was wrong. I promise I won't say another mean thing to you again.

"He did."

He moves then, going around the bed to the other side and pulling up a chair.

"Do you believe them? Do you think she'll ever recover?" I try laughing. "I mean, Piper is pretty freaking stubborn."

He sits down, and I look him in the eye for the first time. Those glacier blue eyes are heavy and filled with something I recognize—pain. "I'm sorry I wasn't here for you."

I open my mouth to tell him I expect nothing from him when he pulls out my sister's hand and kisses her palm before putting it on his cheek.

He was talking to her, not me.

"I'm so, so sorry."

Even I have my limits, and while I don't want Astor touching my sister, I know she would, so I let him apologize and warm her hands on his face until he's finished. "Is it okay if I sit with you for a while?"

It's so hard to take my pain out on him when he's like this. Wouldn't high-class Dr. Astor Potter just take what he wanted? Why is he asking my permission?

I shrug. "I'm sure Piper would like that."

"Thank you." He leans forward with his elbows on his knees. He looks so lost, so bewildered. Maybe he really did love my sister at one time—the time before he knocked her up and hopped on a six-month-long cruise.

"Did you see the baby?" I have to know. Did he love her and want this baby with her or not?

That dark head of hair rises slowly. "The baby?"

I nod. "Yeah, you know that little tadpole you shot up into my sister and then nine—well, eight months later for Piper—a screaming, crying mini-you came out." I flash him a smile that says I know that you know. "That baby. Did you go see her?"

"I don't understand." He stands up, his posture rigid. "Piper wasn't pregnant."

I get up too because he can't be the only one standing. "Oh, she was pregnant with *your* baby! All this is *your* fault. You knocked her up, which gave her myocarditis, which killed her!" I point an accusing finger at him. "Don't act like you didn't know—like she didn't tell you, and then you ran off, leaving her to handle all the morning sickness, all the heart palpitations—" I wrap my arms around myself as far as they will go, letting the tears fall. "We let her struggle. We let her die alone."

I don't even fight when I feel his arms go around me and squeeze. This is the man my sister knew.

"I hate you." I cry into his chest. "I don't want to, but the pain of knowing I wasn't there for her is too much for me to bear alone."

A gentle pressure settles on the top of my head, and I realize it's his cheek as he squeezes me tighter, as if he could tuck me away from the world all on his own.

"I don't want you to be a nice guy." Grief has swallowed me whole. The long nights watching the machines, and talking to my sister, who will never answer, have finally broken me. "Don't make it harder," I plead. "Don't be who she says you are."

"I won't be," he says softly, the warmth of his breath tickling my scalp. "You can hate me. It'll be our secret."

I nod into his chest. "You won't tell Piper?"

"Never."

I don't remember him leaving or at what point I fell asleep.

I woke up in bed next to Piper with a swollen face and… an empty bag.

And the book—the proof that Astor is a lying bastard—is gone.

CHAPTER SEVEN

Astor

Dear Astor,

    I knew you would need proof, especially from me. I violated your trust, and I'm so very sorry.

    But I'm not sorry about this baby.

    With time, I know you won't be either.

    So, go through this book, find your proof, and battle your denial.

    I know this pregnancy is unexpected for both of us.

    But it happened.

    We can do this, Astor.

    We can raise this child together.

All my love,
Piper

No, no, no. "Halle!" I yell, standing up and pacing around my office.

I didn't go home last night after leaving Keagan. I couldn't, not after finding the book peeking out from her bag. I wasn't trying to snoop. I was just getting the blanket to cover her when I saw it. A simple, leather-bound journal with my name on the front, tucked under her purse. A journal that utterly destroyed me.

"Halle!"

A dark head of hair, that is not Halle's, pops into my office. "Vance and Halle aren't here yet." Duke, my younger brother, eyes me with concern. "And from what I see, you shouldn't be here yet either."

I can imagine I look a little insane at the moment. My hair is sticking up like I've been windsurfing. My eyes are bloodshot from the lack of sleep. But probably what sells the look of insanity is that I'm still wearing yesterday's clothes. Crazy is not a good look on anyone. But for me, the levelheaded brother, it's unheard of. I'm never out of control—not in front of an audience anyway.

"I'm fine," I clip. "Just tell Halle I need to see her when she gets in." I look at my watch and note it's only 7:00 a.m. Halle won't be here for another couple of hours.

Duke throws his head back, deep rumbling laughter filling the quiet office. "You really must be out of it." He pushes inside my office, shoves the documents off my desk, and then sits as if I have no available chairs. "Newsflash, brother, I don't fucking work for you. But as your brother, I'll be happy to help pull that giant stick out of your ass." He flashes me a wink. "You know, for company morale."

I could hit him. I'm sure it would make me feel better.

"I'm not Vance. Don't talk to me like I'm not in control."

"Are you sure?" Duke's gaze tracks to the journal. "You aren't exactly screaming stable right now."

I'll lose my shit if I stay here any longer. "Tell Halle to call me." I snatch the journal off my desk and head out. I can't answer any questions until I have answers. And those answers can only be given by one person and she's dying.

I'm halfway across the parking garage when I spot Halle coming in early.

"Astor? What are you doing here?" Vance helps Halle from the car, their gaze laser-focused on me.

Inhaling, I force a smile. The last thing I need is to draw more attention to myself. "I couldn't sleep. Thought I would stop by and check my messages, but I couldn't get into the computer system." Not a lie. My password wouldn't work earlier.

Halle grimaces. "You can thank your brother for that." She shoves lightly at Vance's shoulder. "He upgraded our system while you were gone."

Of course, he did.

"Come on. I'll give you all your new login information." She flashes me a stern look. "But then you're going to go home and rest. You look like shit."

Vance grunts like he agrees, which I don't acknowledge. I simply tip my chin and head back to the office. I don't have the energy to explain or argue. I just need access to prove Piper wrong.

I've been staring at the same document for the past hour. No matter how many times I go over it, I get the same results.

The DNA is a match.

And Piper's note next to the proof brings bile to my throat.

I'm sorry I had to run the DNA against the sample you provided for the incident with Rebekah, but I knew you would need proof. You needed to see I wasn't lying.

Because my ex-wife *had* lied to me.

But unlike last time, I am the father of Piper's child. A secret she kept from her sister. No wonder Keagan hates me. My distrust of women kept her sister from sharing the joy of her pregnancy with the only family she had.

51

Flipping to the next page in the journal, I focus on the white spot on the grainy image.

First ultrasound! Our little miracle is happy and healthy with a strong heartbeat.

I trace my finger along the edge of the image. It's just a blot—a spot barely noticeable to the untrained eye—a baby, my baby, growing inside one of my closest friends.

And she documented it all. So I would believe her. So I wouldn't miss the milestones while overseas.

My stomach clenches as a wave of nausea hits me.

I can't do this. I can't look at any more of this book. It's all a reminder of Piper—the woman who was too good for this world. She sacrificed so much, and what did she get in return? Doubt? Fear? Solitude?

Keagan was right. We failed her. We let her suffer and die alone.

"Hey, you still here?" I look up and find Halle in the doorway, her eyes watchful.

"I'm on my way out." Standing, I grab the journal and offer Halle a gracious smile. "Thanks for getting those logins."

"No problem." She reaches out and places a hand on my cheek. "I say this with all the respect in the world. I don't want to see you for a couple of days, boss."

I chuckle. "Understood." Probably won't happen, but again, I don't have the energy to argue.

"I mean it, Astor, you need rest. How long has it been since you've slept?"

I've lost count of the hours. "I promise, I'm going home." Right after I make a stop.

"Okay." Halle sighs and removes her hand from my cheek. "Call me if you need anything, okay?"

She can't help me with what I need, but I don't want to worry Halle any more than I already have. "I will." I pull her into a side hug. "Keep my brothers in line while I'm gone."

I finally get a laugh out of her. "I'll do my best. Now, go." She pushes me out of the office and into the hallway. "I don't want to see you back here."

That won't be a problem. I have more pressing matters to attend to, like seeing Piper and her sister.

And my child.

The hospital has always been my sanctuary, a place where I leave all my problems and just be. But today, as I walk through the glass doors, all that courses through me is dread. The halls aren't filled with quiet, calm, or new beginnings.

Today, one hallway leads to an end.

An end of a friendship.

An end of a mother.

An end of a sister.

That's not the hallway I dread the most, though.

This hallway, the one connecting to the neonatal intensive care, leads to the end of excuses. It's the beginning of pain and the end of a promise.

"Dr. Potter. We weren't expecting you." A nurse greets me at the door of the nursery. "Do you have a patient with us?"

It's not unexpected that I'm visiting the nursery. I have quite a few babies born with cleft palates that need surgery consults. But it's unheard of that I visit the nursery for a personal matter. "I uh…" I run a hand through my hair. How am I supposed to get this out? "Piper McKellan."

The nurse's face falls. "Such a tragic story. Are you here to see her daughter?"

Her daughter.

My daughter.

"I—"

"Dr. Potter." Carly, another nurse I recognize, appears at the door, placing a hand on the shoulder of the other nurse. "I've got this one, Tiff. The Connors' baby in Pod B is ready for his feeding."

Tiff looks between the new nurse and me. "Okay. Let me know if you need anything, Dr. Potter."

I won't, but I thank her anyway. Carly offers me a sad smile when she's behind the glass doors. "Would you like to see your daughter, Astor?"

No.

Yes.

My heart beats wildly—so hard that the violent pounding steals my breath. "I don't know."

Carly nods her head like she understands my uncertainty.

But she doesn't.

No one but Piper could understand what this moment does to me.

"Why don't I bring her to the glass? Then, when you're ready, you can come in and hold your daughter."

"Is she okay?"

Carly nods, a big smile on her face. "She's doing great. Just a little fluid in her lungs that we're watching. I'm hoping she can be discharged to the regular nursery sometime tomorrow."

An ache spreads across my chest, my eyes burning. *You did good, Piper. You kept her healthy.*

"Dr. Potter? Did you hear me?"

I blink a few times and refocus. "No, I'm sorry. Would you mind repeating?"

Carly offers me a sympathetic smile as she places her hand on my shoulder. "I asked if I could call someone for you? Maybe Vance or Duke?"

I shake my head. "No, that won't be necessary."

I understand Carly's concern. The birth of my daughter came with a price—the death of my friend. Something I don't seem to be handling well, given the reactions I keep getting.

"Okay." She sighs but knows better than to push me. "Give me a few minutes, and I'll bring your little girl to the viewing window."

I don't even thank her. I don't even see her disappear back behind the door.

All I can do is breathe while I focus on the empty spot behind the large window, where Carly reappears moments later, pushing a plastic bassinet.

Breathing becomes difficult. I can't manage to pull in air as I stare at the small body inside. Wires are connected to her chest and heel as she kicks her feet, crying, a sound I can't hear from the hallway. Everything about her is tiny perfection.

I've seen babies before.

I've counted toes and played peek-a-boo.

But I've never done those things to a child that was mine.

Those ten tiny toes I helped create.

Those strong lungs supplying her cries were formed in her mother. A mother that loved her enough to wait on me. A mother that will never see what we created.

Carly pushes the bassinet up against the wall.

My throat bobs, and I try swallowing around the lump as she reaches inside the bassinet.

It takes a moment for Carly to settle the crying baby into the crook of her arm.

A moment for her to move closer to the window.

A moment for my daughter to blink, open her ice-blue eyes and stare right at me.

A moment is all it takes for everything to go dark.

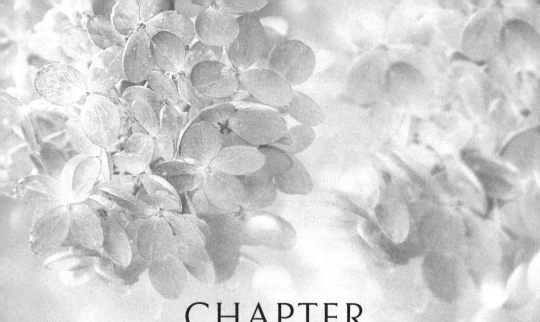

CHAPTER EIGHT

Keagan

Today marks a week since I got the call about Piper, and while I've spent the last twenty-four hours hating Astor for stealing my sister's book yesterday, none of those hours compare to this call I'm having with my boss, Archer. "I understand, sir."

I understand he is a raging, self-serving asshole.

"I'm glad. You know we'll do everything to support you during this difficult time."

I can't contain the eye roll. "As long as I'm not away longer than my allowed three days of bereavement leave."

Archer coughs. I guess he thought I gave a shit about being professional. My sister is dying. I couldn't give eight shits about his feelings right now. "Now, Keagan, that's not what I said."

That's precisely what he said.

"I said you were welcome to take longer, but you would need to call our Human Resources department and file for an extended leave."

"But that leave isn't job-protected. Did I get that part right, at least?" This man thinks he can bully me into letting my sister go and settling her estate, all the while kissing my niece goodbye and leaving her in the arms of a stranger. Yeah, I don't think so.

"Well," Archer clears his throat, "you would need to ask HR. There might be a program that will allow you to keep your job."

"Just not my promotion," I correct.

I'm so tired of the office politics and always being passed over for these men.

"Your new account and project would go to McGee, but you will not lose your promotion unless you're gone longer than your approved leave."

Basically, I will lose no matter how much time I need to help my niece and to mourn my sister. My new project. Probably my promotion—Archer will find a loophole to take it from me—and every bit of progress I've made at *GameTales*. I'll essentially be starting over from scratch—back at the bottom like when I was a college intern. I've clawed my way through a man's playground and finally found a place among them only to possibly lose it.

"Don't worry about your job, Keagan. Focus on your family. We'll deal with the rest later."

He says the words like he's a concerned supervisor, but I know better. Archer wants me to let my guard down—put my faith in him that my job is secure—so when I get back, he can show me a policy I've never seen before and tell me they had to fill my position.

"I'll speak with HR," I tell him, "and see you in a few weeks."

I refuse to lose my sister and my job. Life won't take everything away from me because I won't let it.

"Take care of yourself, Keagan."

I hang up the phone without a parting remark and flip it off. "You hear that, Piper? Ass Face McGee wins again."

Piper coded last night while I was asleep. The monitors started beeping like crazy. Before I even realized what was happening, a nurse ushered me out of the room as half a dozen doctors and nurses filled the room.

They said Piper's heart stopped.

But even as they shocked her body and pumped her full of drugs, I couldn't let her go. Not yet. Instead, I folded over my knees in the hallway and cried until it was over.

Dr. Cox asked me if he could call anyone—someone who could be with me during this difficult time. But there was no one I could name. All the family I had was currently trying to leave me.

I adjust the blanket, tucking it under Piper's hip. "I wish you would wake up and talk me out of going over to *GameTales* and putting eye drops in McGee's coffee. Maybe Archer's too. I think they deserve it, don't you?"

I watch as my sister's chest rises and falls without a sound. She isn't going to wake up and tell me no, that giving McGee diarrhea would be tacky and immature. Never again will she scold me for not taking the high road.

"Fine, be a Disney Princess and wait for Prince Charming to wake you up with a sloppy kiss. Maybe he'll bring back your book so that I can beat his ass with it."

While I appreciate Astor not being a jerk when I last saw him, I don't appreciate a thief. He could have asked me to look at the book. He didn't have to take it when I fell asleep.

"Be honest, Piper, is Dr. Dreamy a terrible lay?" I grab the hairbrush I remembered to bring from Piper's house and run it through her hair. "In my experience, the hottest guys are the worst in bed. It's that whole giving thing they struggle with." Selfish assholes.

"Maybe you should bat for the all-girls team then. I hear they are the more generous lovers."

A voice I'm used to hearing drunk snaps my head up. "Kenny!" Dropping the brush, I sprint to the other side of Piper's room and throw myself at the best bartender friend ever.

"Hey, darling." He smothers a grunt as he catches me, looping his arms around me as I start to sob. "Hey now, none of those tears."

I can't stop the wetness or the heaving breaths as I relish being in the arms of a friend, someone who cares about me. "How long can you stay?"

He pulls in a breath that's basically a sigh. "A couple of days. I didn't want you to be alone when it happened."

When I agree to take Piper off the machines.

I talked to Dr. Cox last night. I told him I would make a decision soon. And Kenny, my dear sweet Kenny, didn't want me to be alone when I did.

"Thank you," I tell him, squeezing him hard. "Thank you for coming when you're allergic to tears." I'm cracking a joke, only because I'm tired of being sad.

Kenny tucks my head under his chin. "You're going to get through this, love. I'll make sure of it."

Grabbing Kenny's hand, I take the pen from Dr. Cox. "Piper has always been the more responsible one, you know. When our parents died, she was the one who stepped up, refusing to go live with our distant Aunt Linda." I chuckle, looking over the document that says I consent to take Piper off the machines. "She stood before Child Protective Services at nineteen years old with a spiral-bound notebook, outlining how she planned to take care of herself and her little sister."

Her plan didn't include her going off to college as planned.

It also didn't include us staying in our childhood home.

No, Responsible Piper packed us up and moved us into a tiny one-bedroom apartment, where she could drop me off at school before heading to her classes at the community college.

Piper loathed community college. For years, all she talked about was going to an Ivy League school and becoming a doctor.

But then our parents died.

And she had to get a GED in order to take care of me and still pursue her dreams of one day becoming a doctor.

Love changes a person.

Humility refines them.

"She would come home every day after six hours of college classes, take a nap, burn our dinner, and help me with my homework before her shift started at an all-night diner."

For four years, Piper the Protector cut costs and saved every bit of our parents' life insurance money.

And then she gave it to me.

"All those sacrifices for it to end like this." I put down the clipboard and blink back the tears. "She deserves so much better than this."

Kenny puts his hand on my shoulder reassuringly. He tried to get me to wait and sign the form, but I knew I might never do it if I waited and he left. Piper does deserve better. She doesn't deserve to suffer—to prolong her life here for my benefit. My sister deserves to be in heaven with the other angels. She was always too good for this world. She belongs there.

"Your sister is a wonderful woman."

I nod at Dr. Cox. "She really is."

"And you're a wonderful sister for making this decision and putting her needs first."

I choke out a laugh. "You might change your mind when I ask you this."

Dr. Cox arches a brow, waiting.

"I want her to hold her daughter." I wipe away the tears. "Piper has suffered too much, not to see the only good thing to come out of her sacrifice. I want her to see her daughter before we let her go. Do you think you can make that happen, Dr. Cox? Can you make sure my sister sees what she did all this for?"

I hear a sniffle behind me.

"I can arrange that," Dr. Cox promises.

I nod, a sense of peace washing over me. "Thank you."

Dr. Cox gets up to leave when one more request pops into my head. "And Dr. Potter. Could you call him? I think she would want to see him too."

Dr. Cox looks confused.

"You know, Dr. Dick, her lover?" I roll my eyes at the thought. "Her baby daddy?"

"I know who Dr. Potter is," he tells me.

"Great. Tell his majesty to get his ass back here and hug my sister goodbye." Or kiss her. You never know. Piper could have a classic case of Princess-itis. She could wake up with one kiss from Lover Boy and be perfectly fine.

"I don't know if that will be possible."

I throw my head back. "Don't tell me…he has a facial scheduled and needs a raincheck?" One good thing about hating Astor is that the tears stop when I think of him sleeping soundly in his posh suburban home. It's easier to be detached from the situation when you didn't promise a lifetime to your baby's mama.

Dr. Cox clears his throat. "Dr. Potter collapsed earlier."

Kenny gasps, just as I jump up from my chair. "What do you mean he collapsed? Is he okay?" I know I hoped Astor had a brush with an STD, but nothing serious. My niece needs one parent to raise her.

Dr. Cox frowns. "I can't violate his privacy and give you details, but he's okay."

The way his voice wavers has me on high alert. "You don't sound like you're sure."

"Everything is fine, Ms. McKellan, I assure you. And when Dr. Potter is stable, I will pass along your message."

"Thank you, Dr. Cox. I'll get back to you with the form." But not until my demands are met. Piper needs her prince and princess.

"Of course. I'll check on Piper again in the morning."

As soon as Dr. Cox shuts the door, I turn and look back at Kenny. "I'm going to find Dr. Dreamy. Are you in or out?" I don't trust Dr. Cox to relay my message fast enough. If Dr. Potter is really fine, he can see my sister and give back the book he stole. My sister has done enough waiting for him—and me—but I'm placing most of the blame on Astor. It's the least he can do before taking the last piece of my sister from me—my niece.

A wide grin spreads across Kenny's face. "Oh, girl. I thought you'd never ask. I'm always down for a manhunt."

CHAPTER NINE

Astor

"Ah, the princess is awake."

Pressure is throbbing between my temples, making it hard to concentrate on Duke's annoying voice in my ear.

"Assstor. Wake up, sugar. You have a lot of explaining to do."

"Fuck off." I groan, covering my face in my hands. My eyelids feel like they weigh ten pounds.

"I would, but since you're having difficulty surviving, you're now under my care for the next twenty-four hours."

Everything hits me at once. The hospital. Seeing my daughter. Her eyes—my eyes.

I jerk upright in bed, my gaze zeroing in on the band secured around my wrist, the words *Duke Potter, admitting physician* glaring back at me.

"Get this shit off of me." I pull at the wires taped to my chest before

I notice Vance sitting in a chair at the foot of the bed. "You think this is fucking funny?" I ask him. "Letting Duke admit me?"

Vance shrugs, fighting off a grin. "You should be thanking me. He wanted to order an enema too."

Gritting my teeth, I address Duke sitting alongside me, his grin more expansive than a canyon. "I'm going to beat you bloody."

"Really?" He raises a brow and then looks back at Vance. "Are you hearing my patient?"

Vance's lip twitches. "I am."

"I'm thinking his behavior is escalating. Would you order restraints?"

Ripping the last wire from my chest, I toss it to the floor. "I wish you would try tying me down."

I'm breathing heavy, already removing the IV in my hand. I need to get out of here and talk to an attorney or to Keagan. Fuck. I don't know what I need. All I know is I have a daughter that needs me.

Suddenly feeling exhausted, I slump over, burying my face in my hands.

This can't be happening. This isn't how I wanted to start a family.

"Hey," comes a sweet voice. "Look at me."

"I just need a minute," I beg Halle.

Shame coats my insides. The last thing I want to do is meet Halle's concerned gaze and explain what a piece of shit her boss is.

"Astor." Vance's hand comes down on my shoulder. "Why didn't you tell us, man?"

I take a deep breath and lift my head. Being the eldest brother comes with responsibility. Vance needs stability with all that's happened to him the past eighteen months, and Duke, well, he just needs to know I will beat his ass if he continues with this doctor-patient shit.

"I didn't know until yesterday," I finally admit to Vance.

"I'm so sorry." Halle wraps her arms around me. "This is such a tragic situation."

The worst.

Piper was a good woman—a good friend. She didn't deserve to

spend her pregnancy worrying if I was going to step up and help raise this baby with her. She didn't deserve to work through all those emotions, only never to see the miracle we created.

Fate is a cruel bitch.

"How are *you* feeling, really?" I look up at Duke. His voice is serious for the first time. "The nurses were concerned. They said you were acting strangely before you passed out."

"I'm in shock." It's partly the truth.

"And suffering from exhaustion and dehydration," Duke adds.

"I told y'all." My head snaps up and locates the voice concealed in the shadows of the corner, a cigarette between his lips. "But I recall you both saying that I didn't know how to diagnose my ass from my elbow." Remington blows out a ring of smoke, watching as it floats in the air.

"This is a hospital," I scold. "You shouldn't be smoking."

"Aww, thanks, Dad, but my other daddy said it was okay. Take it up with him." He blows another puff of smoke toward Vance and grins.

"Seriously, Vance? You said he could smoke?" Out of all of us, Vance is a stickler for rules.

Vance doesn't even have the decency to look ashamed. He merely shrugs. "It's better than him talking. I can only take so much sarcasm before I turn violent."

Remington chuckles.

"Besides, he opened a window."

I roll my eyes. "How considerate."

"The point is, Grandpa," Remington interrupts, "I was right. You hear that, Vancy-poo?" He cups his ear, enjoying fucking with Vance. "Go on. I'm waiting. Tell me I was right, and you were wrong."

Vance flips him off but doesn't engage. Instead, he pins me with a concerned look. A look I recognize, since I was giving him the same look months ago. I groan. "Don't, okay? I'm fine. Nothing a nap and coconut water can't fix."

"Nothing an overnight mandated rest can't fix, you mean?" Halle dares me to argue with her. "Right, Dr. Astor?"

"Shouldn't she be locked in your tower or something?" I ask Vance, keeping my eyes trained on his girl. I know she's just looking out for me, but really, I'm fine. It was just the combination of stress with dehydration that caused the collapse. Nothing serious.

"You should know she never minds her own business."

Pussy has ruined my brother.

"Yeah, well, let me reassure each of you. I'm fine." I look around me, everyone hovering except Remington, who just seems to be enjoying the in-house entertainment.

"That's good to know, but you're still staying here and getting some rest." Halle's expression looks a lot like my brother's. She's been around Vance too long. "Even if I have to sit at the door all night. Do we understand each other, boss?"

I'm exhausted just arguing with her. "Twenty-four hours," I agree, "but not a minute more."

Halle nods, pleased with her leadership skills, but the truth is, being here at the hospital overnight isn't the worst place I could be. It will allow me access to the ICU, where Piper and Keagan are. I need to clear some things up with Keagan. I might be many things, but I'm not a bastard. I loved her sister, just not in the way she assumes.

"Good, now that we have your sleeping arrangements dealt with, we can move on to bigger topics." A smile cracks through Vance's harsh frown. "Like how when Mommy bee falls in love with Daddy bee, and they create a baby—"

The door flies open, and Keagan pulls to a stop when she realizes I'm not alone. "I'm sorry, I thought—"

I motion for her to come in. "They were just leaving."

No one moves or takes the hint they are unwanted guests. I need to talk to Keagan. Alone.

"That's okay." She stumbles out. "I'll come back."

A guy I didn't see before shoves her from behind. Her cheeks turn several shades of pink as she looks at me. "I didn't mean to intrude. Dr. Cox told me you collapsed and well…."

I grin. "And you wanted to kick me while I was down?"

Halle sucks in a breath, and Keagan immediately goes on the defensive. "That's not what I'm doing!"

She looks at Duke, who grins. "It's okay. We wouldn't blame you if you did."

"But I wasn't." Keagan shakes her head and pleads directly to Halle. "I promise, I only wished a little bit of harm on him—nothing bad. My sister would kill me if I wished something worse." She sucks in a breath. "I'll admit, I'm not his biggest fan, but my sister seems to care about him, even when he abandoned her for a cruise."

"Why does everyone think I've been on a cruise?" I can't help the exasperation in my tone. Keagan has a right to hate me for what I did to her sister. But I wasn't on a fucking cruise. I didn't know Piper was pregnant when I left for the Grace of Mercy.

"That's where your office said you were when I called," Keagan says doubtfully, like now she's not so sure.

"Is that true?" I look at Halle for confirmation. "Did you tell her I was on a cruise?"

She shakes her head. "Never. I would never tell—"

"Oh, that was my bad," Remington interrupts, putting his cigarette on the windowsill and standing, his gaze tracking to Keagan with a grin. "You're that chick that called asking for Dr. Bastard, aren't you?"

Keagan's eyes go wide, her cheeks turning an even darker shade of pink. "I was having a bad day."

Remington snorts and flips me off as he walks by. "I covered your phone for a few hours while your brother violated your assistant in the operating room. You're welcome."

I glare at Vance, who just shrugs. "She was on a break."

"For hours?" What has happened to my brother and his rules?

Vance stands and grabs a very red-faced Halle, pulling her to his side. "It was a *long* break." He clasps me on the shoulder. "Rest, brother. I'll be back to check on you in the morning."

I won't be here in the morning. I know I promised Halle, but now that Keagan is here, I have no need to stay once I've spoken to her.

Remington walks backward toward the door, flashing me a wink as he says to Keagan, "There's a vacant alley just a block from here if you need a place to stash his body. It'll be a while before the cops find him."

"Rem!" Halle grabs him by the collar and yanks him from the room. "Feel better, Astor!" she calls from the hallway. "I'm going to call the nurses' station later. You better not try to leave."

Luckily Vance shuffles her down the hallway before I have to lie.

"You okay here?" I glance back at Duke, who's turned serious, likely putting all the pieces together about Keagan.

"Yeah, man. I'm fine. Go home."

He nods, still looking unsure as he walks past Keagan and stops. "I'm sorry to hear about your sister. She's an amazing person." He turns and takes one last look at me. "But so is my brother."

A tear falls down Keagan's cheek. "I know, I'm sorry. I didn't mean—"

Duke puts his hand on her shoulder. "I know."

A few moments after Duke shuts the door, Keagan's friend breaks the ice. "I'm Kenny," he says, stepping forward and extending his hand. "It's nice to meet you finally. I've heard a lot about you."

That seems to snap Keagan out of it. "Kenny!"

"What? He already knows you talk shit about him. It's no secret."

Keagan buries her face in her hands. "This is so not how this was supposed to go down."

Chuckling, I get up and tip my chin at Kenny. "Will you toss me that bag?"

"What are you doing?" Keagan snatches the bag from Kenny. "You're not leaving, are you?"

"Not yet." I pull the bag from her grip. "But I am getting out of this hospital gown." I'll let Halle's extended break go since she was thoughtful enough to bring me a change of clothes.

"Here? You're changing right here?"

I pull the sweatpants from the bag. "Would you prefer I change in the hallway?"

"I prefer you stay in bed and rest like you're supposed to."

"Well, I'm sorry to burst your colorful misperception of me, but

I don't take orders from anyone." Untying the knots holding the gown together, I tip my chin to the door. "So you can either turn around or watch. One way or another, I'm getting naked."

Kenny chokes, his eyes widening before Keagan snags him by the arm. "Turn around. You're not watching."

I fight back the urge to laugh as I watch her cover his eyes, making sure they face the wall while I change. "You can turn around now," I tell her when I've finished pulling on the t-shirt and sweats.

Slowly, she turns around as I sit in the chair Remington vacated. "You should be resting."

"I'm feeling better."

Keagan sweeps down my body with a sharp gaze. "What's wrong with you anyway?"

"Other than the fact I'm an asshole, you mean?"

The comment makes her chuckle, and I swear my chest feels a few pounds lighter at the sound. "Yes. What happened earlier when you collapsed?"

If I didn't know any better, I would say I detected concern in her voice. "Despite what Remington told you when you called my office, I haven't been on vacation. I've been overseas in international waters, operating on children in need."

She swallows, taking a seat on the bed with Kenny.

"Most days, I operated for twenty-plus hours. I didn't take care of myself like I should have."

Keagan is quiet for the longest time, staring at me like she can't decide if she wants to believe me. "No wonder my sister slept with you." She swipes her hand through the air in the direction of my body. "Other than the obvious."

Kenny makes a noise like he can confirm her suspicions.

"Your sister and I were good friends."

"Friends who slept together?" She wants me to prove the rest of her suspicions.

"We were friends who slept together once," I confirm. "We were not dating, nor did I know she was pregnant when I left on my mission trip."

She throws her head back and looks at the ceiling. "A freaking mission trip...."

"Your sister has done several of these mission trips with me. It's how we met."

Tears stream down her face. I can't tell if she's relieved to know I wasn't avoiding her sister or still angry her sister slept with me in the first place. Regardless, she doesn't give me time to figure it out when she stands, walking over and taking my hand. "I need your help."

I nod. "Anything."

"I need you to tell her goodbye."

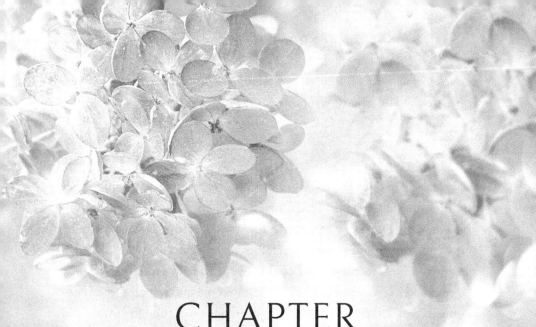

CHAPTER TEN

Astor

Dear Astor,

I tried to wait, but the anticipation was just too much. I had to know if a little girl was responsible for all this exhaustion or if it was a little boy who kicked me all night long. But I should have known that it could only be another McKellan princess giving me this much grief. Keagan would be proud. I can't wait to tell her when you come home. Maybe we can tell her together. She's less likely to kill you if I'm there. Kidding. She'll forgive us… eventually.

When you're ready, we can tell her the whole story.

Stay safe and take care of yourself.

I have our daughter covered.

Ps: I've been researching baby names. What do you think about Tatum? It means cheerful and bringer of joy. I know when you finally get to read this letter, you'll still be in shock, but eventually, I think you'll agree that joy is precisely what this little girl brings us. Think about it.

Piper

Tears drip onto the pages—not mine, but Keagan's. "I couldn't get past her first letter," she admits, swiping at her eyes. "All I could think was you were like every other man I know and didn't believe the baby was yours." She points to the next letter. "I thought they were all letters pleading for you to trust her. I couldn't bear to read more."

It makes sense now why Keagan hated me and left all those hateful messages. "I very well could have been who you thought I was. You didn't know me."

"Yeah," she sniffles, "but I know Piper, and she would never be friends with a piece of shit. I should have trusted her friendship with you."

And I should've called Piper from the ship. I shouldn't have made her feel like she needed to write these letters. We could have talked about all of this. Deep down, I know she did the right thing. Keagan is right, she knows Piper, and Piper knew me. She knew I would need to see the proof for myself. I needed the tests. Piper didn't need me dampening her pregnancy experience with questions and frustrations. I wouldn't have been able to focus on my patients. I would have worried and been overcome with anxiety.

So Piper did what she always does, the right thing. She knew I couldn't leave the ship because all of those patients needed my help. She waited and documented everything, so I would have what I needed when it came time to face reality. "If it helps to renew your hatred, I was avoiding your sister, but not because of the baby. I could have called her or emailed after she sent the first letter, but I didn't. I wanted complete detachment."

"Did your need for detachment have anything to do with the whole story she mentioned in her letter?"

I nod, smoothing out the letter before closing the book. "Yes."

"But you're not ready to tell me yet?"

I force my gaze to meet Keagan's. She's so vulnerable, so hopeful for anything to hold on to. "Knowing the whole story won't make this any easier." It's the truth. Nothing I tell her will change the fact her sister is dying. Her knowing that mine and Piper's relationship wasn't one of unconditional love won't ease her pain. It'll only make it worse.

For a moment, Keagan just stares at me. Not moving, not saying anything, just staring. Finally, she nods. "Okay, I can accept that. But I need to know one thing."

These past few hours sitting with Keagan haven't been as awful as I thought. I fully expected she would grill me with questions while hurling insults, but she hasn't. She simply asked for my blessing in letting Piper see the baby before letting her rest for good.

But now, after we've sat for hours going over Piper's letters, I'm more on edge about what she could want. "What do you want to know?"

She slides the book off my lap and into hers. "I want to know if you'll honor my sister's wishes and name her daughter Tatum." Her lips quiver. "Even though I'm struggling with finding joy, my sister didn't. She wanted that little girl more than anything."

I blow out a breath, fighting back my own emotion. Piper knew once I came to terms with the pregnancy, I would be overjoyed. I just wish that joy wasn't overshadowed by grief. "It would be an honor to name her Tatum."

A tear drips down Keagan's cheek as she smiles. "What about her middle name? Do you have any ideas?"

I shake my head. "I haven't had a chance…" It's not that I don't want to give her a full name, but everything has just happened so fast.

"You have time," she lies, looking over at Kenny asleep in a chair. "At least until tomorrow." When we let Piper go and leave the hospital. The neonatologist said Tatum was healthy and could be discharged as early as tomorrow.

"How long is Kenny staying with you?"

She offers me a sad smile. "He has a shift in forty-eight hours."

"We don't have to do this now," I tell her, reaching out for her hand and then reconsidering. "You don't have to rush this." I don't want Keagan to let her sister go before she's ready because she won't have anyone there for her. "I'll be here if you want to wait."

She side-eyes my hand. "I've waited long enough. It's time my sister got some rest too." She stands and points a finger. "Like you should be doing."

"I told you—"

"Yeah, yeah," she waves me off, "that's not going to happen. I heard you the first billion times. But just know, we don't have time for your fainting spells today. Piper and Tatum need us to be strong." She says the statement like she's trying to convince herself, too. "So, take a nap with Kenny. I'll be back, and then you can take me to meet your daughter." She swallows, the pain behind her eyes evident as she turns to leave. "Before we take her to see her mama."

"Wait." I grab her arm then quickly drop it. I don't know what I wanted to say, but I just couldn't let her go. "Stay."

She turns back and offers me a sweet smile, continuing toward the door. "Get some rest, Dr. Potter."

"It's Dr. Astor." She stops but doesn't turn around. "Only my brother Vance goes by Dr. Potter."

"I've heard people here call you Dr. Potter."

"They do, but the ones who really know me call me Dr. Astor."

"Are you saying I know you now?"

She hasn't left yet. That's a good sign. "I'm saying you know me enough to have the choice."

"And if I prefer Dr. Douche?"

It's like I can feel her smile from here. "Then I'll learn to adapt."

My answer must shock her because she still doesn't leave. "You'd let me call you that in front of people?"

I take a breath. "If it made you feel better, yes."

It takes her a moment before she answers with unsteady words. "And what will make you feel better, Dr. Potter?"

I stand and take her hand from behind. "You can." I swallow, wading through this exchange carefully. "I'll rest if you stay. I'll be strong for Tatum and Piper." *I'll be strong for you.*

I can tell the moment she gives in. The moment she lets down her guard, lets go of her hate, and takes the comfort I'm offering. This isn't about Piper or me. It isn't even about the disdain Keagan has for me. This is about survival. Keagan may think she can handle this all on her own—and she probably can—but she doesn't have to. We can put aside our differences, and I can give her what her sister gave me—a friend.

"Fine," she whispers, "but only because I don't want you falling in love with Kenny and taking him too."

"I'll never take anyone from you again. You have my word." I pull her to the bed and pull the covers back.

Her eyes widen. "I agreed to stay, not sleep with you."

I shrug. "The chairs don't look all that comfortable." Lying down, I scoot toward the edge, leaving her plenty of room, and close my eyes. "But don't blame me if you wake up with a kink tomorrow."

It's so quiet, I think she's left, but then I feel the mattress dip and her back touching mine. There's a comfortable silence between us until she says, "Promise me you'll be there tomorrow."

I don't know if she's asking for her, for Tatum, or for Piper, but it wouldn't matter. "I promise."

I wake to soft whimpers. The mattress does nothing to absorb her shaking as she covers her mouth with her hand. "Keagan?" I sit up, and she springs from the bed, leaving the book she was reading behind.

"I'm the worst sister," she cries, waking up Kenny.

"That's not true, boo," he says, his voice groggy with sleep. "Piper would never think you were a bad sister."

She shakes her head almost violently and points to the book on the bed that contains ultrasounds and Piper's letters. "She loved that little girl so much, and I haven't even bothered to go take care of the one thing that mattered more than anything to her. The one thing she gave up her life for."

Kenny and I both look at one another. Keagan seems like a wild animal. Her eyes are bloodshot, and her face is swollen. I doubt she slept at all. From the looks of it, she sat up all night reading Piper's book— the one she couldn't bear to read before, when she thought it was a book of proof meant for me.

"That whole book is a love story to her daughter." She tries pulling in breaths between sobs. "A little girl that will never know what it feels like to be loved by Piper McKellan."

Kenny gets to Keagan first and wraps his arms around her. "She'll know how much Piper loved her because she'll know what it feels like to be loved by you."

"No, she won't. Because I'm not Piper. I don't know how to love like that. Something is wrong with me."

Kenny shushes her, gently swaying from side to side like she's fragile. And she is, but while Piper and Keagan are vastly different, there's one thing they both love: proving men wrong.

"I'm sure Tatum will understand," I say, breaking through her cries, "you can't help if you live far away and are preoccupied."

Kenny's head snaps up, and I flash him a quick wink.

"We'll still FaceTime you on her birthday, so you can see her."

Keagan's head rises slowly off Kenny's chest. "I hope you don't think that I won't be there for my niece, just because I'm sucky." She wipes angrily at her face and steps away from him, poking me in the chest with her finger. "You promised that you wouldn't take anyone else away from me."

"And I won't." I fight back a smile as determination fills her eyes.

"Oh, I know you won't." She pokes me again, growing stronger with each word. "Because I might be her sucky Aunt Keys, but I'll be the best sucky Aunt Keys she's ever had. And I don't need you or your future trophy wife thinking you're getting rid of me that easily."

I feign shock. "I would never think such a thing."

I promised Keagan strength today, and if that means making her hate me to find her strength, then so be it. She's getting through this day. We're all getting through this day.

"You know what?" Keagan shoves me. "You're already pissing me off this morning." But then she looks down at my sweatpants and grins. "Meet me outside—after you do something with that early morning dong salute. It's time you introduced me to my niece."

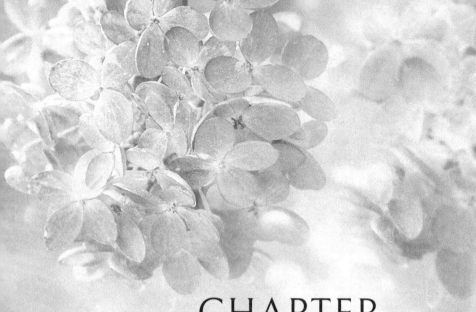

CHAPTER ELEVEN

Keagan

Great. He has a fan club, and Kenny, who decided this was a moment for just Astor and me, isn't here to witness it.

"Dr. Astor, we're so glad you're feeling better."

He's feeling better, all right. It's amazing what a little bit of sleep did for the man, which Piper should thank me for. It's not like I enjoyed feeling his chest rise against my arm where, at one point, he pulled me toward him when I tried to get up. The man needs a teddy bear, like yesterday.

But I did it for my sister and Tatum—took one for team McKellan. They'll need their prince strong today—stronger than me. I didn't mean to have a total meltdown. Hell, I didn't even mean to read so much of Piper's book. But I felt guilty for jumping to conclusions about Astor. My bad experiences with men have turned me jaded. Never did I imagine the reason Astor was on a mission trip was because he was helping children in need. Like, wow.

I thought Astor was another run-of-the-mill pretentious surgeon that Piper knew from the hospital. And while I'm not entirely sold on the fact he isn't an arrogant ass, I'm not sure he's a bad guy either. I read Piper's book, hoping to uncover more of the truth about Astor, more about why she felt she couldn't at least tell me about Tatum. I would have kept her secret; I didn't know Astor. I definitely wouldn't have made time to write him a scathing letter while he was off being a philanthropist.

But there's a reason Piper didn't tell me she was pregnant.

There has to be.

Because I can't fathom my sister keeping the one thing from me that made her the happiest unless... No. Piper would never think I would be jealous of sharing her with a baby or a husband. I would be happy for her. I mean, I would stalk the shit out of Astor first, but when he came back a decent man, I would have let him marry my sister if he wanted.

"Are you ready to hold your daughter?"

I had tuned out the chatter from the nurses who were giving Astor far too much attention, but this question caught my ear, pulling me into their conversation.

"Wait a minute." I grab the back of his t-shirt and tug. "You haven't held her yet?"

The color had returned to Astor's face this morning, but now, looking at him, he's gone pale. "No, there wasn't time," he lies.

The nurse cuts me a look like she wants to inject a word or two, but instead, she smiles when Astor continues talking to her, "I think it's best if Keagan holds her, just in case."

I narrow my eyes. "Just in case what? You run?"

Every time I think he's grown on me, he says something ridiculous and jumps back on my nerve train.

"Just in case I'm still unsteady," he clarifies. "It's safer for Tatum."

"Oh! You picked out a name!" The nurse could blow up a balloon with all the hot air and enthusiasm she's blown Astor's way.

Astor ignores her, though, choosing to hold my gaze in a battle of wills. I know he's lying. He seems perfectly fine and steady, but I can't just call him out in a room of fangirls now, can I?

"Are you going to hold your niece, Keagan?"

Oh, hell no.

No, he did not just challenge me like I'm the one scared to hold her. This man has seen his daughter, but he hasn't held her. Yeah, I'm not buying his lies. He's not weak. Something else is stopping him from holding her, and it better not be doubt. My sister is not a liar, and I am not opposed to using that alley his friend mentioned earlier.

"Yes, I'll hold my niece." I offer him a saccharine smile. "If your friend could lead us to her."

I am so over this parade for Dr. Potter. Did Piper get the same treatment as a woman? I bet not. Though, in all fairness, these women probably care nothing about the fact that Astor is a doctor but rather that they are getting a glimpse of him in gray sweatpants—probably a bucket list item they can now check off.

"Oh, sure, right this way."

Astor sweeps his hand out to the side for me to go ahead of him, which annoys me, but not enough to argue. I don't need his chivalry; I want his truth. What is up with him and my niece, and what in the fresh hell went down with him and my sister? Those are the only two things I need from this man. Not his sweet hugs and endless patience when I need to lash out at someone. I want answers.

But not right now.

Because, right now, the most beautiful girl in the world is lifted out of the bassinet. "Do you want to sit down and hold her?"

I shake my head at the nurse, seeing the dusting of dark hair peeking out from the little knitted hat. "No." I can already feel the tears welling in my eyes. "Just give her to me."

Why did I wait so long to see her?

The nurse places her in my arms, and I lift her to my face, inhaling her scent, drawing the very essence from her little body. "Piper was right," I whisper to Astor, who seems to be frozen beside me. "She is the bringer of joy."

I press my finger to her palm, and she grips it. *Oh, Piper, she's amazing.*

"She's perfect, isn't she?" I look up and find Astor has moved to get a closer look.

I nod. "Piper would so hog her." I try laughing, but it just comes out more like a gurgle. "You wouldn't have to worry about weekends away. Piper wouldn't share her with you anyway. I doubt she would even let me hold her."

My sister would be enamored with this precious little girl. She would love her chubby cheeks and bow lips. She would dress her in smock dresses and spend her days just staring at the sheer perfection of her baby-ness.

"I thought," I suck in a breath and force my gaze to stay on Astor, "I thought if there was any room for a miracle, you and this little one would be it." I force down a sob and hold what I can form of a smile. "I've tried everything I know to get Piper to wake up and smack me, but she remains asleep, just like a sleeping princess."

Astor steps forward, his arms reaching out until I step back. "I hoped she would be that one in a million case—that this was all an over-reaction, and she would just wake up and wonder why she wasn't wearing panties." I shake my head. "But she's not going to wake up, is she?"

Astor moves his head from side to side like it pains him. "No, sweetheart, she isn't."

"So, we're doing the right thing by setting her free?"

I need someone to tell me this is okay, that this is what my sister wanted, even if I'm not totally sold on the idea.

"We're doing the right thing," he agrees. "We're honoring her wishes."

And destroying my heart.

We stayed in the nursery, where I fed Tatum until she was full. Again, Astor managed to remain hands-off with his mysterious man illness.

But I didn't care.

Because I wanted all the baby cuddles.

I wanted all that my sister left behind.

Who knows what will happen after Piper passes? Will Astor take Tatum home, let his big family rally around him and keep her from me? Will he say I'm unstable or not good enough for Tatum—that she needs a normal family and a crazy Aunt Keys who hates men, isn't it? Will he marry someone else? Maybe one of these nurses will become Tatum's new mama. Will Tatum never know of her mama who gave her life? Will she never know about the McKellan traditions of tiaras and ring pops on birthdays? Will she never know me and how I would trade places with her mama in a heartbeat? I would give anything for Tatum to grow up like I had—in Piper's light. She would have been a fantastic mother because she already was—for me.

"Are you sure you're ready for this, love?"

I look at Tatum asleep in my arms and then at Kenny. "I will be."

It's not a yes or a no, but a simple statement. I'll honor my sister's wishes. I'll find the strength to get through this for Tatum. Her life has just started, and while I wish it had started a little differently, these were the cards she was dealt. She has a good father—I hope, who I won't let erase Piper or me out of her life. I'll pick up where Piper left off and love this baby enough for Piper and me. I'll use everything she taught me—everything she did for me, and I'll pour it into this little girl, so she'll know her mother and all her goodness.

Warm hands press down on my shoulders, giving me the strength he promised yesterday.

I might not be Astor's biggest fan, but I'm not silly enough to think I can do this without him and Kenny by my side.

"When you're ready." Dr. Cox stands at Piper's bedside, a nurse next to him. When I nod, they turn off the machines and disconnect the tubes. There's no noise. No audience. The lights aren't dimmed. Everything is just the same as it was. Everyone's lives are going on as planned while mine is being destroyed.

It's a humbling experience—a time where you're reminded that you were once someone's entire world, but to the world, you're just another body.

I'm not special because my sister is dying—that I hold the little girl she's leaving behind. We're no one.

Astor squeezes my shoulders, and I walk forward, past Dr. Cox, past the nurse, straight to my sleeping princess. "Piper," I say, watching as Astor rounds her bed too, pulling back the sheets and making a space in Piper's arms for her baby. "I'm sorry to disappoint you, but I didn't break Mr. Fancy Pants; your daughter did." Astor snorts, but I ignore it, leaning over and placing Tatum in the crook of Piper's arm. "I know, I wish it would have been me too, but I think we can all agree it needed to happen. Someone needed to knock him down a notch or two. He had far too many things going for him. Nothing like a surprise baby to humble a man, huh, Pipe?"

My sister doesn't move at my digs at Astor; she doesn't even stroke her daughter's head. "Look at him, Piper. Look at your prince—at your daughter." My voice rises. "Look at them, Piper! He won't know how to change her diaper or wipe her front to back. He needs a woman to tell him what to do." My words are coming out as fast as my hands are trembling. "We need you!"

I've turned into a full-blown lunatic. I thought I could do this. I thought I could let my sister go calmly, but I can't. My heart is crumbling as her breathing slows.

"Tell her, Kenny! Tell her we need her!"

Tears rain down Kenny's cheeks; he can't even look at me anymore.

"Tell her, Astor, tell her you need her! Make her wake up!"

The nurse must realize this is not going well since she pushes past me and scoops up Tatum. But then I realize when Astor takes Piper's hand, her tattoo mocking me as he brings it up to his lips and kisses her, it's time. My sister is drawing her last breaths. "I can never repay you for the gift you've given me. I can only promise to love her with everything I am. Rest, my friend." He lays her hand down and presses a kiss on her cheek. "I have your girls now."

I can't even digest his words; I can only feel white-hot rage as everyone just accepts Piper dying. "Don't tell her you have it covered! Tell her we need her! She can't leave us!"

Astor moves, his arms going around me in a flash, his embrace immovable, his words leaving no room for argument when he demands, "You can do this, sweetheart. Tell your sister you love her. Let her go knowing you're okay—because you will be okay, Keys. I'll make sure of it."

He's wrong. I won't be okay. Not without Piper.

Astor can't fix the broken. He couldn't fix my sister. He won't be able to fix me.

Shrugging off his embrace, I do what I've done for years and crawl into the bed next to my sister. Hugging her with all my strength, I offer her the only thing I have left as she takes her final breath in my arms— one last *I love you.*

CHAPTER TWELVE

Keagan

Red-streaked eyes and a steady throbbing in my temple is all that remains of my meltdown and goodbye to Kenny. He wanted to stay longer, but I wasn't very good company. Besides, he had a shift soon and a long drive ahead.

It's better this way anyway.

Something inside me changed when Piper left this world—something irrevocable.

I'm not the Keagan Kenny knew anymore.

Even walking down the hallway, not hearing the laughter from the nurses' desk or my feet touching the floor, feels strange.

Some would say I'm numb.

But I disagree.

I'm empty.

My body. My heart. My soul. Is utterly empty.

Piper took it all when she drew her last breath.

I am truly alone.

It's not the same as when my parents died.

I remember crying, but what I remember the most was my big sister pulling me close, rocking me back and forth, petting my hair, and promising me it wasn't the last time we'd see our parents.

I believed her.

I let her promises settle around me, warming me with thoughts of hope and a brighter future. One that she shattered in a single breath, leaving me cold, empty, without a family. Now, her promises are giant balls of pain. How am I supposed to leave here? How am I supposed to go back home to my life of writing game content and barhopping with Kenny? How can I create a happy ending when I have no happiness to give?

Everything I was rested in her arms.

Piper was my human.

My best friend.

My family.

My entire heart.

And now, all those things have been ripped away. I wasn't ready. All the days I spent by her side were merely a blink of an hour. I needed more time. I needed her to wake up and tell me what to do. I need to know how to go on when I have nothing left to live for.

"Ms. McKellan?"

I turn around and find a nurse standing outside the nursery door. "Is something wrong with Tatum?"

She's quick to reassure me. "Everything is fine, but…."

But is never a good word. "But what?" What in the world is wrong with my niece?

"We're having a hard time consoling her. I thought maybe you or Dr. Potter would like to try some kangaroo care with her, that often helps settle down the newborns."

"I don't know what kangaroo care is, but I'll get Astor." This is his job now; he'll be the one who needs to take care of her.

"We called him," she says gently. "He said we should ask you."

My eyebrows shoot up, and she hurries to explain. "I'm not sure what's going on with him. Dr. Astor is the best when dealing with children, but he seems terrified of his daughter for some reason. He won't even come close to her."

Well, we can't have that now, can we? I promised my sister that I would make sure Tatum is happy, and she can't be happy if her daddy is a scaredy-cat.

"Show me what to do."

I find him right where the nurses said he would be—in an empty hospital room on the couch, folded over his knees like a beautiful angel.

"Hey."

Astor lifts his gaze, his stunning blue eyes streaked red like mine. "Hey."

I nod to the tiny newborn in my arms. "The nurse said she was being you and upsetting everyone." Tatum decides to confirm by crying. "I thought you might like to feed her."

I'm not going to call him out just yet. Piper treated him delicately at the baby shower. Maybe he has a thing about kids. Maybe Piper took his secret with her?

Either way, no matter Astor's secret, Piper would want Astor to have a healthy relationship with their daughter no matter what.

Astor clears his throat, casting a wary glance at Tatum. "You can feed her. Piper would want that."

Okay, so he's going to continue to be difficult. Let me try a different strategy. "I think Piper would choke you with her purse strap if she heard your tacky refusal."

He shakes his head, a silent plea in his eyes. "Please, Keys. Please feed her."

And Tatum, just like her aunt, expresses her disappointment with the food delay by wailing. "Fine, but only because I don't think all three of us should be crying. Someone must be the comforter in this shitshow."

He's quick to correct me. "I wasn't crying."

I take the seat next to him on the vinyl sofa, not bothering to give him space. Instead, I slide right up next to him, so he's forced to smell his daughter's soft skin and see her eyes staring sleepily back at him. "Sure, you weren't, champ. But don't worry, I promised Piper-doodle I would stop giving you a hard time."

Surely, she'll forgive me if I fudge a little on that particular promise. She knows Astor can induce violent behavior.

Settling Tatum in the crook of my arm, I flash Astor a smile. "Last chance. Are you sure you don't want to pop the seal and feed the little gremlin the first of a gazillion bottles?"

He doesn't hesitate. "I'm sure."

"Have it your way." *Don't say I didn't try, Pipe.*

One-handed, I unzip my hoodie as the nurse instructed and pull down the neck of my sweater, exposing some bare skin on my chest.

"What are you doing?"

Is that shock or fear I hear in his voice? "I'm doing kangaroo care with Tatum. The nurse said it's important for infants to have skin-to-skin contact after birth. Did your fancy medical degree not cover that topic?"

He moves his head side to side, stunned.

I roll my eyes. And Piper thought this man was a score.

"Well, I suggest you pull out your phone and google it since your medical skills leave a lot to be desired. Doctor, my ass...."

"I'm not a neonatologist," he snaps back, "and it isn't like this whole thing hasn't been traumatic for all of us."

True, but... "I know becoming a father is a surprise. I get that. And becoming a single father is even more of a shock. Losing my sister and becoming a surprise aunt isn't my ideal vacation either. But this isn't about us anymore. Tatum is the only one who matters right now. Mine and your trauma will just have to wait. My sister would dig a tunnel through heaven to help me if I needed her. I'm going to make sure her daughter knows that we will too. We're all she has now. It's our job to make sure we don't fuck her up worse than Piper would've."

I hold out the bottle. "Now hold this for a minute while I attempt being a kangaroo for *your* child."

Astor swallows, his fingers absently wrapping around the bottle as his gaze tracks my hands, unwrapping his daughter (effectively pissing her off) and placing her baby skin onto mine. "Okay, give me the milk."

I don't miss the tremble in his hands when he passes me the bottle, which is so confusing. Why would a surgeon who specializes in kids be terrified of his own? Did he watch *Chucky* growing up, or does his mom have a doll collection that terrified him on stormy nights? What could possibly make a grown man scared of a helpless infant?

Sliding the nipple past Tatum's lips, she latches on and sucks aggressively, making her Aunt Keys proud. "Attagirl. You're going to hurt all the little boys' feelings at the bar one day."

A noise, much like a shocked scoff, comes from my right, making me turn my head to the source. "Are you opposed to her making boys cry?" I narrow my gaze at Tatum's father.

Please tell me Piper didn't pick a pussy to be her baby's daddy.

"No, not the tears," he corrects, arching a brow, "just the bar."

I rear back. "What? You want her to grow up frugal and drink at home?"

What the heck? She'll never 'bust all the balls' as long as she's locked up in her apartment.

"I'm so not allowing you to raise my niece to be a smoking-hot cat lady."

A deep and crazy-sexy laugh rumbles from Astor's chest. "A cat lady? Is that really what you think about me?"

"Can you blame me? You seem a little too put together." Except for this whole shy around Tatum thing, but I don't say that. "And put-together people breed put-together children. But since you'll be raising Tatum without her mother, I can only imagine the whole protective dad ideology where you lock her away for safekeeping so no man—even boring ones like yourself—can taint her. Aka, you'll create a very hot and introverted cat lady."

I roll my eyes at his frown. "Cat ladies are amazing. I'm not talking down about cat lovers. Hell, my sister was Queen Cat Mama sans the cat. She couldn't help that she was beautiful and shy—she worked hard on that patio garden at her house—which I killed, by the way. I can barely remember drinking water myself, much less water plants. I'm just saying, Tatum, here, has my genes in her too."

Astor narrows his eyes, his lip twitching at the corner.

"Don't look at me like I don't know what I'm talking about. I've flipped past the Discovery Channel before. I know Tater-bug shares like a millimeter of my DNA. Therefore, with my involvement in her life, she'll be more like the hot dog lady at the park who yells profanity at the geese when they get carried away with that quacking while she's trying to write a love story about magical trolls under a shaded willow tree."

I'm panting by the time I'm finished with my declaration, which apparently amuses Astor, if his smile is any indication. "I see."

He fingers the blanket delicately, almost touching the tiny baby foot hanging out the bottom. "I'll be sure to write that down with all the other things I don't know."

"You think I'm lying to you about kangaroo care? Because I will find the nurse and have her…"

Astor's finger grazes the bottom of Tatum's heel.

Holding my breath, I watch as Astor becomes braver, moving his finger across the sole of her foot. "She really is beautiful," he muses softly. "I'll never be able to repay Piper for the gift she's given us."

I notice he says us and not him.

"Yeah," I sigh, "Piper is obnoxiously thoughtful." It takes me a minute to realize what I said and the crushing weight from earlier returns. "I mean, she *was* obnoxiously thoughtful."

Is this what I have to look forward to for the next year, as I painfully grieve my sister? Learning to refer to her in the past tense and not the present. She wasn't so thoughtful about that. Piper knows I only write in the present tense. She's changing up my whole brand—my whole life. What was she thinking, helping everyone her entire life and then up and dying on me without so much as a farewell card?

I didn't even realize I had started crying until I feel Astor's finger swipe along my cheek, catching a betraying tear.

"You don't have to do that," I tell him.

He sits back against the sofa. "Do what?"

"Baby me." I don't mean for the words to come out harshly. "I'll be fine. It's Tatum that needs you."

Ugly much, Keys?

"Who says I'm babying you?"

Was that a laugh? Did he just laugh at me? "This is a serious conversation. Stop trying to make it sound like I'm being ridiculous."

"Is that what I'm doing?"

The smile he flashes is not cute. As a matter of fact, it only pisses me off more.

"Um, yes. Clearly, only one of us in this room is ridiculous, and it isn't the one kangarooing a baby on her chest—which is so what her father should be doing right now, but he's scared."

Somehow, Astor manages to make me feel guilty when his smile fades into a tight frown.

"I'm not..." He swallows and glances at Tatum squirming against me.

"Scared? Sure you are, but let's pretend you aren't until the hospital discharges her." He'll have to hold her then.

Like I just told him I had lice, Astor springs up from the sofa, tugging at his hair while he paces, talking to himself? Us? Who knows? "I don't know what I was thinking. I can't do this. A baby?" He looks over at us and groans. "Babies need their mothers. I can't..."

His gaze looks far away as he stares absently out the window. Maybe I was wrong. Maybe Astor isn't scared of breaking Tatum. Maybe he's scared she'll break him.

"Don't worry. You have a big family, right?" I've had too much heartbreak this past week. I can't sit here and watch this man crumble.

"Just brothers," he mumbles, not taking his eyes from the window.

"But those brothers have wives, right?" I saw one girl in the room with him the other day.

"Not wives. Just an assistant girlfriend."

He's not making any sense. Not that he usually does, but now it's really bad. "You have a girlfriend who's also your assistant?"

He shakes his head. "My brother, Vance. His girlfriend is my assistant."

Don't be relieved, Keys. This is not your man. You do not care if he has one girlfriend or a hundred. He's Piper's baby daddy—and right now, a very broken one.

"Ah. I gotcha." I try infusing a little excitement into my words. "See? You have lots of help. Brothers and girlfriend assistants are notorious for being the best at child-rearing."

His head snaps back to me, any hope for lightness disappearing with the sharpness of his tone. "This is not a joke."

"Agreed. It would be in terrible taste, but then again, Piper always lacked a funny bone."

"Keagan," he barks, making my stomach respond by doing this tingling thing, which I quickly force down.

"Hate to break it to you, As," (It should be spelled Ass) "but this isn't the ideal situation for me either. As much as I love Tatum and want to do right by her, I'm not the ideal parental candidate. I still eat Froot Loops out of my ice bucket rather than wash dishes." I shrug. "Neither of us are gonna win any parent of the year awards, but I'm sure Piper only expects that we keep Tatum alive long enough until she can tell us what to do next." Seriously, this kid has Pipe-tastic's genes. She's going to rule Astor—and likely me—by the time she can form complete sentences.

"So, you plan on staying a while?" he asks.

I pause, leaving my mouth open mid-argument. "Not a while." Archer and Ass Face pop into my head. "I don't have much leave at work."

"You still need to settle Piper's estate, right?"

Right. Her estate. I forget my sister is the responsible one. She likely has a will and all that mumbo jumbo. "I don't know how to settle an estate. Do you think she left instructions?" Or a timeline on how long that will take? If I go to battle with Archer and HR to keep my job, I need to know how much time it'll require to settle everything.

I don't know if my face or the crack in my voice betrays me, but the big, annoying man sits down beside me, raising his arm as if he's going to hug me before patting me on the back in a very underwhelming and awkward manner. "I'll help you sort it out."

For once in my stubborn life, I don't turn down an offer from a man. "I appreciate it."

For a moment, all we do is sit in the small room, staring at the wall.

We're two strangers forced together by life-changing circumstances.

Dr. Astor Potter is the father of my sister's legacy—the only family I have left.

Piper would expect me to do everything in my power to make sure this little girl had a normal, happy life, despite growing up without my sister's love and patience. The same love and patience that I will miss with a passion. But I'm not handicapped. Piper gave me all the tools.

She gave me the greatest gift—her memory.

And it's my job to make sure I pass those memories and traits on to her daughter.

Keys, the Ball-Busting-Man-Hating Phenomenon, is gone.

In her place is Aunt Keys, the Ball-Busting-Baby Daddy-Tolerating Phenomenon.

I can be the responsible human Piper tried to raise.

And my first duty as a responsible adult starts with helping the man next to me. "I'm gonna need you to take your shirt off."

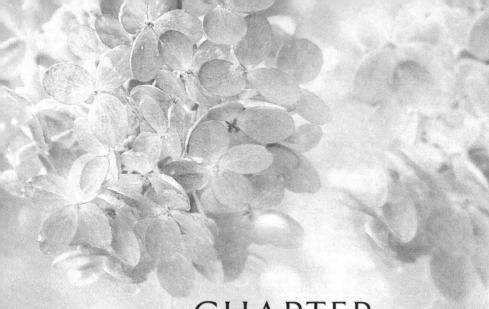

CHAPTER THIRTEEN

Keagan

"Pardon me?"

Did he—This man did not just say the word *pardon*.

"Hold on." I slip my hand into my pocket, pulling out my phone. "I need Google Translate. I don't speak old."

Astor pulls my phone away with a sigh, leveling me with this parenting stare that's impressive for a first-timer. "Why do you need me to take my shirt off?"

I startle Tatum with a deep belly laugh that makes her cry. "Don't flatter yourself, your highness. I'm not trying to hit on the elderly."

"I'm thirty-seven—far from old."

"If you say so." I shrug. "Just letting you know that I have a vibrator that you can't compete with, and sugar daddies aren't my thing, so no need to fret. I'm all settled with the single life, thanks."

"I'm not old," he repeats, seeming slightly offended, "and vibrators are for the timid."

I gasp. Did he just say what I think he said? "I'm not timid."

And like he knows I can't hit him with a baby in my arms, he offers me a shrug and a smirk. "If you say so."

Okay, I've had all I can take of this bonding session with Piper's one-night stand, baby daddy. "As enlightening as this conversation is, take your shirt off or the next time Tatum needs to be fed, I'll tell the nurses to bring her to you."

Total lie.

I'd never let the poor little thing starve, and reluctantly, I can't bring myself to see Dr. As-tronomical Pecs suffer either.

"I don't think it's—"

"—a good idea. I know, but I promised my sister that I would pass along her goodness, and she wouldn't let her baby's father go one more minute without holding his daughter." I flash Astor a severe look. "Your daughter needs you. Let her hear your heartbeat. You're all she has left in this world."

I nod slowly, watching Astor's gaze as the fear is gradually replaced with determination, his fingers going to the buttons of his shirt. "Let her know she isn't alone. Let her feel the power of being wrapped in your arms. Let her know she'll always be safe with you."

Astor has the first four buttons undone, and I've almost convinced myself that I need a hug from this man. "She needs her daddy… even if she confuses him with her grandpa from time to time."

I chuckle as Astor's hands stop. "I'm kidding, jeez. This poor kid will need Auntie Keys to teach her what a joke is. Clearly, she's not going to be exposed organically."

Shooting me a glare, Astor shrugs off his shirt. "I have a sense of humor."

I can't even find it in me to argue.

Because damn.

All I can think is…

Pecs.

Abs.

Ripples of flesh that my imagination can't even make up.

This man's body is divine. "Not wrinkled," I find myself muttering.

"Hate to ruin your joke and remind you that *all* of me is thirty-seven."

I nod, unabashedly staring. "You'll have to fix that. You're a dad now. All dads must have dad-bods. It's a rule. All the parents talk about it in online forums. You'll be cast out of the club with those things." I point at the hills of muscles on his stomach. This man definitely doesn't eat Froot Loops out of an ice bucket.

"I bet they'll let me slide this one time," he teases. "Since I'm a new father and all."

The nerve of this man leaning back against the sofa with the smuggest smile in the entire universe. It's like he's enjoying making me…bothered? No, I'm not bothered. I'm unimpressed. Yes, that's it. I've seen an amazing male body before. Astor's is nothing new.

Been there, rode that.

Okay, I likely flipped *that* off, but he doesn't have to know all the depressing details of my single life.

Sitting up, I turn serious, hitching Tatum up my chest. "You're not gonna puke on her, are you?"

It's as if Astor forgets what a monumental moment this is and stops, sucking in a sharp breath. "I won't throw up."

His words hold a finality about them. Honestly, I wouldn't have even questioned him if he hadn't gone pale when I shifted. But I feel deep in my soul that whatever scares this man about his daughter, he won't allow it to bring any harm to her. And I can live with that security.

"I'm going to put her on your chest now." I nod in the direction of his exposed chest, just in case he's forgotten exactly where that might be. "Right on top of your heart."

He doesn't nod or acknowledge me in any way. He simply locks his gaze on the infant in my arms as I stand, dragging in a shaky breath, just as I bend over and lay her over his heart.

It takes me precisely six deep breaths before I start crying.

And it's all Astor's fault.

As soon as I placed Tatum on his chest, his arms went around her. She looked so small, so protected in his bulky arms, that I couldn't stop the overwhelming feeling of joy as I watched Astor's eyes glass over as he lowered his cheek to her tiny head. But it was his body that sent me over the edge as he cradled his daughter and silently sobbed.

It was the first time I've seen him truly lose control.

He wasn't the put-together surgeon who promised to be strong.

He was simply a man.

A scared father who held his daughter for the first time.

I've never witnessed a moment as powerful as watching Astor hold his daughter skin to skin. And standing here—alone—as Astor loves on the only connection I have left of Piper, I can't help but revel in the beauty of the bond of a new family and drown in the pain of never having such a bond again.

My family is gone.

My bond is gone.

My girl is gone.

I'm full-on silent-sobbing, too, when Astor's voice breaks through the pain. "I need you, Keagan."

I raise my head, clearing my eyes and see true pain etched on Astor's face.

"I'm sorry?"

He clears his throat, taking a moment to settle himself with another breath. "I said I need you."

"You need me for what?"

I've found jumping to conclusions with Astor doesn't serve me all that well.

"I need your help with Tatum."

At first, I think he's just being nice and trying to include me in their little family bond, but then he takes my hand and squeezes. "I know you think I should be qualified to care for a child, but I'm not." He shakes his head. "Your sister knew I couldn't…" His voice trails off like he didn't mean to say all that.

"My sister knew what, Astor? That you work too much? That you're never home?"

Suddenly, leaving Tatum doesn't seem all that settling.

Astor inhales and looks me in the eyes. "I owe your sister a promise."

Ugh. I thought this was something juicy. "Don't we all." I wave away his concern. "Trust me. She expects us to back out of 99% of those promises. Piper knows we suck."

Just like Piper knows I'm not going to be nice to Astor forever. The honeymoon phase will wear off. He need not concern himself with that.

"No, before I went on the mission trip, we made a deal."

"A deal?" I arch a brow. "What kind of deal?"

He looks at Tatum on his chest. She's abandoned the bottle, preferring to sleep contently on her Hulk of a daddy. "A deal that I realize I want to see through."

Ugh. Why is he so annoying?

"Are you going to tell me what this deal is, or should I just get used to you speaking in code?"

The faintest smile appears on his face. "Do you trust me?"

That's easy. "No."

"Do you trust Piper?"

"Of course."

He nods. "Then help me honor my promise to her."

Does he not hear himself? "A promise that you won't tell me."

"A promise I won't tell you yet. But I will. I just need to make a few calls first."

"But then you'll tell me?" I arch a brow. "After you call some people?"

He pulls in a deep breath, seemingly finding his conviction. "Yes. When I get things settled, I'll tell you the whole story. I just need you to stay. I don't know what I'm doing with Tatum, and I could use your help."

He just had to dangle the baby and a mystery in front of me.

"I must admit your negotiation skills are quite impressive." I shoot him an unamused glare. "You know I would do anything to find out your dirty little secret." Even if it meant spending more time with him.

He flashes me a sly grin. "That's not why you'll do it."

Listen to him acting like he knows me. "Be careful, Dr. Potter. I'm not my sister." His cuteness won't work with me.

"Exactly."

After making a deal with Manipulative Dr. Potter, he left the hospital, leaving me to entertain Tatum. Tatum's doctor said she was doing amazing (I expected nothing less out of a McKellan woman) and would be discharged tomorrow, meaning she's going home. Given that Tatum was a surprise for Astor and me, we had nothing whatsoever in terms of baby supplies to care for the little gremlin.

But Piper did.

When I went to her house to shower, I noticed she had a whole nursery set up in what was once her guest room.

Tatum will never sleep in the nursery my sister designed, but Astor and I agreed she could use everything her mother bought. Piper would most definitely want that.

I just couldn't be the one to do it.

But I should have known Prince Astor would try to get on my good side and volunteer to take down the nursery and move it into his house.

In the coming days, I will need to pack up all my sister's things and decide what to do with all of it, but today is not that day. I was happy to send Astor to do what I couldn't.

I don't know how he will accomplish moving an entire room in one night, but he has brothers and money. I'm sure they'll pay someone to get it set up before we bring Tatum home tomorrow.

"Ms. McKellan?"

"Yes?" I glance up and smile at Tatum's nurse, Carly. Unlike the other nurses, Carly seems immune to Astor, so, right now, she's my favorite.

"I see you got her quiet." She nods to the little girl on my chest.

Apparently, Tatum loves this kangaroo care. I'd even say she loves kangaroo care more with me than with Astor. "Yeah, she wasn't all that impressed with Dr. Dad's rock-hard pecs. She prefers more of a pillow top."

Carly laughs, and I almost tell her I'm lying. Tatum was perfectly content on Astor. What pissed her off was him handing her off to me, so I could be the bad guy and change her diaper. The kid would rather be wet than disturbed.

"This is the quietest she's been." Carly touches the top of her knit hat. "I think she just needed her family."

Her family.

Me and her doctor daddy.

"I think she's just enjoying the bourbon we slipped into her bottle."

Carly pauses. "I'm kidding. She just likes me. I don't know what's wrong with her."

She may have also melted my heart with the sweet coos and nasty looks she gives. This little girl might just be the only thing that has kept me from breaking completely—her and her manipulative father.

"Well," Carly chuckles lightly, "I brought Astor's copy of the birth certificate. Can you give it to him? I'm off duty in another hour."

She extends the paper to me, and I hesitate to take it. "Is he supposed to do anything with it?" I don't know how these things work. Hopefully, Astor does.

"We'll file everything with the state. This is just a copy for his records."

Seems simple enough. "Okay," I say, taking the paper. "Thank you— you know, for everything. You've been very kind to us."

Without warning, Carly leans over and hugs me right in the chair. "You take care of yourselves. We're rooting for you." And like she just didn't say she was rooting for me like I was in the Olympics, she walks off.

I look down at Tatum, who hasn't bothered to wake up. "Your father brings out the silly in people," I tell her. Why else would Carly say something so weird? Only thoughts of Astor make people go squirrely. "Let's see if she wrote her number down on your birth record."

I said Carly was my favorite and acted the least wowed in Astor's presence, but she could just be a great actress. I don't put it past anyone.

Scanning the form, I start at the top and go line by line.

I don't get far because Tatum's name is at the very top.

Her full name.

Tatum Ruth McKellan Potter.

Mine and Piper's tattoo...

Astor knew the significance.

And he kept the tradition.

And my sister's last name.

CHAPTER FOURTEEN

Astor

"**S**omeone has to do it."

I'm fucking exhausted, so I don't mean for my words to come out clipped at Halle. "No."

"Astor," Halle's arms come around me in a hug, "I know you guys have been through the pits of hell the past week, but not only do I think Piper would want this, I think you both deserve this little piece of normalcy."

I stare at the wheelchair. Its very presence disturbs me. "Nothing about this situation is normal, Hal. Let's not pretend otherwise."

"Fine," Vance clips, stepping in, "how about you sit your ass down anyway. We'll stop pretending, and you'll stop being an asshole." He pulls Halle away from me.

"I'm sorry, Hal. I didn't mean—" I run my hands through my hair. "I just have no idea what to do right now."

Halle offers me a soft smile, her gaze drifting to Keagan at my side.

"I get it. This isn't a normal situation, but you can salvage this small moment of joy." She reaches over and takes Keagan's hand. "You might not have birthed this little girl, but you're the only family she has. She's going home with both of you, where you will love her unconditionally, right?"

Keys nods, a lone tear sliding down her cheek.

"One day, when the pain isn't as raw, she'll want to see pictures of this moment. Are you ready to tell her you didn't take any? That you couldn't muster up the courage to show her that even though you were in a tremendous amount of pain, you remained joyful when you left with her in your arms." She pulls Keys in for a hug, squeezing her tightly. "I know this is hard, but you guys are strong. You will teach this little one that she was the light in this dark moment."

This dark moment…

A moment where Keagan will walk out of the hospital without her sister.

A moment where I will walk away as an undeserving father.

Neither of us knows what will happen once we leave these doors.

Apart from each other, we're respectively alone in this.

We're the only ones who can understand what each other is going through.

We're dysfunctional enemies who've been thrust together, fate demanding we become a team.

We're all each other has.

"It should be you." I step back, placing my hand on Keagan's lower back, gently pushing her toward the wheelchair.

She flips around, swiping angrily at the few rogue tears. "You should do it. I'm not her mother."

"Neither am I."

She looks at me like everything she's ever hated stands before her.

I don't blame her.

Fate is cruel.

Fate left her alone in this world.

Fate left her with me.

"You're her father." She grits her teeth, each word coming out like

103

a hiss. "You should carry her out. She'll want to see you holding her in the pictures."

Someone—likely Vance—sighs.

"I'm serious." As she stares at Tatum in the hospital's bassinet, Keagan's voice trembles. "I need you to do it."

Because she can't.

"I—"

Before I can tell Keys that she can do this, I feel a wheelchair hit the back of my legs. "Sit down, Astor, and take your daughter home."

Vance.

I look at Keagan, her eyes silently pleading with me.

I can't let her not be part of this moment.

I can't let her walk out of the hospital alone.

"We do this together," I offer. "Me, you, and Tatum."

Her lip quivers, and I can tell she's torn between knowing what we should do and what she can handle.

In these moments, someone finds the courage to do the unthinkable.

It's in this moment, Keagan is brave.

"Okay," she concedes, fighting back the tears.

Everyone is quiet as Keagan takes a few hesitant steps toward me.

I lower into the wheelchair and reach for her hand. It's shaking when I wrap my hands around it and tug her forward. "We can do this."

Keagan lets out a small whimper, blinking twice before looking up at the ceiling, finding the last of her strength to take the final steps into my arms.

I smile when she glares at my thighs widening.

There's my girl. Find that hate and use it to drive away the pain.

"If anything pokes me, I will cut it off." She looks at Halle and flashes her a tight grin. "After the pictures, of course."

Halle belts out a laugh, easing the tension just a little. "That's all I'm asking."

Keys nods, pulling in a deep breath as she flashes me one more warning look before she removes her hand from mine and turns around.

Placing my hands on her hips, I guide her down onto my lap. She's stiff, and it's not easy for us to get comfortable. But then again, nothing about this situation is relaxing.

"Alright, Auntie, scoot back."

Keagan and I tense as we watch Halle scoop Tatum from the bassinet and walk over. I take a deep breath. This is it. I'm leaving with my daughter—away from the woman who gave her to me—away from the woman who sacrificed everything for this moment.

I pull Keagan into my chest, my arms lying over the tops of hers, interlocking our fingers. "Thank you," I whisper. "Thank you for doing this with me."

The only response I get is a squeeze from her hand. We're barely holding it together. While I'm thrilled to be a father, I'm not happy about how I got here. I'm also not over the shock of how drastically my life has changed over the last few days.

And Keys, well, I'm positive she loves Tatum as much as I do. But for her, she's leaving what family she had here. She doesn't know how this will work with Tatum and me. How often will she see her? Will we both adjust to our lives without Piper? Does Keagan go her way, and I mine, sharing the occasional picture of Tatum?

We both are blindly walking into futures we never considered. Our old lives have been obliterated—our futures changed with the last hope we had for Piper's recovery.

All of those things must be mourned.

But when Halle places Tatum in Keagan's arms, both of our arms cradling around her, I know in that instant that whatever future we have, we'll always be bonded by this moment—one filled with bittersweet joy as my brother pushes us out to the car, smiling as the cameras snap picture after picture. But it's behind those smiles, where the pain still bubbles up to the surface, where we fight.

To take the moment back.

To make it ours.

I hug Keys and bury my face in her neck, taking her strength as she smiles and coos at Tatum. The world has taken so much from her, but she's still here, sitting with my daughter in her arms, sacrificing herself. For her sister. For her niece. For me.

Keagan McKellan is a fucking hero. She just doesn't know it.

Our moment of joy doesn't last long.

"No."

I tap my fingers on the steering wheel. "Why not?"

"Because, unlike my sister, I'm not wowed by you. Nothing on this shitty planet would convince me to stay with you tonight." She glares out the window, watching the scenery. I might have missed the turn to Piper's house and suggested that she just come home with us for a little while.

"I didn't wow your sister," I argue. "But even if she was, I'm merely asking you to take a detour. Let me get Tatum settled. Then I can take you to Piper's."

"Why not take me to Piper's now?"

Because I didn't miss the tears she swiped away a few minutes ago. She shouldn't be alone. And, unfortunately, apart from a newborn, I'm all she has left.

"Because I don't like driving around with Tatum in the back seat during rush hour."

I cock a brow, daring her to argue with me that the twenty minutes of traffic we just sat through is safe enough with the infant in the back. You never really think about how unsafe the road and the world are until you have a child in your back seat. My worries have changed in a matter of days. Traffic would usually only serve to annoy me. Now, it makes me feel like catastrophe is waiting, just outside my window, for the worst time to strike.

I catch Keagan glancing in the mirror. Like me, she doesn't want Tatum in this car any longer than she has to be. "Whatever, but you're taking me home. I'm not staying. Don't even try to bribe me with more hints and promises about your secret."

"Believe it or not, I'm not thrilled to let you in on my 'secret,'" I counter. "I'd prefer to handle it alone, but I can't. I need someone."

She may say the hints won't sway her, but they redirect her anger into curiosity. "Why not ask your brothers?"

"They don't know." Nor will they, if I have any control over it. "The deal was between me and your sister." And I was going to back out of it as soon as I saw Piper again. But now, after everything that's happened, I can't.

"And now me—once you tell me, that is?"

"Correct, but I still need to make some calls and get Tatum settled first. Do you think you can be a little more patient? I promise, I'm not trying to keep you here longer than you want. I just need a little time to acclimate to being a new father and—"

"—making those calls. Yeah, I get it. Just know that my patience is much shorter than Piper's. So don't go thinking about trying to charm your way into my good graces, just because you picked out a great name for my niece."

I raise my brows. "Is that a back-handed compliment I hear?"

"Don't be cute. It won't work on me. I'm immune to your charm."

I can't help the laugh that escapes me. It's a welcome reprieve from all the pain. "Oh, so you think I'm charming too. And here I thought you hated me, Keys."

She fights back a smile. "Hush, before I end up hurling in your car."

It's not confirmation that we're friends, but it's close.

Somewhere during the last fifteen miles of traffic, Keys fell asleep. I thought she would wake up when I pulled into the garage, but she didn't. The girl sleeps like the dead.

So I take Tatum in first, setting her carrier down on the floor while I carry her insane aunt into the house wedding-style and into the guest bedroom, laying her gently on the mattress. Keagan's eyes flutter open as she looks at me, leaning over her. "I can't even be shitty to you right now, and that's more upsetting than it should be."

I grin, grabbing the throw blanket at the foot of the bed. "I'm calling that progress."

"Don't be a good guy, Astor." She pinches her eyes shut. "It just makes my heart hurt worse."

Pulling the blanket over her body, I kiss the crown of her head and whisper, "Sometimes, healing hurts worse than breaking."

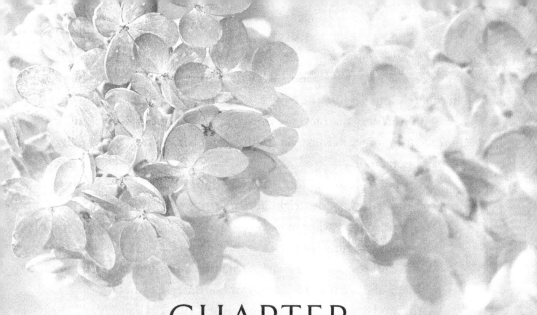

CHAPTER FIFTEEN

Keagan

It's midnight, and Tatum is already about to be fatherless.

"You said you'd take me Piper's"

Astor has the audacity to be lounging in his pajamas. His pajamas! Like he's getting ready for bed and not getting ready to take my ass Piper's like he promised.

"Good evening to you too. Would you like a drink to take that attitude down a notch?"

What would take my attitude down would be wringing his neck, but since that isn't going to happen, I grab the drink from his hands and down it in one gulp. "Thanks, now, can we leave?"

Unbothered, he takes the glass back. "It's midnight. Tatum is already asleep."

"She's a week old. She's always asleep. That's not an excuse to keep me prisoner."

I've resorted to theatrics.

Sleeping in Astor's guest bed wasn't the worst thing I've experienced lately, but I'd like the time to scream and cry in private. Being here with him only distracts me from thinking about my sister. And I don't want to forget her just yet. I don't want her memory to fade like my parents' memory.

"A prisoner?" Astor quirks a brow, fighting off a grin that I'm sure my sister thought was downright adorable.

"Yes, a prisoner. I want to leave. Now."

He stands, pushing me back a step. "And do what?"

Well, I can't just say *have a meltdown* now, can I? "I need to pack my sister's things and see if she wrote down her funeral wishes."

Astor nods, pushing past me toward the kitchen. "We'll go tomorrow."

My mouth drops open. "There will be no we. You either take me to Piper's right now, or I'll call an Uber." Just who in the hell does he think he's talking to? No man runs me. No matter how sweet his intentions might be.

He grins, completely unfazed. "Can I make you something to eat?"

"Are you planning on ignoring my demands?" Gah, has no one ever told this man no?

"I plan on making you something to eat. You haven't eaten all day, and before I drive you home, I want to make sure you've at least eaten something."

Ugh! "I hate when you do this!"

"Do what?"

Now he wants to be charming. He knows exactly what I'm talking about, and you know what? I refuse to play into his games. If he wants to play nice guy, I'll let him. "Fine. I'll eat. What are you cooking?"

For once, he looks sheepish. "How does casserole sound? Halle said the ladies at the office baked enough to keep us fed for a couple of weeks."

He says *us*, like Tatum will actually eat solids. Because I know he isn't saying *us* as in him and me. I agreed to stay and help him with Tatum. I didn't promise to play house with him. "How considerate of your employees."

"They are. Especially the ones trying to get in good with my brother." He spoons out more food than I'll eat in a week.

"Sounds like a firing offense to me." This is why women get a bad rep in the workplace. The last thing I want to do is flirt with the men in my office. Smother them, maybe, but definitely not flirt. I can't even imagine baking Ass Face a casserole.

"For being nice?" Astor chuckles. "Seems like a PR nightmare waiting to happen."

He pops the plate in the microwave and sets the timer.

Unfortunately, I've taken several steps closer, looking like I'm actually interested in this conversation. "I mean, they are flirting in the workplace."

He cocks a brow. "Have you never kept the day interesting with a little flirting among coworkers?"

The words, *like you did with my sister,* are on the tip of my tongue, but I hold them back. I'm tired of hating the world—hating Astor—who is making it seriously difficult to continue to do so anyway. "The day I flirt with the men at my office will be when I drown myself in a gas station sink. There is no excuse for flirting where I work."

I admitted too much. I realize it when Astor's brows nearly reach his hairline. "I don't know if I should be shocked you have a punishment already planned for yourself or the fact you're so passionate about it."

Let me clear this up right now. "I don't like men, especially ones at my office."

"Any particular reason?"

I pull out a chair and roll my eyes. "Is there any particular reason you're prying?" My sister may have shared all the pillow talk with this man, but I will do no such thing.

"Just curious where all this hostility comes from."

It comes from always being the one who worked weekends and nights just so she could pitch an idea to the boss and have him take the credit.

It comes from the guy I slept with in college only using me to get the answers to the midterm he didn't study for.

It comes from the boy next door who asked me to prom only to spread a rumor about me when I wouldn't show him my tits in the back seat.

It comes from my TA at college who proposed I drop under the desk and blow my way to an A.

You could say I've been burned by men, Dr. Potter, and so far, I'm not impressed with the overall species.

Except for you.

You seem to be the cool weirdo in the Dong Association.

"I'm just an asshole." It's partly the truth. I've been an asshole to him and Ass Face and others. It's safe to say I'm not at a sweet phase in my life.

Walking over, he places the food in front of me. "I highly doubt that. I've met assholes before. You aren't one of them."

I don't know what to say to that, so I shovel in a massive bite of food. "Ow!" I mumble around the scorching hot pasta.

"It's hot. I'd let it cool off if I were you."

Now he tells me.

"Here." He picks up the plate and blows.

I swear my eyes widen to the size of the plate itself. This man—this surgeon—is blowing on my food. Like I'm a child.

"Now," he places the plate back in front of me, "try it."

Now try it.

Like it's the most normal thing for two strangers to do. I don't even have the heart to say something snarky about the likelihood that he just spit on my food. All that courses through my body, heating my fingertips, is the memory of my sister doing the same thing when I was sick, and she made me chicken noodle soup.

This can't be healthy, right?

I mean, surely Astor does this for everyone. It's not just me. I'm not special to him. He feels sorry for me and is trying to do for me what any big brother would. Like Piper, he can't help himself. Doctors go into the field of medicine to help people. They have God complexes.

Yes, that is all this is. Astor is being nice to me because it makes him feel better.

"Thank you," I manage to choke out.

He tips his chin, a slight redness flushing along his cheeks. "I don't use the microwave very often."

Is this his way of saying he's sorry for nuking dinner and burning the roof of my mouth?

"I eat out most nights."

I take another bite—which is actually really good. "It's okay. I eat out most nights too." I shrug. "It's not worth the dishes."

I think of the takeout containers probably growing mold in my refrigerator. "Piper hated eating out. She thought the portion sizes were too big."

Astor throws his head back and belts out this deep belly laugh. "She was so full of shit. You've never seen her at the taco bar. The woman ate until she was sick." He folds over his knees and shakes his head. "She was a beast with chimichangas."

The way he talks candidly and lovingly about Piper has me smiling. "You didn't see her with those little peanut butter Easter eggs. I swear she only bought them for me, so she could eat them."

Astor lifts his eyes to mine. "You don't like peanut butter?"

His eyes feel magnetic as they pull the explanation from me. "I like peanut butter fine, just not eight pounds of it."

His freaking smile…

This is how Piper caved to his advances.

"Did you love my sister?" The question explodes out of me, and I almost take it back when I see his face fall into something that resembles pain.

He pulls in a breath, his gaze going to the ceiling before answering. "I will always love your sister for many reasons, but not the one I think you're asking."

Somehow, his answer doesn't crush me. If my sister loved this man like that—like that unconditional, crazy type of love, she would have told me about him. She wouldn't have been able to keep him such a secret. "So, you didn't love her as a girlfriend?"

Cautiously, he moves his head to the left, before slowly moving to the right. "Like you, I have my issues too."

"And also, like me, you're an asshole?"

He barks out a laugh, easing the tension of our heavy topic. "Exactly."

"So, you and Piper were truly just friends?"

He tips his chin. "Amongst other things."

Heaven help me decipher this man's explanations. "Other things like what? You being her Tuesday night hook-up?"

"Your sister wasn't a one-night stand." His voice holds finality. "Our relationship was more than when we… conceived Tatum."

It's interesting that he doesn't want to admit he and my sister had a sloppy hook-up.

"I'm not judging," I try explaining. "I'm proud Piper pulled a one-nighter. It likely was the only time she did." A pain settles in my chest as I think of all the other firsts Piper won't have. "There's nothing wrong with having a standing guy friend for those lonely nights."

Not that I know anything about that life, but if there were ever a man I could tolerate longer than five minutes, I would most definitely work out a similar agreement.

"But that's not what our relationship was." He pours another drink, like this conversation is too much for him to handle right now.

I take another bite of the casserole and give him time to settle himself before I add, "I'm sorry. I didn't mean for it to sound like you were my sister's whore. When I'm upset, especially at men, I lose my verbal filter—not that I was trying to be insulting. One-night stands are totally acceptable in my book." Nothing is coming out right. "You know what? Never mind. I'm just an asshole, and I'm sorry. I'm sure whatever you and my sister had was beautiful."

I stand. There's no reason I need to stay here any longer. All I'm doing is offending this man, who has been very kind—to my sister and me.

"Your sister was my doctor."

I pause.

"I, uh… I'm not ready to explain everything, but I want you to

114

know that your sister was helping me through something, and we...." He shakes his head. "We had a few drinks, and things got out of hand."

His forehead creases. I recognize that pain. I know that pain. "Well, that makes so much more sense than her just taking a ride on the Dr. Potter train for fun. I should have known she felt sorry for you."

He barks out a laugh. "Are you saying I was her pity fuck?"

I shrug. "If it wasn't a relationship or a one-night stand, as you said, it doesn't leave room for much else."

He nods, seemingly amused with my definitions. I'll be honest. For some crazy reason, I'm relieved to know Astor and my sister weren't a regular thing. "Okay, I'll agree to that definition of what happened."

I smile, but only because he is, and if I let the worry I suddenly feel about this man seep through, he might backtrack and never tell me more. What happened to this man that my sister would feel sorry for him? Not that I think it was a hardship to sleep with him, but why? Piper would never cross the doctor-patient relationship line unless she had good reason.

And that reason, I'm betting, is why they made a deal. The one he feels the need to follow through with even after my sister is gone. This man isn't just a pretty face with an MD behind his name. This man has demons he's ignoring right now by taking care of his daughter and *me*.

Maybe it's time someone took care of him.

"It's late," I say. "Would it be okay if I just stayed here tonight?" The least I can do is let him get some sleep while he can. "I can help you feed Tatum throughout the night and leave in the morning." Piper's funeral arrangements aren't going anywhere. "Would that be okay?"

He flashes me a smug grin.

"Don't. If you make one sarcastic comment about how you were suggesting that earlier, I will walk home."

He puts his hands up. "I didn't say a word."

"But you wanted to."

"But I didn't," he counters. "See how that works?"

Did I just say someone needs to take care of him? I changed my mind. "Don't get on my nerves, Astor. I'm just starting not to hate you."

And like Tatum knew she needed to break this up, she cries.

"I got her," Astor tells me, that big, stupid grin still on his face. "I'm sure she just wants to be held. It isn't time for her bottle. You finish eating, and I'll bring back something for you to sleep in."

He sprints off before I can even correct that delusional thinking of his. In no universe will I be wearing Dr. Potter's t-shirt to bed. I'm sure it's comfortable and probably smells divine, but it's the principle of the matter. I can sleep in my own t-shirt just fine.

But thirty minutes go by, and Astor never returns.

Surely they're okay, right? I mean, Tatum isn't crying anymore, but what about Astor and his pajama plans for me? He wouldn't have forgotten, right?

What if he collapsed again like before? He seemed okay, but... You know what? I'm just going to check on him. If he catches me, I'll say I was looking for those damn pajamas he promised me. This man has already seen me at my worst. I couldn't possibly seem any crazier at this point.

Walking down the hall where Astor disappeared, I peek into a couple of rooms that aren't Tatum's. One is an office that barely looks used, and another is a home gym that looks really used. It's not until I'm at the end of the hall that I find Tatum's room.

A room that steals my breath.

A room that is identical to the nursery my sister had at her house. The wall art, the bedding... Even the rocker is the same. I thought he would just take the furniture, not move the entire nursery. The room is a replica, and there, on the floor, propped up against the crib, is a sleeping Astor.

I don't know what Piper was doing to help him, but I can see why she wanted to. No matter how much I despise men, I don't hate this one. I want to, but he just won't let me with all his love and thoughtfulness. What man would do all this? Who would make sure his dead friend's sister ate, that the nursery she took great thought in creating was used just how she wanted? He could have driven me to Piper's without an argument. He could have hired a fancy designer to decorate

Tatum's room in light gray, so it went with the overall color scheme of his house. But he didn't. He hung every piece of pale yellow and pink on his walls for her.

This man is honorable.

I can see that now. I can see why he mattered to Piper—why he matters to me.

I take a few steps inside the room, careful not to wake him, and peer over the crib's rails, noting a little girl fast asleep, her father at the foot of her crib like a sentinel. He shouldn't sleep there; he'll wake up with a kink. But he looks so peaceful. They both do, like they just need to be in each other's presence to rest—something I haven't done in a week.

Before I realize what I'm doing, I'm sitting on the floor next to Astor, my back against the crib just like his.

I tell myself it's just sleep I need when my head goes to his shoulder.

And it's just comfort we seek when his hand takes mine.

CHAPTER SIXTEEN

Keagan

I wake on the floor covered with a blanket.

At first, I thought my sore back was what startled my eyes open at the butt-crack of dawn.

But then I hear…

Gagging.

Astor is… oh my gosh.

"Keys! Please!" Astor begs from the changing table in Tatum's room. "I need your help."

I'd like to tell you I'm a better person and didn't laugh.

But that would be a terrible lie.

I start laughing. "I can't—"

I can't even respond as I watch Astor's big back heave forward dramatically. This grown man—a doctor no less—is retching like he's drowning in a porta-potty. It's absolutely hysterical, and I can't do anything but fold over my knees and laugh harder than I have in weeks.

"I'm serious, Keys. I'm going to be sick." He gags some more. "Do you want me puking on the baby?"

Now he's being *really* dramatic. "She weighs six pounds," I say, pulling myself from the floor. Last night's sleeping arrangement ended with my head slipping down Astor's shoulder and into his lap. I don't remember him moving or even getting up to change Tatum. I must have slept hard. Who knew Dr. Potter was more comfortable than a Sleep Number mattress? "What could possibly come out of her that is so revolting?" I tease, standing and taking time to stretch the muscles in my back. Didn't I tell Piper he would need help with diapers?

Astor coughs, trying to mask another dry heave.

"Really, Dr. Potter, I'm disappointed in your lack of professionalism. Surely blood and bone smell worse than baby poop." Not that I know if a bone has a smell, but Astor doesn't deal with guts, so a bone was the first thing I could think of.

"They don't, I assure you," he fires back.

I would shoo him out of here and handle it if I were my sister.

But I'm not.

Astor Potter is not using his man card to get out of changing his first poopy diaper.

"Well, now you can tell all your doctor friends that baby shit smells worse than blood and bone." I tease. "I'm sure they'll all be impressed you could withstand such a harsh working environment."

He dry heaves once more, and this time, I'm concerned he might actually barf on Tatum, but then he says, "Your sarcasm is not helping."

I step up to the changing table and see a little girl naked and likely confused. "Oh, I didn't mean for you to think I was trying to be helpful." I grin, leaning over and kissing the top of Tatum's sweet baby head. "Tatum looks appalled by your reaction to her natural bodily functions."

Astor flashes me a glare that I'm sure he means. "She's not appalled. She's getting cleaned up. She's happy."

I shrug. "True, even if you are taking half an hour doing so."

Gah, if I had my phone to document the eight thousand wipes he's used so far…

"Please, Keys."

He's resorted to panting out breaths. "Please. Just take over." Aw. He's begging. How the mighty have fallen with a bit of baby poop.

"Can I make you something to eat?" I wink, hoping my words remind him of last night when he ignored my pleas to go to Piper's. "I want to make sure you've had breakfast before I leave."

I swear he whimpers—a tiny little sound, I'm sure he hopes I didn't hear.

"Just keep breathing." I pat him on the shoulder and walk to the door. "And make sure you wipe her front to back. I'll start breakfast."

"Keagan, please." His plea shoots straight into my soul and shatters the ice there. "I need your help."

Dammit. "No, you don't. You're a doctor. You can certainly change a diaper."

His head drops to his chest, and he blows out a breath. "I probably can, but I'm asking for help anyway."

Don't you do it. Do not flash me that broken man look.

He does.

And those eyes, that stiff jaw looking intense and vulnerable…

"I *want* your help, Keagan. I want it."

Damn him. Damn him and that cute little bundle of kicking feet staring up at him like she already loves him more than milk.

"Fine," I relent, "but you have to promise never to look at me like that again." Or say that you want me. It does something to my heart that won't be healthy for either of us. He's Piper's baby daddy. I can't fall in love with him. That would be weird, and Tatum has had enough challenges already.

"Look at you, how?" Bless his heart. He genuinely looks confused. Like he didn't know he was using a look to melt the ice around my heart. "I looked at you how I always do."

That little line on his forehead isn't cute. Neither is his denial.

"Just move." I wave him away with my hand, completely ignoring his frown. I can't help it if the man doesn't realize just how sexy he is or how he, inadvertently, found the back door to my cold, dark soul. I don't have time to explain it. A little girl is tired of being cold, waiting on her daddy to figure out how to change her.

I manage to get Tatum cleaned up and changed into a new outfit, all in minutes. All the while, Astor just stands there, staring. "Now, class, can you tell me what you learned today?"

Astor's nostrils flare, that sexy hard line of his jaw prominent as he tries to look serious.

"Oh, come on. It wasn't that traumatic. Don't act like you're scarred for life."

Men are such wimps. No wonder God let women carry the children. Men wouldn't survive morning sickness.

"Shut up."

I burst out laughing. "Oh wow. *Shut up*. You have officially crossed over into the land of immaturity. Welcome, we're glad to have you here."

Elite my ass. Astor Potter might be the patriarch of Potter's Plastics, but a six-pound little girl brought him down to normal-people level. That's definitely the blood of a McKellan.

"Anyway, are you hungry? How do you feel about eggs over easy?" I tease. "Or is anything runny too soon?"

"It's too soon," he clips, never taking his eyes off me.

"Oh, well, maybe you'll feel better once you clean the glob of poop off your shirt."

I really do try to hold back my laugh, but it just erupts out of me when the color drains from his face, his eyes doing a slow sweep of his shirt until he gets to the hem.

"How the—never mind."

He reaches behind his shoulder and, in one manly motion, pulls the shirt over his head, leaving us both in a trance as I stare at his rock-hard body, and him at the shirt now on the floor.

My oh my, this man and his abs. "Do you ever just lie in bed and stroke yourself?"

Astor chokes, and I realize how that sounded. "I meant your abs, not your...." I wiggle my fingers at his pajama pants. "Not that. I just thought if I had abs like yours, I would lie in bed and just run my fingers through the ridges. It's like a roadmap. A very hard, very sexy roadmap."

I think Astor realizes I'm likely sleep-deprived and talking crazy since all he does is grin. And then ruins it. "I do believe that's another compliment, Ms. McKellan. Admit it. I'm growing on you."

I narrow my eyes. "Don't try and be cute. I just saw you cry over a dirty diaper."

"I was not crying."

"Sure, you weren't." Shrugging, I turn, walking back to Tatum's crib and laying her down. Looking at Astor's body clearly makes me stupid.

"I wasn't."

Those damn abs appear to my left, and I have to take a deep breath before standing up straight and facing them again. "Fine. You weren't crying. You were whining."

His jaw twitches, which only enhances that flexing muscle in his neck that—"Oh, no."

I cover my mouth, trying to smother the laugh bubbling out. "What?"

Oh my gosh. "You have a little—" I can't hold in my laugh as the color, once again, drains from his face.

"Please tell me it's not what I think it is," he begs, his eyes closing like this is the worst day he's had in a while. And dammit, if it doesn't hit that exposed piece of my heart.

"Stay here."

As funny as this whole morning has been, I have to draw the line somewhere. The man has suffered enough.

Hurrying over to the changing table, I grab fresh wipes before walking back over and pausing as I stand in front of him, realizing that I'll have to touch him. Memories of his hand rubbing my back as I laid my head in his lap come flooding back from last night. I don't even know if he managed any sleep, but he didn't move. He just sat there, the warmth and pressure of his hand soothing me into a deep sleep.

This man has made sure he's taken care of me, even when I've hated it.

I take a step toward him, his chest rising and falling in a way that lures me in closer until we're hip to hip. Neither of us makes a sound or a snarky remark when I raise onto my toes, my hand going to his shoulder and his to my hip, holding me steady. I ignore the slight tremble when I press the wipe to his neck and drag it across his skin a couple of times, making sure I got the small spot Tatum left behind.

But what I ignore the most is when I drop the wipes to the floor and throw my hands around his neck. His arms immediately go around me and hold me tight against him. I don't worry about where the sudden urge to hug him came from. I'm sure I'm lonely and just need human contact, but then again, maybe it's because I don't hate him like I do every other man. This man gets me. He's patient. He's kind, and just this once, I want to be there for him.

"Thank you," I whisper into his neck. "I don't think I've told you that, but I couldn't have made it through this without you." I would have died right along with Piper in that hospital bed.

His voice sounds different, thick and raspy, like he's been asleep. "You're stronger than you think you are."

Oh, this man wants me to be president of his fan club.

I tighten my hold, squeezing him one last time before pulling back and pressing my lips to his cheek. I can feel his chest, his heart beating faster as I drag my hand over his heart, my lips lingering on the slight stubble of his face. His body is warm, and the rhythm of his breathing seems to bring me peace. It's funny. I'm never at peace. Not with anyone.

Only Piper McKellan could make me feel like I belonged—like I was cherished. And here I am, soaking up the comfort from her child's father. I don't know if that makes me the worst sister in the world or simply human. But one thing I do know for sure is that I can't stay here.

Astor Potter isn't mine.

He was Piper's, and now he's Tatum's.

I push against his chest, and he lets me go.

This isn't healthy. We're both grieving. Nothing but pain can come from this situation.

So, for the first time in my life, I behave responsibly.

"I need to go."

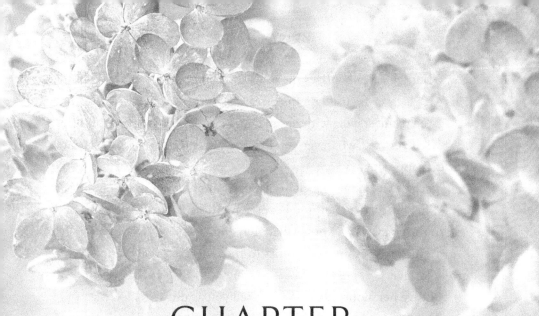

CHAPTER SEVENTEEN

Keagan

I should have known Astor would be a pain in my ass.

"What are they doing here?" I try smiling, but through clenched teeth, it probably looks more like I'm growling in Astor's ear.

"They came to watch Tatum."

"And why would they need to watch Tatum? All I asked for was a ride to Piper's. You only need to put her in the car seat while you *drop me off*."

Astor doesn't even bother looking at me. "We need to make funeral arrangements today. Tatum will be more comfortable here."

"What would make her even *more* comfortable is if she was here, *with her father*. Her Auntie Keys doesn't need any help with funeral arrangements."

"Well, her Auntie Keys doesn't get a choice in the matter."

I didn't appreciate the teasing tone in his voice when he said Auntie

Keys. But what really pisses me off is the fact he still won't look at me. His gaze is laser-focused on his brothers.

"You're not staying with me all day." I nearly growl for real this time.

"Tell yourself whatever you need to get through this, sweetheart, but it's happening."

Fuck it. I'm about to kick his ass in front of his entire family. I don't care if his brothers are arguing over something in the living room. I'll add to the chaos. "You know what? I'm gonna—"

Astor shushes me and points to the living room as Vance's voice grows louder.

"Leave her alone, Duke. I won't tell you again."

Duke stares his brother down, his jaw twitching. "This is none of your business. I wasn't asking for your permission."

"It's all our business! You will destroy our entire practice if you go through with this insane idea."

I elbow Astor in the ribs as the tension rises. "It's probably best you stay and break this up. I'll call you later." I use the opportunity and step back, but I'm jerked to a stop, noticing my shirt is gripped in Astor's fist. "Let me go," I whisper-growl. I'm not above getting louder and in-terrupting this family squabble.

"No." His voice is clipped, but his gaze is still focused on his brothers.

"You need to handle that," I suggest, hoping to redirect his atten-tion to someone other than me.

Astor leans down to my ear and drops my shirt, seeming to agree, but then he says, "Do not attempt to walk out of this house because I will chase you."

"Are you threatening me?"

I narrow my eyes to slits, just as he fingers a lock of hair before moving it off my shoulder. "I'm promising that we'll put on a show for the entire neighborhood if you disobey me."

Oh hell no. "I'm not your daughter. You don't tell me what to do." I don't know what happened in that shower he took earlier, but clearly the hot water washed away some brain cells. *Disobey me…* Have you ever? This man is delirious.

I lift my gaze and find him staring right at me, his jaw hardened, but what concerns me is his smile. A smile that I haven't seen on him before. A smile that screams danger. "Then run. Let's see who prevails."

Then run. Those two words manage to send shivers throughout my body.

I cannot with this man. "Crazy is not a good look for you, Dr. Potter. I suggest you tame that before you remain a bachelor forever."

What am I supposed to do with that statement? Test him? He seems quite serious that he has no problem looking foolish by chasing me through the neighborhood. And while I'm never one to back down from a challenge, I'm not in the mood to end up on the news and mortify Tatum when footage shows up years later of me and her father weaving through the bushes of million-dollar mansions while screaming profanities at each other.

I'm not saying I *won't* act crazy—especially if Astor keeps up his bossiness. I'm just saying I'm not in the mood right now.

So, I'll let this one slide.

We're both tired, and Astor is likely suffering from PTSD after the poo incident this morning.

"Go," I shoo him away, "and handle your brothers. I'm ready to get this day over with." I refuse to acknowledge the smug victory smile he shoots me before tipping his chin and walking away from me and toward his brothers.

Fucker. Just when I think he might not be so awful.

"It's good to see him smiling again."

I glance beside me and find Halle, the freaking ninja assistant, next to me. "Yeah, well, my client list is exclusive. My mission statement has always been to return surly surgeons back to their former charming selves. You can expect him back at the office very soon."

I can never just deal with uncomfortable situations in a normal manner. I always need to crack a joke, but Halle laughs more than she should at my lameness.

"Oh, you sweet girl."

Halle definitely doesn't know me well if she thinks I'm sweet.

"I remember those days of denial like it was yesterday." She leans in closer. "A lot can change in three months."

"Three months?" What is she talking about?

Her eyes widen. "You didn't hear?"

Apparently not.

I shake my head.

"Dr. Astor isn't returning to the office for another three months. He's taking paternity leave."

Oh, whew. "Good for him." My sister would be proud that he's staying home for an entire three months to be with his daughter.

Halle nods like she knows something I don't. "You both need the time to heal."

"Oh, I'm not staying," I correct her. "I don't have that much leave. After I settle my sister's estate, I'll be heading back home."

Her face falls, which is concerning.

Did she think I was staying with Astor? Did he make it seem like we were taking this leave together? Surely not.

"You're not going to stay here with Tatum?"

I shake my head. "I can't. My job isn't as lenient as Astor's. I'll have to go back to work if I plan on eating again." I shrug. "It's not an ideal situation, but I'm glad Tatum has Astor. He's a good father."

Halle nods like she understands, but she couldn't possibly. "What about family? Do you have support in Fairfield?"

Suddenly, Astor grabs Duke and hauls him away from Vance. "We'll discuss this later," he says all authoritative-like, which shoots tingles straight to my toes.

Vance, however, ruins the feeling when he grits out, "You aren't included in this." He pauses and flashes me a look. "You have enough to worry about. I said I'll handle it." Astor doesn't respond; he simply works his jaw like he's about to crack a tooth, so Vance continues, pointing at Duke, "And you'll stop whatever you're planning. She's not yours anymore."

Duke is in his face in seconds. "She's always been mine, not his."

Ah. I should have known they were arguing over a girl. The question is why Vance cares and what does this girl have to do with their medical practice.

But whatever. I don't have time for their drama. I just need Tatum's diva daddy to take me to Piper's, so I can make funeral arrangements for my sister.

"Well," I say, walking away from Halle and her uncomfortable questions, "now that that's settled, Grandpa and I have funeral arrangements to make. If you'll all kindly keep my niece alive and keep the emotional damage to a minimum, we'd appreciate it."

I grab Astor's arm and pull him toward the front door. "You sure Tatum will be okay with them?"

He pauses a moment like he's not as confident as he was a few minutes ago.

That's answer enough for me. "Stay here. I'll call you if I need anything." Which I won't. I can handle the arrangements without help from a man. I always have.

A hand clutches mine. "Not a chance. Let's go."

Piper's house feels like a museum. I'm scared to touch things, even the cup she left on the counter. All that's floating around in my head is that my sister touched that glass for the last time.

Grief is debilitating.

"I can help you search her files." Astor's voice breaks through my wandering thoughts. "See if she left a will."

I wave him off. "Knowing Piper, she had a will, and likely has it filed and labeled in her office. She was always the overachiever."

Astor tips his chin, his body seemingly tense since we walked through the door. "I'll be outside then."

"Okay."

I wait until Astor disappears out the back door, before I set my purse down on Piper's antique coffee table and breathe.

I can do this.

I can follow my sister's final wishes.

I can pick out the dress she'll forever wear, the barrette she always wore of Mom's most definitely needs to go in her hair, and her shoes… I don't know about her shoes. I vote she go barefoot. But, likely, Piper would want something casual yet stylish. She was the opposite of me; yet, we fit together. She was the yin to my yang… in perfect harmony with each other.

Fighting back tears, I walk toward Piper's office and stop.

Astor is in the backyard.

His shirt is off, and the muscles in his back flex as he cranks the push mower. Each pull is the catalyst of rippling muscles as they pull taut and release. It's like a dance, a ridiculous sexy dance made of only man and sweat.

Who knew the surgeon knew how to do yard work. It seems so beneath him; yet, he finally gets the lawn mower to crank, walking up and down Piper's small backyard. I don't know how often the grass needs cutting, but I'm sure Piper has a lawn service that will handle it, especially when I list her house for sale.

Like he knew I was watching him, Astor turns and levels me with a stupid grin that causes my hand to spasm and drop my phone on the floor.

I don't need it anyway.

I need to finish what I started and find Piper's will—in her office, and not by the French doors where her boy toy is mowing like a freaking gentleman. What is with the men in Bloomfield, Texas? Why aren't they shitty like Ass Face and Archer? Why do they make sure you eat, and that your sister's grass is mowed, even though she isn't there to complain about it?

It's a freaking mystery. Knowing men like Astor exist disrupts every factual conclusion I've drawn about men over the years. Men are selfish, arrogant, and entitled—especially at *GameTales* where I've done most of my research on assholes. They don't do nice things for women, unless there's something in it for them.

What's in it for Astor to cut Piper's grass? To help me make funeral arrangements?

I seriously can't find a reason he would do such things. He already knows I would never sleep with him, nor do I like him. (Okay, I like him a little, but not much.) It's baffling. I don't understand his motives and it's killing me.

It's like when he insisted on coming here to help me look for the will; he could have stayed home with his daughter and family. He could have caught up on sleep or answered emails. He literally could have done anything other than come over and help me dig through files.

He makes absolutely no sense.

Unless… Maybe he loves my sister in all those "other" ways he mentioned. Maybe whatever they had meant more to him than any other relationship? Maybe the people of Bloomfield are just nicer and have less to do than those who live where I do in Fairfield?

All I know is I've never seen a surgeon (other than Piper) be so giving—especially to someone like me, who pushes people away like it's a sport.

Astor Potter is a freaking mystery—a hot mystery, but a mystery all the same.

Pushing open the door to Piper's office, I take in the wall-to-wall bookshelves, brass wall lighting, and centuries-old furniture. Piper had such grandma-taste in decor. I swear, if our grandma was alive, she would be so proud of Piper's design choices.

Ignoring the open book on her desk, I head to the cabinet in the corner, pulling open the top drawer. It takes me all of two minutes to find the file I'm looking for: Last Will and Testament. She even labeled it in a pink folder, just like I said she would.

Oh, Piper-weanie, I would say you're predictable, but you ruined that by surprising me with your secret side-beau and a baby.

Sliding to the floor, I open the file, but then my phone rings from the living room. And to my ever-loving horror, I hear the back door open, and Astor say, "Hello?"

I spring up and dart into the living room with the file clutched in my hands. "Hang it up," I whisper-shout.

Astor gives me his back—his sweaty, muscular back.

I'm frozen to the floor. If I grab for the phone, I might accidentally touch him, and we all know that accidentally touching a man when he's shirtless always leads to crazy aftermaths—like reverse cowgirl on the kitchen island.

No one needs those kinds of memories haunting them when they are home alone and perpetually single.

"I'm sorry, she's in the middle of something. Can I take a message?" Astor carries on with the phone call like the world's hottest secretary.

"I beg your pardon?"

His body tenses.

Oh shit. "Hang up the phone," I beg. "Just hang up." It doesn't matter who's on the other end. They can thank me later, since Astor looks seconds away from punching something.

"I see," he says flatly.

Only Ass Face or Archer can cause rage like that. Kenny would have recognized Astor and the threat in his voice, only Tweedle Dee and Dumb would keep poking the bear. (Well, and me, but we're not talking about me here.) Screw it, sweaty or not, I can't allow Astor to ruin one of the only stable things I have left—my job.

I jump for the phone, but Astor holds it above his head, his angry eyes narrowing on me. "You let this asshole talk to you like this?"

"Which asshole?" I jump again, and he snags me around the waist, clutching me to his chest in a tight hold.

I give up fighting because, well, I'm just physically and mentally drained. If Astor wants to rip someone from work a new asshole, then who am I to stand in his way? For just this once, I'll let him be the buffer.

When Astor realizes I've stopped fighting, he pulls the phone back to his ear.

"I'll tell you what, Alan—"

Alan? Does he mean Archer?

"—you'll keep her job secure or her attorney will file motion after motion until your company goes bankrupt from legal fees."

I can't help it; I hug this mammoth of a man. No one has ever talked to Alan—who I'm one hundred percent certain is Archer—like that for me. I don't particularly need Astor's help with Archer, but I'm not all that turned off about it like I thought I would be.

"In the meantime, I suggest you email her for anything else you require in her absence. She'll let you know about the project."

He hangs up the phone and slams it on the island, his chest expanding and contracting with harsh breaths. I almost smile at how upset he is, but then he pulls me away and looks me in the eyes. "I better never hear him speak to you that way again." He leans down and ever so casually kisses my forehead, his lips moving against my skin with his words. "Handle him or I will. I won't warn you again."

CHAPTER EIGHTEEN

Astor

K eagan has hardly spoken to me since I threatened her about her boss a few days ago. "I'll take care of it" was all she said before she disappeared back into Piper's office, slamming the door and locking it behind her.

I was no longer a welcome guest. I had crossed the line and interfered with her job. But some things you can't look away from, and that dickhead, Alan or Asher, whatever his name is, is a prime example. How dare he call Keagan and leave a message with me that if she didn't get her ass back to the office next week that she'd be fired. What kind of man—what kind of boss—gives a grieving woman that kind of ultimatum?

A broke one.

At least he will be when my attorney is finished with him.

I have no qualms about going after a man that abuses his power. That's not the kind of boss we need around our wives, daughters, and mothers. This man needed to be put in his place. So, I don't care how pissed off Keagan is at me, it had to be done.

"Duke said he found her."

I nod at Halle by my side and point up the hill at the woman dressed in green. But it isn't her flowy jade dress that stands out amongst the throngs of people walking back to their cars in their funeral-black ensembles.

"What are you going to do?"

Halle pats Tatum on the bottom, attempting to stop her fussing. It's as if Tatum knows this is a day of mourning for her too.

"I don't know." I sigh, looking at the top of the hill where Keys sits—up in a tree, her legs dangling off an oak branch.

Piper's funeral was a beautiful yet ugly reminder that life is short and unforgiving. Piper deserved many more years on this earth, not just an elegant funeral that Keagan spent several days pulling together. She obsessed over her clothes—even the flowers. Keagan handled it, all just as Piper would have wanted. And it was stunning. The perfect sendoff for a beautiful soul.

I hand Halle my car key. "Will you take Tatum home and watch her for a couple hours?" Keagan never makes things easy, and I'm under no fantasy that she'll come down without an argument.

"Of course," she says, pulling me in for a hug, "take as long as you need."

"We won't be long." Today wasn't easy to endure. The last thing I want is to be away from my daughter longer than I need to be. "Tatum will need a bottle in an hour."

Halle flashes me a sad smile. "I'll take care of your little girl. Go take care of Keagan. She needs you."

I don't correct Halle. Keagan needs her sister, not me. All I seem to do is upset her more. "I'll be home soon. Drive safe."

I watch as Vance guides Halle and my daughter to the car, handing Remington the keys to his car, so he can drive the girls. It's times like this that remind me how fortunate I am to have such a big family—a family that is there for me, even when I might not always want the help. I don't know that I could have handled this all alone.

The cemetery has thinned to only a couple of people by the time I trek up the hill, heading toward Keagan. I can see her staring at the casket where her sister rests, her gaze far away from here, but I can't tell if she's crying.

"Don't come any closer," she warns.

Looking up, I find her gaze now on me. "Oh yeah? What are you going to do?" From this angle, it doesn't look as if she has any weapons or objects to throw.

"Go away, Astor. I'm not in the mood to see you in hero mode."

I choke on a laugh as I circle the tree, looking up. "Hero mode?"

Even this far away, I can see her roll her eyes. "Don't act like you don't know what that means."

"I don't," I admit honestly. "You'll have to excuse my lack of knowledge about gaming modes. I spent more time with books than video game consoles."

"I bet your parents are proud." It's not a compliment.

"They aren't—my parents, I mean. They're proud of Vance, not me." I slip off my suit coat and lay it on the grass. Keagan doesn't look as if she's coming down anytime soon, and Texas, even in late October, is still sweltering.

"Why not you? Aren't you and Vance both plastic surgeons?"

I nod. "We are, but my father doesn't judge success by how many lives we touch, but rather by how much money we can make touching lives."

"And your Grace of Mercy cruises don't bring any money into the practice?"

I smile. "You catch on quickly."

She looks away like she didn't mean to be caught staring. "How does Vance feel about your philanthropy?"

I find a low hanging branch and pull down on the limb, testing its strength. "Vance isn't my father. He's always supported my charitable work."

"Sounds like Piper," she muses. "She always supported my dreams, even when she didn't understand them."

"She didn't know what a game writer was?"

"She knew the basic concept of writing the storyline for video games; she just didn't understand why I didn't want to write novels or screenplays instead. Video game stories seem like the generic version of a writer."

"Is that what Piper really thought? That you were the generic version of a writer?" I find that hard to believe.

"No, she didn't. Well, at least I don't think she did. Piper was always supportive." She chuckles, wiping under her eyes. "She even played a few of the games I helped write."

"What? Dr. McKellan played a video game?" The thought makes me smile.

"Crazy, right?" Keagan shakes her head. "She never made it past level one, but she tried, and that meant more than any promotion I could ever receive."

Her sadness seems to saturate the air around us.

"I just keep thinking that I'll never get another excited squeal or bone-crushing hug from her. It's like my whole life revolved around wondering what Piper would think of this?" She twirls the tweed bracelets on her wrists. "I sort of expected her to rise from the dead and tell me that you can't wear green to a funeral." She scoffs, but it sounds more like a muffled cry. "But I didn't pack anything black. I didn't know when I left home that I would need to prepare for my sister's funeral."

"You look beautiful—that's what your sister would have told you if she were here." I move closer and hold her teary gaze. "She would have said you brought the light to a dark time."

She shakes her head. "I told you not to turn on hero mode."

I reach up, grazing her ankle with my fingertips. "This is friend mode, I'm no one's hero."

Her lips purse. "You're lying. You're a doctor who spends half a year on a boat, treating poverty-stricken children for nothing, not even for praise in the newspaper. If that's not a hero, then I need to brush up on my definitions."

"I enjoy children," I correct her.

"Is that why you had a baby with my sister? Because you both wanted a child?"

My neck feels warm as if the sun is beating down on it. "Not exactly."

"Not exactly?" Her eyes widen. "What's that supposed to mean?"

I grin. "I thought you were good with definitions?"

"I'm also good with aim." She breaks off a small twig like she might chuck it at me, but I already anticipated her threat.

Latching on to her ankle, I give her a tug. "I sure would hate for you to fall into my arms."

She scrambles to hold on to the branch above her. "You wouldn't dare."

I shrug, tugging once more, just so she doesn't drop her guard. "You said it yourself, I like hero mode. Nothing screams hero like a damsel falling straight into the hero's arms."

"Now you're just being annoying."

But she isn't seeming so lost. Her fire is back, even if it's directed at me. "Well, I tend to get annoying when I'm hungry."

She doesn't miss a beat. "Then go get something to eat. No one said you had to wait on me."

Dropping her ankle, I sit, leaning back against the tree trunk, making a show that I don't intend on going anywhere without her.

For a moment, we both simply relent, and relish the peace with the birds chirping overhead. The world doesn't know of our pain, it simply keeps spinning, keeps growing. We're the only ones on pause.

"Why are you up in this tree anyway?" I finally ask after a moment. "Don't tell me, you were a tree climber as a kid?"

There's a beat of silence before she sucks in a breath and speaks. "No, I wasn't a tree climber. Piper was. She started after our grandma died." She breathes in and out like she's trying to keep calm. "Dad noticed it too and built us a treehouse, but Piper would never play in it. Instead, she climbed the tree next to it." I gaze up and see her staring out at the men filling the grave with dirt. "I asked her once why she'd rather sit on a limb, and she said it was the closest she'd ever get to Heaven—to grandma." Keagan shrugs, swiping under her eyes. "Since I know Piper is with the angels, I wanted to be as close to her as I could. She's not in that grave anymore."

I stand, dusting off the back of my pants, and reach out for the lower limb.

"What are you doing?"

Gripping the limb, I hoist my body up, making sure my foot is secure before grabbing hold of the next limb. I don't need to tell Keagan what I'm doing, she knows. Very carefully, I adjust to lean against the trunk. I don't know how sturdy the branch is, so I keep my distance, searching for another.

"Astor!" She raises her voice like that's going to make a difference. "Get down! You're going to hurt yourself."

"I thought you said I was a hero?"

She cuts me a sharp look. "You're going to be a hurt hero if you don't cut it out. You're a doctor for goodness' sake. I bet you've never even climbed a tree before."

I would never admit that she's right. My father made sure our outdoor time was kept to a minimum. Potters studied; they made good grades and stayed focused. There was no room for imagination or free time.

"I can climb a tree just as well as the next man," I argue, snapping a branch.

"Oh my gosh! You're going to fall!"

Finding a better angle, I adjust my body and wedge myself between the limb and the trunk. I flash her a wink. "Can you hush? I'm trying to enjoy the peace up here. You're making it quite difficult with all that worrying."

She looks aghast. "Me? You're—"

I hold my finger to my lips and shush her. She wanted to be close to her sister, and I want to be close to her. She needs to know she's not alone—I'm with her, even if she'd rather I not be.

I don't know how long we sit in the tree. Halle texts and tells me that Tatum is sleeping and not to rush home. So I don't. I sit until my legs grow numb and my stomach growls.

"You should eat."

I glance over at Keagan. "I'll eat when you do."

She rolls her eyes. "I'm not hungry."

"Neither am I."

"I literally just heard your stomach growl," she argues.

I shrug. "I'll be fine."

The leaves rustle and I have to force myself to keep still.

"Come on, let's go feed you. The last thing I need is you passing out in this tree and breaking your neck. Tatum would never forgive me."

I watch as she carefully slides down the branch, wedging herself in next to me. She smells of honeysuckle and sunshine.

"Why are you looking at me weird?"

How am I looking at her?

Smiling, I reach out, and surprisingly, she allows me to tuck a wayward strand of hair behind her ear. "Thank you for letting me sit in your tree."

At first, I think she's about to tell me to shut up, but then she sighs, and leans forward, looping her arms around my neck. "Thank you for not leaving."

Balancing my weight, I keep one hand on the tree while the other pulls Keagan closer to my chest. Her nose goes to mine, her eyes downcast as we both just breathe. Here in this tree, close to the Heavens as Piper said, we're in our own world. The pain inside us fracturing our very souls, but we're still standing, with each other.

I don't know who moved first, maybe it was her, maybe it was me, or maybe the ground shifted and gravity pulled her closer. Either way, her lips part on an exhale and I press my lips to hers.

Body trembling, Keagan's hands move up the back of my neck, knotting in my hair. We don't overthink it, we simply give way to our bodies, to our grieving hearts, taking what each other desperately needs—love. In this moment, exploring the taste and feel of each other, we simply exist, soothing the pain in one another. In this tree, with our lips moving frantically, we find peace.

Keagan pulls away, her breath ghosting over my lips. "We can't do this," she explains. "You're Piper's."

Inhaling, I lean my forehead against hers. There's no need in arguing that I never belonged to Piper. Keagan needs a reason to keep this barrier up between us, and unfortunately, I'll do anything she needs to help her through this.

Pulling back, I offer her a smile. "Come on, let's get you something to eat."

"No." She shakes her head. "I can't betray my sister."

"You're not—"

She doesn't give me time to finish before she jumps down to the ground and walks away.

Sometimes you know when someone has shut down, and Keagan has not only shut me out, but she's also barricaded the door.

CHAPTER NINETEEN

Astor

Keagan refused a ride home.

What's worse was seeing her get into an Uber with shaking shoulders. She was sobbing from kissing me. I don't know what made me feel worse, the fact that I didn't regret kissing her or the fact she did. Mine and Piper's relationship was based solely on friendship—a complicated friendship—but a friendship, nonetheless.

But explaining it to Keagan will open wounds that I'd still like to ignore a little while longer. I made Piper a promise, and while I had planned to renege on that promise, having Tatum and losing Piper put things back into perspective. Piper was right; I was allowing social norms to control my reaction—to control my life. If I want to achieve my goals, then I need to humble myself. I can't allow pride to control me any longer—well, any longer after a few more days. I'm not quite ready to spill everything to Keagan.

Keys thinks she wants to know the arrangement between me and her sister—and she does for the most part. Piper was my friend and my doctor, what we agreed when Tatum was conceived is where I lock down the sharing circle. I just need a few more days to sort things out and make arrangements for Tatum, and then I'll tell Keagan everything. Right now, it's best if she focuses on healing, which I don't know if she's doing because she wouldn't answer her phone or come to the door when I checked on her.

The kiss upset her.

I get it, and if I'm honest, it was poor timing, but it happened, and I regret nothing. Piper wasn't my girlfriend or my lover. She was my friend. We didn't hang out and get naked on the daily. We had sex one time in the heat of the moment, which resulted in Tatum. She didn't expect or want an engagement ring out of the deal. Like me, Piper was singularly-focused on her career—though Tatum changed that for both of us.

The point is, Piper would be the last one to be upset that I kissed Keagan. Our relationship wasn't like that.

Now, would it be weird if Piper was still alive and carrying my child? Most definitely. But if Piper wouldn't have died, I wouldn't have gotten to know Keagan like I have, nor would we have spent so much time together.

Piper's passing brought Keagan and me together.

And while I swore off relationships years ago, I'm not all that opposed to see where this is going, which, I suppose is nowhere since Keagan still won't answer her phone.

I tried to play fair.

I called several times, sent several texts, and knocked on her door. She ignored me.

Therefore, I'm resorting to more drastic tactics that some would define as low.

Call it what you want, but I refuse to lie awake all night, worrying if Keagan is all right.

Me: *I can't get Tatum to stop crying.*

Which is the truth. I couldn't *earlier*. I'd been rocking Tatum in the glider for two solid hours. She wouldn't take a bottle, pacifier, or anything.

Keagan: Did you change her diaper?

Me: Of course.

Keagan: Feed her? Burp her? Rock her?

Me: Yes, yes, and yes. I even enlisted the help of Vance, which shows my desperation.

Also, the truth. When I couldn't get Tatum to sleep, I broke down and called Vance, thinking something was wrong with her. We went over her symptoms and vitals and agreed I should take her to the hospital, but then Halle came on the phone and asked if I had tried talking to Tatum.

Vance and I both snorted.

But Tatum… completely hushed as soon as she heard Halle's voice on speaker.

"*She's used to hearing her mother's voice in the womb,*" Halle had said. "*Talk to her, Astor, she'll learn to get used to your voice too.*"

My heart shattered inside my chest.

Rebekah was right—I couldn't be a good father, even if I wanted to be. I didn't know how. My daughter was living, breathing proof of that fact.

Tatum needed her mother.

She needed her mother's words—her comfort.

I was never going to soothe her like Piper.

I can never give her the comfort of her mother.

But Keys… she could try.

But she wasn't speaking to me.

Until now.

Keagan: And what did he suggest?

Me: You.

Several minutes go by before she responds, but when she does, a tremendous weight is lifted off my chest.

Keagan: *I'm on the way.*

Half an hour later, she's knocking on my door, looking disheveled and exhausted.

"Hey."

She's also been crying—a fact I'm quite sure she wants me to ignore.

"Hey." I open the door wider, allowing her to step inside. "Tatum is in the bassinet—crying. Again. All that kangaroo care has her thinking she's supposed to be held all day."

A slight smile appears through the obvious pain on Key's face. "Only weak men complain."

Ah, there is the Keys I'm used to. For a moment there, with the wild hair, smeared mascara, and tear-stained face, I thought she might be lost forever.

Clearly, my concern was unwarranted.

"I'm not complaining, just merely pointing out facts," I argue.

She brushes past me and smacks my chest. "Sounds like a whole lot of excuses to me."

Chuckling, I close the door, watching Keys scoop Tatum out of the bassinet, cuddling her to her chest and placing soft kisses to the fine dusting of dark hair on the top of her head.

"Halle said Tatum probably misses Piper's voice and…"

If it wasn't quiet in the house, I would have missed the faint whimper that escapes Keys as she cuddles Tatum closer and whispers, "You and me both, kiddo."

I don't know what it's like to lose a sibling. I can't imagine the thought of losing one of my brothers, not having them available to answer my calls, talk shit to my face and call me out when I'm being an asshole.

I've taken my family—my brothers—for granted for so many years.

At any moment, I could lose the very people that made me the man I am today. And it sickens me to think of the possibility. And here Keys is, enduring that exact pain, pulling herself out of the pits of despair to help me.

"Can I get you something to drink?" I offer, needing one myself.

Keys swipes her cheek along her shoulder, drying the tears there. "I'll take whatever you're having." Offering me a smile, she sits down on the couch. "Do you mind if I turn on the TV? I can't take the silence anymore."

"Not at all." I try not to think about her sitting alone in Piper's house with nothing but stillness and memories. "I'm pretty sure Tatum prefers the news."

She shoots me a severe look and then laughs. "I bet she does, but Auntie Keys is here, so Tatum will just have to endure a feel-good rom-com for tonight."

We both know we're not talking about an infant's channel preference.

I groan at the thought of sitting through a cliché whirlwind movie romance with silly dates that would never happen in real life. "I haven't watched a chick flick since I was in college."

Keagan arches her brows. "Let me guess, you only watched them then so you could score after the ending credits."

"Perceptive," I muse, "and spot on. Women were much easier to please back then."

"Women had simpler lives in college," she counters. "Before their careers and responsibilities sucked their souls dry." She stares at the TV, like she's searching for something she lost in it. "Men like to call you a bitch when you try and take your life back, but what they fail to realize is that if we don't adapt to our new lives, we'll drown."

I pour us each a glass of orange juice—it's all I have other than booze. I don't eat at home often, and if I'm going to drink, I generally prefer something a little stronger. But the juice was in my refrigerator, along with several fruits and vegetables with a note from Halle, telling me not to forget to take care of myself too.

I hadn't opened the juice until now.

Sighing, Keys exhales a long breath and then shakes her head. "Never mind. Ignore me… I'm just…" She gazes down at Tatum, giving her a long look before continuing, "All I ever wanted to be was the best game writer at *GameTales*—to beat Ass Face with his subpar penis."

Just as I take a sip of the orange juice, I choke. "What does his penis have to do with anything?"

Walking over, I set her cup of juice on the coffee table and sit in one of the chairs across from her.

"Men just have it so easy, you know?"

I nod, there's no denying that fact. Unfortunately, her sister was a prime example. I knew Piper worked harder than most surgeons; yet, she was the last one to be added as a partner in her practice.

"Like our kiss…"

My gaze snaps up. I felt sure she wouldn't mention the kiss.

"No one will judge you for kissing me. It's like men get a free pass to do whatever they want. But women? Me? If someone saw us kissing at Piper's funeral, they would burn me like a Salem witch. Whatever transpired between us today can't happen again. I can't taint my sister's reputation and ruin mine." She says the words like she's trying to believe them too.

Flipping the channels, she goes on like she didn't just admit her struggle out in the open—something I don't know how to do.

"Go get some rest," she insists, after I continue staring at her.

This woman is so different from her sister—so different from anyone I've ever met. She's open, honest, with a spirit so bright, I doubt she could hide it under thousands of those boho bracelets she wears.

"Please." Her whispered plea has my head snapping up and meeting her eyes filled with tears. "I don't want you to see me like this."

I can respect that, even if I don't agree with it. Kissing Keagan was not a mistake. We've developed a friendship and, as crazy as it sounds, a relationship too. I care about her. And I know if it weren't for the fear

147

of tarnishing her sister's reputation, she would admit she cared about me too.

Something between us is brewing, and it's only a matter of time before it boils over.

"I'll leave," I agree, standing, "but only because you've had enough emotional turmoil for one day."

She opens her mouth to argue, but I cut her off.

"This discussion is *not* over…" I take a long look at my daughter cradled in her arms and shake my head. "Not by a long shot."

I have made a lot of mistakes in my life, Keagan will not be one of them.

"I'll give you tonight," I tell her, "but *only* tonight."

Fortunately, she didn't need the night—only an hour.

"I changed my mind. For just this once, I want a free pass to do what I want."

And then she closes my bedroom door behind her.

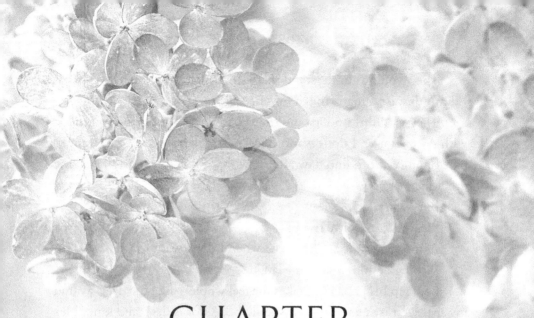

CHAPTER TWENTY

Keagan

I tried.

I tried to hate him.

Tried to make excuses.

But I'm lonely.

And he's familiar—the only person who knows what I'm going through.

But people *would* talk. All my sister's colleagues would view her in a cheap light. They'd throw away all the noble rumors they might have conjured up while she lie dying after having Astor's baby. They'd congratulate Astor like it's a reward to knock up a woman, but Piper, they'd say she was just a conquest. Then whatever she and Astor really had between them would be overshadowed by lies.

They'd think I played with Astor's emotions. They'd say I took advantage of his delicate state. They'd say I betrayed Piper.

But they didn't *feel* what happened when he pressed his lips to mine.

They wouldn't understand that I finally felt warm and alive—that I didn't despise a man's touch for once.

They wouldn't understand that I hate myself for being enamored with Astor Potter. I don't want to feel better in his presence. I want to hate him. I want to find flaw after flaw that proves he's just like all the other men I know.

But I can't.

Heaven knows I've tried.

Astor makes me smile—even when I don't want to.

Picking on him makes me laugh.

Being in his presence makes me feel whole—like the deep wound my sister left isn't as open as it should be. Astor is deep and kind. He's not a playboy surgeon that spends his time chatting up women who mean nothing to him.

This man spent six months not making money at his private plastic surgery practice to donate his services to children. Children! Not adults who wanted face lifts. Children! And then he took off twelve weeks to spend time with his daughter. He's a man who climbed a tree to sit with me in silence. He's made sure I've eaten and had his hand to hold while I perused a room full of coffins, trying to pick the perfect one for my sister.

He held up dress after dress while I cried and screamed. He dug through a box of pictures, pulling out the most recent ones of me and Piper. He laid them out on the table and asked me to tell him the stories of each of them. When I was through, he slid the picture of me and Piper at my college graduation, right before I got her shitfaced with tequila shots, over to me.

"You smiled the most in this one," he had said. "Perhaps she could wear the dress in this picture?"

The man is unbelievably patient. He's not bothered with my outbursts or my need to keep everyone at a distance. I feel alive with him. I don't feel like a burden or even an unwanted guest. Astor treats me like he's known me forever. Things are just comfortable between us.

And. I. Want. Him.

I'm tired of denying myself. I'm tired of making excuses. I want Dr. Potter more than I've ever wanted a man.

"And what is it that you want, Keagan?"

Astor hasn't moved since I came into his room and closed the door behind me. He's still sitting on his bed with a book in his hands.

"I want you," I say firmly.

He shuts the book and sets it on the nightstand. "And what about what people will think?"

"They won't know. You're good at keeping secrets, right?"

Let's not forget that. While Astor makes me come alive, he still harbors needed information about his relationship with my sister.

"I can keep a secret," he says softly, standing and making his way to me. I push my back flat against the door, frozen by the heat in his eyes and the determined set to his jaw. "But I don't want to keep secrets from you anymore. You deserve to know the truth."

He pushes his fingers through my hair. There's no denying that this attraction we've smothered between us has been flickering. All we needed was to light the fuse.

"You shouldn't have kissed me today." I breathe along his lips as they move closer to mine.

"You're right," he agrees, tilting his head, "I should have kissed you yesterday."

I thought it could have been a fluke—a feeling that came on because of grief, but now, when Astor crushes his lips to mine, his tongue parting the seam of my mouth, that earlier feeling is amplified by a million. My knees weaken and I feel my body sliding down the door until Astor's strong hands find my bottom and hoist me up to his waist.

"Wrap your legs around me."

Oh no. Am I really not capable of remembering how this works or has Astor just rendered my body useless? I don't think I want to know.

"Don't drop me," I whisper, searching for his lips again as my legs wrap around his waist, once again providing me an anchor.

"I won't let you go, I promise." One of his hands slides up my back, bringing the hem of my shirt with it. "Can I take this off?"

I nod, not giving myself time to change my mind.

It doesn't matter what arrangement he and Piper had.

He said they weren't together—they weren't in love.

And for some strange reason, I believe him.

Astor moves us to his bed, single-handedly removing my shirt before my butt hits the mattress. "You sure you want to do this?"

I take a breath and sigh. "Can you not just take advantage of me like a regular guy? Must you ask me like a gentleman?"

The grin he flashes me would have sealed the deal if I wasn't already sure I wanted to do this with him.

"I don't want you to have any regrets." He says all the right things, but his eyes say something totally different—something primal.

"I won't regret it." At least I really hope I don't. I can't be sure, though, since this is so unlike me.

He nods and takes a step forward, his palms going to my knees. "And when I tell you what happened between me and Piper, will you then?"

I shrug.

Their little promise or arrangement, whatever they want to call it, could be anything. I can't promise not to get pissed off about something I don't know yet. But what I can do is live in this bubble just a little while longer.

"I don't want to talk about you and my sister right now. I want to ignore whatever happened between you two," reaching out, I pull him by the waist of his sweatpants, "and focus on what's happening between me and you."

He tips his chin. "I can do that."

We'll deal with his promise later, but for now, he's not my sister's baby daddy or one-night stand.

He's just… mine.

"Can I take these off?" I tug at his pants.

"No." He takes a step back. "In here, you don't make the rules."

I wasn't aware that I made the rules outside of the bedroom, but his comment has me thinking he gives me a lot more leeway than he does most people.

He reaches behind him and grabs the back of his shirt, pulling it over his head in one motion.

"Unhook your bra. I want to see all of you." Normally, I wouldn't be able to stand such barking demands, but the way his jaw ticks like he's doing all he can to restrain himself is a powerful feeling. It's weird knowing that the mere sight of your body can cause a man to lose con-trol—to lose his so carefully crafted composure.

"And if I say no?"

I think the corner of his lip twitches, but I can't be sure because he moves so fast. Pushing me back, his mouth sucks a nipple through the fabric of my bra, forcing me to close my eyes and cry out in pleasure.

The pressure of his suction, the torturous motion of his tongue has me arching underneath the weight of his body. "I'll take it off," I beg, needing to feel him without anything between us. "I'll take off my bra."

"Too late," he clips out, right before he bites the edge of my bra, his teeth grazing my heated skin in the process. Using only his mouth, he bares my breast by pulling the cup to the side. I don't even care if he ruined the elasticity of a good bra because his mouth closes over my nipple, nipping, sucking, and driving me out of my mind as he massages the other one with his hand.

I'm on fire, squirming, likely grinding against him as he brings me to the cusp of madness. "My pants," I beg, wrapping my legs around his waist, trying to push his pants down with my feet. "Take off my pants."

In this room, I'm not proud.

I'm starved for this man.

I'm starved for his attention—his devotion—his love.

Everything Astor Potter is, I want.

"Take off your pants and do what to you?"

I could hit him for removing his mouth, but since I'm throbbing and needy, I'll let it go. "Take off my pants and fuck me."

I expected a different reaction, not him clucking his tongue and standing up, unwrapping my legs from his waist and pushing them to my chest. "We don't do that in here." His finger finds my slit covered by my leggings.

"Do what?" I gasp as he makes strong strokes up and down, increasing the pressure of his finger when he gets close to the sensitive bundle of nerves at my center.

"Fuck," he answers, finally stopping where I want him. But he doesn't apply pressure. Instead, he reaches between my legs and grabs me by the chin, forcing me to look him in the eyes—eyes that hold a finality about them. "I'm not going to fuck you, Keagan."

Oh, well, that's disappointing. But I should have known better. He can fuck—

He yanks my legs flat and pulls me toward the edge of the bed, lying over me like a sexy weight. "I'm not going to fuck you… *yet.*" His mouth presses against mine, his tongue slipping in like it's familiar— like we've done this a million times. This is what he does to me—he makes me feel like I've always belonged by his side.

Without pause, Astor's hands drift down my body as he rises ever so slightly, his thumbs hooking my waistband, his mouth parting from mine as he slides the leggings down to my knees. But then he stops.

"What are you doing? Finish taking them off." I kick at the fabric preventing my legs from wrapping around him.

Of course, Astor ignores my pleas, looking down at my boob pulled out of the bra cup, my hair likely disheveled from his hands, and yanks me down the mattress. "I think I'll take you like this."

No wonder women get pregnant around him. I'm already close to a roaring orgasm, just by looking at his muscled torso looming over me. He may think I'm joking, but this man has hero mode in spades.

"Look at me, Keagan." His voice leaves no room for arguing.

My chest rises with each panting breath. "I see you."

"Do you?" He grabs the center of my leggings and lifts my legs. "Do you really see me?"

I nod, not sure exactly how deep he's taking this conversation.

He lifts my legs off the bed, slipping his body between my thighs, the leggings catching at the back of his neck, rendering me immobile as he lowers to his knees on the floor. "I'm not the man you want me to be," he warns, "but I am the man you need." He tugs me closer, lining my center with his mouth. "Stop fighting me, Keys."

I don't know what he means by fighting him nor do I have time to really think about it because his finger is at my slit, gathering the wetness that he caused earlier with that same finger, and his mouth… his tongue circles my clit.

My head hits the mattress while my stomach clenches, my legs snapping closed on instinct. I can't remember the last time someone went down on me, but I can assure you, it never felt like this. It never shot pleasure up my spine and made my toes curl and my womb ache. My body craves this man and mourns his absence when he lifts his head, grinning wide. "Hold your knees apart."

Heaven help me, I do it without argument. I'm desperate to feel him inside me.

"That's my girl," he praises, a sly grin gracing his face. "Now, keep them open."

I hold my legs tighter, just because the way he said to keep them open sounded more like a challenge and less like a demand, and I'm always one to take on a worthy opponent.

When Astor's satisfied that I'm ready, he presses another finger to my slit, wetting his fingers and pushing them inside. My breath catches as he bears down on the rippled, sensitive flesh. My legs tremble in my hands and it takes all the strength I have not to let them clamp around him.

Easing in and out, Astor quirks a brow. "Can you handle more?"

"I want you—all of you." My gaze drifts lower, telling him exactly what I'm ready for more of. It's been a long time since I've got the recommended dosage of vitamin D. I'm prepared to spend the night giving my body some much needed nourishment.

Astor lowers his head, his fingers pushing in farther, and then he attacks. His teeth rake across my clit, his lips closing over me, sucking me, torturing me with every slight movement of his tongue. "Astor." I almost cry at saying his name. "Astor, please." He's not giving me enough to tip me over the edge into orgasmic territory. He's priming me, and at this point, I'm not above begging. "Dr. Potter, I need you!"

His mouth releases. His fingers stop. Time seems to stand still as I release my legs and clasp his cheeks in my hands, lifting his eyes to mine. "I don't need many people, but I need you right now."

I try not to read into why I phrase my sentence that way, or why I'm even on my back in this man's bed. I only focus on how he makes me feel.

Without another word, Astor stands, slipping my legs over his head, and pulls my leggings off. He takes a longer lingering look while he reaches over and plucks a condom out of the drawer in the night-stand. His pants are pushed down to his thighs and his cock sheathed a moment later. "Are you sure?" He stares down at me, so strong and confident, and I grab my legs, holding them like he instructed earlier.

"Ye—"

He doesn't let me finish before he impales me with his cock. There's no other word for it as the intrusion steals my breath and sets my body on fire as it works to accommodate him.

"Oh, shit," he breathes, his hands going to my tits.

"Oh, shit is right," I agree, dropping a leg and trying to wiggle slightly to the left to find some relief that just won't come. Astor is consuming me from the inside out. I can't breathe without feeling his presence inside me. It's a delightful fullness that warms me down to my toes.

I'm held still, a delicious bite at my center with his movement. "I told you not to let go of your legs."

No, he did not just scold me when he's the sole reason I'm squirming.

"Well, if you—"

He pushes a finger into my mouth, making me taste myself. "The time for talking was earlier when I texted you." His hips roll and I groan at the pressure. "When I called you." He shoves another finger inside my mouth. "When I showed up at your doorstep and knocked." This time, he pulls almost all the way out and thrusts back in.

I bite his fingers, breathing through the waves of pleasure.

"That won't happen again, Keys. Do we understand each other?"

He doesn't remove his fingers for me to speak, so I nod instead.

"I don't care if you don't want to talk to me—you will, even if you need to scream at me to get it out. You will not ignore me."

He pounds into me hard enough that I drop a leg again.

"Never again, Keys."

Finally, he pulls his fingers out, hitching the leg I dropped with one of his hands. I can feel the primal need to dominate consume him as he looks at me for an answer.

"Never again," I promise with a whisper.

It's all he needs to thrust into me, hitching my leg higher, pounding that sensitive place inside me. One of us shouts or cries, I can't tell who through the blinding rush of euphoria as Astor lifts my ass off the bed, owning me and ruining whatever is left inside me.

He took my body.

He took my soul.

And when he kisses a rogue tear on my cheek, holding my eyes and finding his release with me, he takes my heart too.

CHAPTER TWENTY-ONE

Keagan

A week later and I'm still sore.

I think Astor might have poked a hole in something. Seeing how he is a doctor and all, I asked him if it was possible that he punctured something—which only led to him scaring me into climbing on the table, so he could take a look.

I realized, only when my legs were spread, and he was grinning, that the famous Dr. Potter was scamming me. The terrible comedian took an exorbitant amount of time exploring me with his mouth and fingers, only to tell me that vaginas were like a new baseball glove—they needed to be broken in. I might have smacked his chest and let him lube me up to prove his point.

But I'm still sore, and not from the first time we had sex.

Astor and I have found a way to deal with our grief. We have sex when Tatum is asleep, and then feed, rock, and change her when she's awake. When those things are done, we're both able to pass out and sleep, at least until Tatum wakes again.

It's been the best few hours' sleep I've had since learning of Piper's prognosis.

But since my time away from work is counting down, I need to pack up Piper's apartment—alone.

No matter how much I want to stay with Astor and Tatum, I can't.

Because this thing between me and Astor is just comfort—it's not real. And it will serve me well to remember that.

Relationships like these never work out—it's not possible. Everything built between the couple is reactionary.

Would Astor have slept with me before Piper died? Doubtful. I wasn't all that warm and fuzzy back then either. The difference is, we shared a trauma, which put us in each other's path. We needed comfort, and only the two of us could understand that need.

It's not that I want to push aside the feelings I have for Astor but right now, things are too complicated—too raw. I can't make any decisions when my life has been uprooted. I'm highly unstable.

Besides, my history with men isn't all that great, and once I go back to work, Ass Face will be happy to remind me why I avoid the male species altogether.

Not to mention when Astor goes back to work, he'll be flooded with lunch offers from all the single female doctors.

They won't hate men like I do.

They won't be suffering from grief like I am.

They'll offer to watch Tatum for him so he can sleep in on Sunday mornings. Then he will be reminded of all the nights he spends alone, rocking a baby who has no mother, just an aunt who lives three hours away that he only sees on the occasional weekend.

Mine and Astor's relationship is doomed—a disaster waiting to happen.

So, I'm doing the responsible thing and putting distance between us.

Besides, I need to clean out Piper's house and maybe find a

mortgage statement. A payment is probably due, and the lender needs to be notified that Pipe is paying rent to Jesus now.

It should be easier than it sounds, considering Piper is an organized adult. But I'm on the second drawer of Piper's filing cabinet and all I've discovered is that she needed an intervention.

Two drawers—I repeat, two drawers—are full of inappropriate birthday cards I sent Piper over the years. Most have terribly embarrassing pictures of her asleep with her mouth open with sarcastic verbiage along the lines of, *Men won't care how many wrinkles you have with a mouth circumference like yours. Happy Birthday to the oldest sister I know. I love you more than raw cookie dough.*

Granted, I was likely buzzed and feeling frisky coming up with that gem, but my crazy sister saved every last card, like a mom saves her kids' artwork.

A mom.

My sister deserves to be here, celebrating Halloween tonight with Tatum, and handing out candy in her picturesque neighborhood. Instead, Tatum is home with her orgasmic daddy, and I'm here, devouring the two Reese's cups I found in Piper's desk.

What a life I have.

I wonder if Kenny is manning the bar tonight. Maybe he could at least sneak some pictures of the crazy costumes for me. I've always loved Halloween. I can remember holding Piper's hand as we walked around our neighborhood, collecting as much candy as we possibly could. When we got home, we'd dump it all out and start sorting it by favorites. Piper was the chocolate hog, and I loved anything that would pull out a tooth filling.

We were simple people.

At least we were back then. Piper jumped on the complication train with Astor and whatever that drama is. Astor tried telling me one night after we had sex, but it just never feels like the right time to discuss whatever he and my sister had going on. I think I'd rather just not know. It's safer for my heart that way.

I stare at one of the sloppy hearts I drew on a card and smile—I remember drawing it while I pressed down on Kenny's back like a make-shift table. Piper was leaving for the Grace of Mercy, and I had forgotten she wouldn't receive it if I didn't send it early. Kenny and I were at a weekend concert, sharing a tent, when I rummaged through our bags, found our packing list, and wrote:

If you weren't so old, you would be here, puking in the bushes.
We miss you!
Happy birthday, Granny.
Love you lots!

Ps: You'll be on a ship with no exits... I'll be upset if you don't come back with at least one pregnancy scare. Live like you're twenty.

Keys

Who knew just a few years later, my sister would do just that, but instead of a scare, she went all the way and had a baby. Told you, she was always the overachiever.

I'm sliding the card back into the folder when I hear a strange noise coming from the hallway. It's either a snake or my imagination. Either way, I'm not all that happy to drag myself off the floor and walk down to the end of the hall to the closet where the hissing noise is coming from.

I swear if it's a snake, I'm just gonna burn the place down. Piper would understand. I can handle a lot of things, but animals that slither are not one of them.

Grabbing an umbrella from the hallway, I ready my swing as I push the closet door open and find water on the floor. It's like a roaring waterfall coming out of a pipe.

"And this is why I'm not a homeowner," I mutter, assessing the damage, then realizing the water is seeping out into the hall.

Oh, no. The water will ruin Piper's hardwood floors.

I don't remember grabbing my phone. I don't even realize I've called Astor until he answers, his voice reaching through the phone and finding that hallow part in my chest, filling it with something I don't want to acknowledge.

"Keys? You all right?"

I blink back tears. Why am I tearing up? Surely, it's not because I missed the sound of his voice?

"I need a life jacket," I stumble out. At least I didn't admit that I missed him. This conversation could have started off a lot worse.

"What do you mean, you need a life jacket? Are you swimming?" It's cute that he thinks I would actually be doing something productive like exercising.

"Where would I be swimming?" I can't keep the exasperation out of my voice. "Do I strike you as someone who takes joy in drinking other people's urine?"

That sexy little chuckle he releases does not make me smile. Fine, it does. I hope he's happy that he's broken my hate of men and dongs.

"You've gotta help me out here, sweetheart. I can't bring you a life jacket if I don't know where you are."

Oh hell. He called me sweetheart. Worse yet, my heart did a little fluttering thing in response. No. No way. I'm just overly tense with the possibility of ruining Piper's floors and not being able to sell her house. Not that Tatum needs the extra money when both of her parents are (or were in Piper's case) doctors. The kid's kids are probably set for life.

But still.

I shake off the tingling in my stomach and suck in a breath. Astor can help or he can at least call a local plumber. "I'm at Piper's and there is water shooting out of this round thing that won't stop and..." my voice wavers and the tears threaten to fall again, "...and the water is going to ruin Piper's floors."

The line goes silent for a moment and then Astor clears his throat. "I'm on the way. Can you look around the 'round thing,' which I suspect is the hot water heater, and see if you can find a shut-off valve?"

The relief that shoots through me is masked by the overwhelming shock that Astor knew what the round thing is called. "How do you know it's the hot water heater? You're a doctor, not a plumber."

I hear his SUV rumble to life. "Believe it or not, before I was a doctor, I was just a man. And sometimes, men know things. Not a lot of things, as you well know, but some."

I pause my search of the mysterious valve and narrow my eyes. "Now is not the time to be sarcastic."

"Yet, it was a few minutes ago when you claimed you needed a life raft."

This man. "I said I needed a life jacket, not a raft, and the comment is defined as dramatic, not sarcastic. But I'm guessing they don't stress language arts all that much in med school anymore."

"No, just the saving lives aspect." I can hear the humor in his voice, and unfortunately, it makes me smile.

"Are you really going to be able to fix this?"

He might be a man, but does he really know valves and pipes? I mean, other than my pipe? Clearly, he has that one mastered, but then again, the man knows his anatomy.

"Probably not, but I can call someone who can clean floors. Men know how to make calls, too, you know."

Now he's just trying to be cute. "You're already getting on my nerves. You better hope I calm down before you get here. Otherwise, I'm liable to drown you—floors be damned."

He snorts. "How's it going with the packing?"

My mouth snaps shuts. "Great. Almost done."

"Can't wait to see all the progress."

He knows I've been avoiding him. I'm sure of it.

"Goodbye, Astor."

I hang up with him as he enjoys a deep belly laugh at my expense.

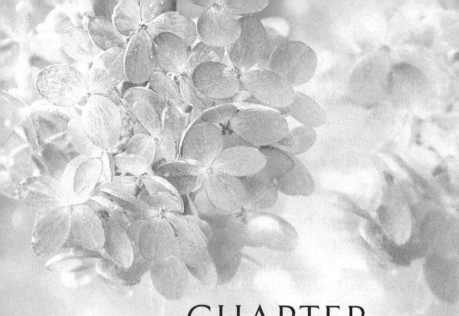

CHAPTER TWENTY-TWO

Keagan

He rings the doorbell, looking like a supermodel who had ten hours of sleep and a team of people who made him look like he was fresh, even though he had only gotten two hours of sleep.

"I brought coffee instead of a life jacket. Hope that's not disappointing."

He thrusts the cup into my hands, only allowing his eyes to linger on my chest for a full minute before I remember that I am still bra-less—no one pretends to pack boxes in a bra, give me a break—as well as soaked from head to toe from looking for that damn valve.

"What's disappointing is that you're not covered in baby puke. Tatum and I are going to have a long talk about what is expected of the McKellan women." I grab the carrier from him and it's not nearly as light as he makes it look. "Hope all your man knowledge kicks in because that valve is not there."

The corner of his mouth tips up. "Would you like to make a wager on it?"

This is my problem. I never can back down from a challenge. Especially from a man who thinks he's smarter than me. Okay, well, Astor is *probably* smarter than me. I doubt I could have passed rigorous medical boards, fellowships, and a million years of school to become a doctor. But I'm just saying, Astor is no more a plumber than I am.

"What are the stakes?"

Astor pushes inside and closes the door, his fingers already clutching the bottom of his t-shirt. "I'm thinking a night out."

I scoff. "That's easy."

"Alone."

Alone? "Like a date—without Tatum?"

He nods. "You scared to talk to me without our buffer?"

This man knows how to push my damn buttons. He knows I'll have to prove him wrong. "I talked to you before Tatum, remember? I've also slept with you. Several times, I might add." Has he forgotten all those nights?

"Not since things have changed between us."

I scoff, hoping my cheeks don't redden and betray my lies. "Nothing has changed between us. We slept together, that's all."

He shrugs a shoulder and then rips the t-shirt from his body, revealing those glorious packs of muscles.

I swallow, forcing my gaze to the ceiling. He's just trying to prove a point, Keys. Don't fall into his hotness trap.

His cool fingers grasp my chin and pull my face down, so I'm looking him in the eyes—those crystal-clear blue eyes that almost seem inhuman. "If nothing has changed between us then a date shouldn't create a problem for you."

Oh, it's definitely creating a problem, especially if he keeps up with this behavior. But if I'm going down, so is he. "Deal. Find the valve, Dr. Potter."

Without another word, I take Tatum to the back bedroom and guzzle most of the coffee until I'm calm enough to change clothes and risk walking back to the closet where Astor is kneeling, his jeans darker from the water. I don't notice how they cling to his thighs and how his forearms flex as he reaches behind the round thing. "The plumber will be here this afternoon, and the cleaning crew thereafter, but I recommend we get most of the water soaked up before the wood floors have a chance to absorb more."

I appreciate that he doesn't rub my face in the fact that he found the sacred valve and has shut off the spraying water. "Okay. I'll grab some towels and a mop."

I don't give him time to answer because I need a minute to myself. Should I have known he would find the valve? Probably. Should I feel bad for thinking this man couldn't find something if I couldn't? Yes. And I do. But what bothers me the most is that I agreed to an actual date with this man, where neither of us can use the excuse to change a diaper or put the baby down when conversation becomes too uncomfortable.

Sure, we'd talked in the hospital, but that was a different time. A time when we were both scared and in a tremendous amount of pain. Now, we've had time to lament on Piper's passing and the fact that we are basically raising a child together.

We've had time together.

We've experienced grief and joy together.

But never have we ever just experienced each other.

Alone.

Without any excuses or sex between us.

I grab a stack of towels and head back into the hallway, where Astor is standing, water dripping down his pecs like it was purposefully done. But I know this is no fairy tale and the tightness of his mouth is due to a look of concern, not sex appeal. "Do you know if Piper has a dehumidifier? I'm thinking we should run it with as many fans as you can find, so the floor dries faster."

I wait about three seconds, making sure he's absolutely serious before I cry, drop the towels and throw my arms around him like an absolute fool. I don't say anything, I just hug every hard inch of muscles my arms wrap around. This man needs to go home and sleep like yesterday. Yet, here he is, tired, likely rundown thanks to Tatum's circadian rhythm, and he's worried about saving Piper's floor. He could have answered the phone this morning and responded with, "Man, that sucks. I'll have my assistant send you a list of reputable plumbers. Ciao!" But he didn't. Instead, he brought me a coffee, got sopping wet and called people who would help me, but not before thinking about how we could salvage these floors before help arrived.

Ass Face wouldn't have done that.

Hell, Kenny wouldn't have done that. Kenny would have come, but there is no way he would be elbow deep in water he didn't know where it was coming from. Astor Potter has rocked my world and created doubt in my cold heart that all men are not created equal.

"Hey." He shushes me while rubbing soft circles on my back. It only makes me cry harder. This man's strength—his comfort—is something I will never get used to. I lap it up in gulps, remembering his stern voice demanding I tell my sister goodbye and that I was going to be okay. At the time, I was so mad at him. I knew I wasn't going to be okay. I wanted to be selfish and make Piper open her eyes and comfort me, but he wouldn't let me. He made me take his strength and lie to my sister that I was going to be okay.

And clearly, sobbing into this man's chest over some water-logged wood floors is not okay. So really, it's his fault he's in this position.

"The floors will be fine." He tries lying to me, which I appreciate, but we both know the floors won't escape this incident without scars.

Just like us.

And that makes me angry. I have enough scars; I don't need Astor Potter, Man Extraordinaire, leaving more. "Would you like to make a wager on that?"

I might be upset, but stupid I am not. I lost a bet; doesn't mean I can't make it right with another one.

Astor chuckles, and I feel it vibrate my cheek. "Never. You're not getting out of our date."

It's not like I haven't been on awkward dates before. "Whatever, it's just a date. I've ruined enough of those before."

He pulls me back and presses his lips against mine. "Not just any date. We're going trick-or-treating."

"So, the packing..."

The plumbers arrived faster than I expected. So did the cleaners, which resulted in an awful lot of free time that Astor used to snoop around, noting that I hadn't packed one single box, before shuffling me into the car. The cleaners needed us to clear out, he said, lying through those straight white teeth.

"I've been busy," I cut him an exasperated look, "offering up my vagina to you."

Grinning, he grips the steering wheel, adjusting in his seat like the thought of my pootnanny conjures up stiff thoughts that manifest in his pants.

"And what a succulent offering it is," he teases.

I roll my eyes. I find this cute, teasing side of him rather hot. And while that's all fun and games in the bedroom, I'd rather he keeps that contained to only the sexy times. Astor acting all adorable in the daylight just makes me want to keep him—and that can't happen.

"Stop before Tatum's first words are something obnoxious like succulent."

"Tatum doesn't understand what we're saying." He glances in the rearview mirror, like he's making sure she hasn't grown into a toddler in the last five minutes.

"Yet," I amend. "In a few months, we'll need to watch what we say around her."

I realize before it's too late that my comment makes it seem like I'll still be around in a few months—and I will. I'll always be there for Tatum; I just won't be there most days of the week, like I am currently. Again, Astor and I live separate lives three hours apart from one another.

"Where are we going anyway?" He said we were going

trick-or-treating earlier, and I'm trying not to get excited about it. The last time I went trick-or-treating was when I was probably twelve. I don't know who told Astor that it's cool for adults to still participate, but I'm not questioning it. Maybe it's something that only rich people can do, though Piper never mentioned it. But, then again, Piper was a martyr and would have likely volunteered to work, so all the moms could take their kids.

Don't think about Tatum dressing up as a princess, never getting to hold her mama's hand as she goes from door to door.

I force the thought from my head, glancing up to see Astor staring at me. "You all right?"

"Yep." I let the P pop, just so my lie is a little more believable. "Would you like to answer my question?"

"Would you like to stay in this universe when I repeat it?"

I cock my head to the side. "You answered me?"

"Yep." The sarcastic jerk pops the P, too, grinning like he needs to be kissed.

"Well, then, my apologies for dozing off, Gramps. Would you mind repeating yourself?"

Astor chuckles, completely unbothered by my age comment, which is simply a running joke at this point. "I said we're stopping by Vance's so he and Halle can watch Tatum."

"And then?"

Please still say trick-or-treating.

"And then we're going by my office."

"Your office?" I try not to sound severely disappointed. "I thought you took a few months off."

"I did."

I don't like the look on his face—it screams, *I have a secret and you aren't going to like it.*

"So why the pitstop?"

He flashes me a wink. "You'll see."

CHAPTER TWENTY-THREE

Keagan

"You have lost your mind."

The laugh that bubbles out of me is as ridiculous as the two outfits hanging from each of his hands.

"I don't know much about video games, and I didn't want to dip into cosplay territory, so I thought why not dress up as the ultimate video game couple?"

I burst out laughing. "And you thought Mario and Princess Peach was that couple?"

I never thought I'd see the day when Dr. Potter blushed. "Mario was the only video game I knew."

Eliminating the space between us, I wrap my arms around this ridiculous man. "Oh, Papa. You really are old."

The costumes, still hanging in his hands, close around me while he hugs me back. "Maybe you can show me some of the new things you kids play now."

We're teasing. Astor is far from old. There may be ten plus years between us, but nothing about this man—other than his video game knowledge—is old. "Nah. You don't need to keep up with the kids. I rather enjoy keeping you a classic."

He chuckles, as the weight of his chin drops to my head. "You ready to go trick-or-treating?"

Stepping back, I look up at those icy blue eyes that I once thought were cold and detached. "You're serious? We're really going to go trick-or-treating?"

"Are you too cool to knock on doors?"

I nearly snort. "No, but you are, Dr. Elite."

He pushes the pink ballgown into my chest. "I'll have you know I never miss a Halloween. It's my favorite time of the year." Without another word, he turns me around where I face the bathroom door inside his office. "Get dressed. We can't be late."

I feel like a real-life princess.

"One day, I'm going to grow as big as you." I gaze at the little hand clutched in mine. Her name is Hannah, and she's six and a half years old—her words not mine.

I wasn't shocked when Astor—who looks dapper in his overalls and plumber's hat, impersonating the hottest Mario I've ever seen—pulled into the Children's Hospital parking garage.

Apparently, he and other clinicians put on a trick-or-treat parade for the children spending Halloween in the hospital. The ones who are well enough to walk or ride in wagons and wheelchairs go from floor to floor, stopping at offices and nurses' stations collecting candy and prizes. The children who aren't well enough to participate in the parade await all the staff (Astor and me included) to come to their rooms with baskets of goodies.

It's the sweetest, most thoughtful Halloween party I've ever been to.

Squeezing Hannah's hand, I respond, "I think you're gonna grow much bigger than me, and you know what happens when girls grow tall?"

That sweet little face grows curious. "No, what?"

"They become models."

"Really?" Her excitement grips my heart and squeezes. "You think I could be a model?"

I touch the tip of her little nose. "Without a doubt."

Hannah, her mom told me, recently found out she has a rare blood cancer. What was supposed to be just a simple sick visit to the urgent care turned into a month stay at the Children's Hospital. But apparently, Hannah, dressed in her adorable pumpkin pajamas and knitted hat, has kept her positive attitude. Her mom says that if it weren't for those little girl giggles and smiles, she would have crumbled when the doctor first broke the news.

It's funny how children seem to look at adversity and act like it's simply a bad hair day. They don't allow it to cripple them the same way adults do. They live every day like it was the day before. They truly are examples of innocence and purity.

"You guys ready to get some candy?"

There's a little boy on Astor's shoulders, and he's wearing his Mario hat.

"Lucas here says he's going to get more candy than me." He jostles the boy, making him giggle. "But I told him that I was the best at tricks, so there was no way I wasn't coming out of this the Candy King."

Oh, he's the best at something all right, but it's not tricks. This man and his hero mode have my womb aching with a primal need I never knew I wanted.

"Don't worry, Lucas," I say, finding my composure. "You can stay with me and Hannah if Dr. Potter ends up with a few doors slammed in his face."

Though, no one would dare turn Astor away.

In fact, this is one time I think Dr. Potter will have no problem beating me. He looks hot and ridiculous dressed as a video game plumber, but he has this boyish smile, and a child on his shoulders.

He's a single woman's fantasy.
And he's *mine*.

I've smiled so much my cheeks hurt.

Racing Astor down the hall in wheelchairs with Hannah and Lucas on our laps was better than any night I spent at the bar with Kenny. The kids chanted as Astor and I rolled the wheels as fast as we reasonably could, with sick kids on our laps, until we reached the end of the hallway.

We called it a tie, but I saw Astor slowing down toward the end. Hannah and Lucas didn't care. All they wanted was the bag of goodies waiting for us at the finish line.

It was a Halloween night I would never forget.

"It looked like you had a lot of fun out there tonight."

We're headed back to Vance and Halle's to pick up Tatum-Bug.

"I did. Thank you for taking me. It was a Halloween like no other."

Astor, still in his overalls, cuts me this ridiculous grin that if I wasn't on birth control would have me ending up pregnant. "The kids really liked you."

"They liked you more." The nurses and parents too. Astor looking like a real-life video game hero, running up and down the halls like a big kid was straight-up mommy-porn.

"Nah. I bribed them with extra candy."

He lies. This saint of a man is lying. You can tell he loves children. "It's funny to me that it took you so long to actually knock up a woman." I chuckle. "Clearly you love kids."

Astor's smile fades. I'm not sure which part of what I said upset him. I've always joked about him knocking up Piper. What's changed?

"I just never met the right woman, I guess."

Until my sister.

But I don't say that. Astor doesn't seem to be in a teasing mood about his accidental pregnancy, which, if I'm being honest, is played out.

Shit happens. Astor and Piper probably were at some boring conference and passed the time playing with each other. Who could blame them?

"Well, you'd do the world a disservice, Dr. Potter, if you stopped with Tatum."

He flashes me a smile but I can tell it's forced. "I'll keep that in mind as I approach forty."

"In three years," I remind him.

He grins. "Tatum might need a puppy just in case."

And a mommy, but neither of us mention that as we pull into Vance's driveway.

"You up for one more house?"

Astor puts the car in park and hops out, coming around in nearly a sprint to open my door. "You're in hero mode again," I remind him. Though, I'm starting think Astor's hero mode is really just Astor's normal play mode. The man is just otherworldly. "But yes, I'm up for one more house."

"Good, because it's not this house." He snatches me from the car and flips me over his shoulder like some kind of firefighter.

"I thought we were getting Tatum?"

"Nope." He swats my ass. "We are kissing Tatum goodnight while she stays with Uncle Vance and Aunt Halle for the night."

"What? No. She's too little to be away from us."

Astor tightens his hold on my legs. "She'll be fine. We'll come back first thing in the morning."

We get to the front door and Astor rings the bell.

"What if she cries?" I ask while we wait.

"Then they'll feed her."

I hate that he sounds so confident.

"What if the bottle doesn't stop her crying? What if something goes wrong?"

Astor shifts me on his shoulder. "Then my brother, who's also a physician, will assess her and call me."

"How convenient that you can always pull the doctor card."

He slides me down his chest until my feet hit the ground. "Tatum is in good hands. I would never leave her with anyone who I didn't feel was capable."

"But—"

He presses his lips to mine, taking care to kiss the side of my lip as he withdraws, his icy blue eyes holding mine. "I want to focus only on you tonight. Will you let me do that?"

"That's not fair." It comes out sounding more like a whine.

"Sure, it is." He brushes the hair back from my face and adjusts the crown. "If you really don't want to leave Tatum tonight, we won't. But I'd very much like to spend some alone time with you, Ms. McKellan."

Fuck. Me.

No woman in her right mind would turn him down, right? Like no one.

Looping my arms around his neck, I pull him closer. "You play dirty, Dr. Potter." But I kiss him anyway.

"Is that a yes?"

He knows that's a yes; he just wants to hear me say the words. "That's a yes, Astor. I want to spend alone time with you too." More than I have ever wanted with any other man.

With a victorious and smug grin, Astor reaches behind me and rings the bell, at least ten times, before someone finally flings open the door.

"Trick-or-treat!" Astor elbows me and I repeat the phrase at the guy who is not Vance at the door. He's eating a small bag of chips and looks at the sack of candy in Astor's hand.

"I hope you get laid for this." Then he discards his bag of chips inside our candy bag and turns around walking back into the house.

Astor throws his head back and laughs a boisterous sound.

"Remington! Did you not give them candy? That was your only job!"

Halle runs to the door with a bag of candy and a grin, offering us her apologies for ruining the surprise by dropping a few pieces into our bag. "Astor wanted you to have one real house to actually trick-or-treat at."

Something deep inside my stomach clenches.

You can't keep him, Keys. You. Can't. Keep. Him.

And apparently, I can't even manage to answer her without crying stupid tears. If Piper were still here, I would be calling her from the car and telling her all about this unusual and wonderful date. I'd make her ask me questions, so we could analyze every single behavior. Something has to be wrong with him. He can't be this perfect. Well, he's not perfect, but he's pretty darn close.

"Come on." Halle takes me by the arm and pulls me inside. "Tatum will be happy to see you. Although, she seems pretty fascinated by Remington."

"He's not smoking around her, is he?" Astor says from behind me.

"Oh no, he wouldn't dare." Halle shrugs. "We also hid his cigarettes, which is why he's in such a delightful mood."

Halle leads us through the open floor plan to the den, where Vance sits in a leather chair reading. Remington, the guy who answered the door, is in one of the other chairs with my precious girl in his lap.

"She was crying," he says by way of greeting.

Halle looks at me and grins, mouthing, "He won't put her down. It's so cute!"

"Shut up, Hal."

Ignoring Remington, I walk over and scoop my munchkin from his arms. Her eyes open and I swear she smiles. I know it's probably gas, but there's something exciting about thinking this tiny human will one day be genuinely happy to see me. I don't want to miss one of these smiles or her first steps or when she rolls over or throws up on her daddy. Just thinking of how many milestones I'll miss by moving back home is enough to bring tears to my eyes.

Not only do I realize how much I love this little girl, but I also realize that I like her daddy... a whole lot.

CHAPTER TWENTY-FOUR

Keagan

Alone time with Astor was nothing like I imagined.

"Seriously? You did this in college?"

His lips are slightly swollen from the intense make-out session we had in his driveway. "Why do you think I'm such a prude?"

I shrug, plucking the full syringe from his fingers. "I've just never met a man like you before." Pressing the tip of the needle into the gummy bear like he showed me, I inject the vodka. "It confuses me sometimes."

Before I can reach for the injected gummy, Astor swipes it and tosses it into his mouth, swallowing after only a couple chews. "Do I confuse you in a good way or—" He presses his lips to mine, and I need no coaxing to open, letting the taste of Astor and vodka flood my tastebuds.

Gah, I love the way my stomach flutters every time he's inside me. Whether it's his fingers, his tongue, or his cock, my body responds with a frenzy of feelings, sending my stomach tumbling over itself.

I've never felt this way before. Not with high school boyfriends or even that one dude in college that I allowed to take my virginity after a lackluster conversation at a frat party. I never once considered intimacy or a man's touch as something pleasurable.

Being with a man has never been an enjoyable experience. I didn't want to hear them talk or placate me with lies of how they could make my body feel good. It was all a ruse to get what they wanted—a quick poke.

But Astor... His touch feels like it's part of me—like it's a necessary process for things to run smoothly. Things like feeling wanted, cherished, and revered. Astor caressing me like he has all day, is nothing short of a long, naked hug.

I want him to do it again. And again. And again.

What is wrong with me?

A small voice inside my head says something that I already know. I might be falling in love with Dr. Potter.

I don't know how I should feel about that. Am I betraying my sister by falling in love with her daughter's father? Am I making these feelings up because I'm lonely and Astor has been here for me in my darkest hour?

There are so many reasons, other than love, that I could be feeling this way.

But one thing is for sure, I enjoy the feeling.

I enjoy being the object of Astor's time and affection.

I adore his touch and the way he looks at me when I'm talking. The way he'll stop what he's doing and absorb every word as if he's committing it to memory.

"Are you not going to answer me?" He nips at my ear and chills break out along my arms but then again, maybe the chills are from only being in my bra and underwear.

Arching my back, I give him better access to more sensitive parts of my neck. "Depends. Is this your way of convincing me?"

He chuckles. "Hmm... maybe we should try a different tactic, then?"

He pulls back, and I whimper. "I thought we were spending quality time together?"

"We are." I watch with rapt fascination as he picks up the syringe and injects another gummy bear with the precision of a surgeon.

"I don't know if anyone ever told you this, but it's super sexy when you do that." I mean, a compliment is a compliment, no matter how weird it might sound.

Astor snorts. "Filling candy is sexy? I think I have the definition of sexy all wrong."

I narrow my eyes as he walks over confidently and, if possible, even more alluring. "It's the syringe and how you insert it like you're…" Okay, well, now I really am making it weird.

Astor's brows arch. "Like I'm what? Making love?"

I shrug, trying to seem unimpressed. "Or just sticking your dick in slowly because you're too old to pound it fast anymore."

I knew those were fighting—I mean fucking—words when I said them. So, when Astor snatches me off the island, and flips me over his shoulder, all I can do is laugh when he carries me into his bedroom and tosses me on the mattress like a rag doll.

"Slow, huh?" Those sexy sweatpants of his are off before I can even get my bearings. "I guess you'll have to help an old man out and do all the work then."

He pulls my underwear off (we both knew where the vodka would take us) in one go, leaving me bare from the waist down.

"You forgot something."

I pop my bra strap, and a devilish smirk pulls onto his face. "I didn't forget it. You're going to take it off for me while you ride my face."

My mouth drops open. "Did you say—"

Astor climbs onto the bed, his glorious body toned from all the hours I've yet to see him spend in the gym, and lies down. "You like to take charge, don't you, Ms. McKellan?" He places his hands behind his head. "Especially with powerful men. Does this suit you—me being beneath you?"

Oh, hell. Oh, sweet holy hell. This man wants me to orgasm just from his words.

"I don't mind a man in charge, Dr. Potter, as long as he's a good man."

Astor's cocks a brow, his face alight with eager anticipation. "And if he's a good man who wants to do bad things to you?"

I'm liking where this game is going. "As long as he can back up all this shit-talking, I think I could be game." I crawl over Astor's hips, straddling his narrow waist with the heat of my bare pussy coming in contact with the heat of his skin.

We both groan at the contact.

"I want you to pleasure yourself on top of me—show me what that vibrator does that I can never live up to."

I vaguely recall telling him something similar in the hospital. At the time, I wasn't wrong. The vibrator was amazing, but not as amazing as Dr. Potter and his magnificent penis have been. "I might have been wrong with that statement," I admit.

He moves his hips up, grinding his hard cock into my sensitive clit. "Bare yourself to me, Keagan."

It wasn't a request.

He's not giving me control—not fully anyway.

And I think I'm quite okay with that.

Astor has never been an entitled man like Ass Face and Archer, and because of that, I want to please him. I want him to take control of my body.

Reaching behind my back, I unlatch my bra, letting the material slide down my arms, baring my breasts to him. This moment feels like more than just sex. It's trust built between two people—submission— as I let him know that I'm opening myself up to more than I ever have before.

"That's my girl." His arms twitch, but he keeps them tucked behind his head. "Tell me what you need."

I need him, but I don't say that. Instead, I pull my arms out of the bra strap and toss it to the floor. "I want your mouth," I tell him, feeling powerful when his cock jerks against my ass.

"Where?"

I drag my finger down my chest and circle my nipple. "Here. I want your mouth here."

His tongue snakes out, wetting his lips. "Put it in my mouth."

Chills break out along my skin as I follow his directions, placing my hands by his head and lowering my chest to his mouth. The sensation of heat, followed by the pressure of his mouth, bucks me forward as he nips and sucks my breast.

"You follow directions well, Dr. Potter."

My head drops to my chest. I'm struggling to keep from collapsing onto his face, but the view of this powerful man setting my body on fire with just his mouth is tantalizing torture, especially when I crave more.

"I want…" Sweat dots my forehead as I pant out breaths, trying to remember what I need to say.

"What do you need, Keagan?" Astor licks my nipple, moving his head to the space between my breasts and inhaling. "Tell me."

I almost admit that I'd rather he flip me over and pound me into oblivion, but then there's this other part of me that wants to play this naughty little game with him. "I want you to lick me… lower."

Astor leans back slowly, a stupid-sexy smirk on his face as he drops his head back to the mattress. "You know what to do."

Put my pussy on his mouth.

I don't know if I'm the weirdo here, but I have never ridden a man's face. I would argue that it seems demeaning to the person on the bottom, but then again, maybe that's the point. Submitting yourself, putting your pride aside to make someone feel good is the greatest show of love and devotion.

Astor isn't a man that should be on the bottom. He's the type of man that I imagine women drop to their knees for, yet, here he is, lying beneath me, his sole intent to pleasure me.

There's a reason some men make women stupid, and Astor is exhibit A.

Inhaling, I gaze into those beautiful eyes, he's waiting, giving me time to make the first move. He's submitting to me, and he's waiting for me to do the same. It's a pivotal moment in our relationship—one I no longer want to ignore.

Inching up his body, I hold his eyes until they disappear between my thighs. He doesn't give me time to settle, his arms come out from behind his head and clamp down on my hips, his tongue slipping inside me in the next breath. At first, it's a gentle caress, much like how he used the syringe with the gummy. Softly and confidently, he eases in and out of my body, filling and retreating, so that I recognize the emptiness, the need, the hole he leaves when he's gone.

My hips buck, but he holds me down, making me feel everything, even the rush of wetness that's likely dripping on his face, but he doesn't seem to care. In fact, the noises he makes while he nips and tastes me have me thinking he's enjoying himself even more, knowing I'm losing control.

And the more he teases, the more I find it difficult not to smother him. "Astor," I beg. "I need—" At this point, I don't have time to play the "tell me what you want" game. "I need you inside me. Now."

His mouth stops immediately, and later, I'll think about how stupid he made me, because I don't think about a condom. I simply slide down his body, take his cock in my hand and lower myself onto him.

The muscles in his neck flex, his swollen cock demanding entry while my opening stretches around the welcome intrusion. It's the biting pain that tells me when I'm fully seated and full of Astor Potter's cock. It feels like he is everywhere inside me, but maybe that's just him, demanding space in my heart too.

Exhaling, I try relaxing as his palms slide up my thighs to my hips. "Set the pace, Keys."

With a slow roll of my hips, I do. I take everything I need from this man. His power. His strength. I use it all as I work us into a needy frenzy. "I need you to finish."

Because as much as I like to be the woman in charge, I enjoy Astor being the man in charge more.

I should have known he was hanging on by a thread, because the man needs no other instruction when he growls out, "Hang on."

And then he grips my hips, slamming me down on his cock, moving my body to the speed of his liking.

I can't breathe as he thrusts inside, hard and owning. Astor Potter is making sure I know that he's the only one to ever own my body. When he thrusts for the last time, pulling one final scream from me, I realize that I am completely and utterly in love with him.

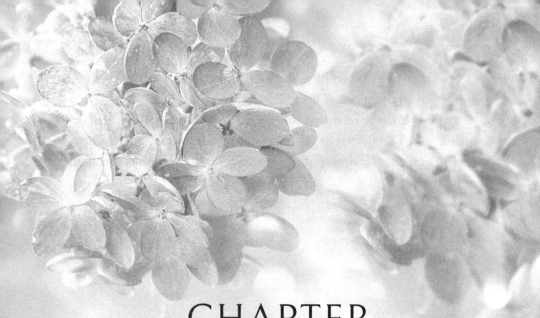

CHAPTER TWENTY-FIVE

Keagan

"What is on her head?"

I pull Tatum from her car seat and grin. "It's a bow. Don't you think she looks adorable?"

Astor's gaze tracks from the olive-green headband with a bow, which I'll admit, is pretty large for her little baby face, to the matching headband in my hair.

"I think she is adorable," he says in a flat voice, his eyes never leaving me. "I didn't realize she favored the boho chic look already."

I tuck the little nugget in the sling and turn around so Astor can tighten the buckle at my back. "Yeah, we talked about it the other day when you were napping."

"Oh really?"

His thumb grazes the base of my neck as he moves my hair off my shoulder to get to the ring, pulling the fabric of the sling. I swallow, feeling the warmth of his hand as he pulls me against him, tightening the last of the straps, reminding me of last night when I realized I was in love with Tatum's father.

"Yeah, Tatum and I decided that you and Piper have the worst taste in clothes," I recover quickly. "If I didn't step in, she would end up being the only kid in daycare wearing a Vera Wang pants suit when you go back to work." I turn around and teasingly straighten Astor's collar as an example. "Someone had to put a stop to this madness before it got out of hand. Besides, we can't have the kid going into the grocery store, looking like she's going to a Milan fashion show."

Not that Astor has dressed her like that yet—she's too little, but he will, I just know it.

"So you both decided boho bracelets and oversized linen bows were the right grocery store attire?" Astor's lips twitch, fighting back a smile.

"Yeah, we did. Are you trying to imply that we have no taste in fashion?" I glance down at my own pair of linen pants and white crop top.

Clearly, Tatum had no say in this matter, but I'll be leaving soon—the least I can do is impart some style on the girl. It's not that I want to leave; I don't. But I can't put off Archer much longer. He's resorted to sending me emails instead of calling. My guess, he doesn't want to risk Astor answering again.

"Not at all." He chuckles, shaking his head. "Just making sure I understand."

"Good, I'm glad we have that settled. I'll stock her closet full of acceptable outfits and bows before I leave. If you think they are too big, you'll know they are just right."

I swear Astor's eyes flash quickly with something like anger, but it's gone before I can be sure. Was it because I mentioned leaving?

"Got it," Astor states dryly. "The bigger the bows, the better."

"The motto all women should have," I agree with a grin, totally taking this discussion to the gutter, and hoping to return some lightness to our conversation.

Surely Astor understands that no matter how much I love him and Tatum, I have a life back in Fairfield—a career that I've worked years to achieve. I can't be another love-struck woman and throw all of that away just because I fell in love. I will never be solely dependent on a man. Not that I couldn't learn to trust one—especially Astor—but I want to work, and right now, that work is in Fairfield, three hours from Astor and Tatum.

But we have time.

We'll figure something out.

We have to because I'm not sure that I can live without them.

Shaking his head, Astor places his hand on my lower back and guides me into the store, effectively ending our conversation.

Once inside, Astor grabs a cart and starts pushing it alongside me. "Did you bring a list?" he asks.

I stare at him and blink slowly. "When did you allow time for a list?"

The man kept me in bed until it was time to pick up Tatum, and then we stayed and chatted with Halle and Vance a while before coming to the store.

He at least looks sheepish for forgetting the list. "We'll just go down every aisle and whatever we miss, we can order."

"Do you know how to order groceries?"

He grins. "I'll learn." Those bright, unnaturally blue eyes hold mine. "I can take notes when I'm studying the grocery store dress code for future visits."

I jostle Tatum, laughing so hard. "Stop. You're gonna wake her up," I scold, but I'm still giggling.

"Looks like she's happy right where she is."

We both look down at the little girl sleeping peacefully against my chest.

My little niece.

The only family I have now.

"Don't worry," I clear my throat, forcing back the emotion. "You'll grow boobs in no time. I heard children always pack the pounds on you."

Astor flashes me a look that clearly relays that he's not concerned in the least about packing on any future pounds. Which he should be, he can't stay this hot forever. Eventually his prime will end, and he'll be like all of us regular people.

"Okay," I try shifting his focus onto something else, "what aisle do we start with?"

He tips his chin to the bread aisle and starts walking.

I must say, it might look like this man is about to walk a runway in his expensive suit pants and button-down shirt, but those forearms with the sleeves rolled up as he steers a grocery cart to my favorite food—bread—relay something totally different. Those forearms say they held me up by the ass while he fucked me hard against the wall last night.

Oh my gosh.

I cannot get wet in the grocery store.

But muscled forearms with prominent veins just bring out the horny ho in me.

"You alright over there?"

I didn't realize I've been staring hard at his arms—like crazy person hard.

"Yeah, I'm fine." I rip my gaze away. "Are you fine?"

He nods, watching carefully as his lips tip up into a smile. "Is something on my arm I should be concerned about?"

"Nope, just that arrogance."

Heaven help me.

"Arrogance, huh? I don't—"

"Astor?"

A feminine voice stops him cold. Like he freezes mid-step, his posture stiffening with the grip he has on the cart. I'm concerned he's cutting off the circulation in his hands.

"Rebekah," he says tightly, forcing a fake smile that I haven't seen in a while now. "How are you?"

This 'Rebekah' with her copper hair, green eyes, and buttoned t-shirt dress has the nerve to give me a cursory glance before pushing closer to Astor. "I'm well." She points to the little boy in her cart. "As you can tell."

As he can tell?

What does the toddler have to do with Astor knowing she's well?

187

"He's handsome," Astor says, sounding like someone else is speaking the words for him—like that old Astor when I first met him.

"Isn't he?" Rebekah smiles, and it makes me ragey for no rational reason.

Who is this woman, and why does it seem like Astor would rather run through this grocery store naked than keep talking to her?

"His sister is at home with the nanny."

Ooh, the nanny. Isn't she flashy rich?

"Congratulations. I didn't realize you had another."

Just tell her to go back to the country club, Astor. Jeez. She's already annoying me in the first two seconds of meeting her.

"Yeah, Ashlyn has been such a welcome surprise in our life." Rebekah cuts her eyes to the carrier on my chest, addressing me for the first time. "Is she yours?"

Is she mine?

I look at Astor and mouth, *what the fuck?* What is this, a high school reunion on aisle six? "No."

I'm in no mood to be polite to people who make the man next to me revert back to the ice king.

"No?" She chuckles. "Well, she certainly isn't Astor's," she looks over at Astor and blinks her fake eyelashes, "unless you decided to adopt."

Oh hell no.

She did not just insult this man.

Does she not know the hell he's been through these past few months?

"I need you to take Tatum," I tell Astor, keeping my eyes trained on the bitch in front of me.

I've dealt with people like this before. Ass Face trained me well. And while I would normally never resort to violence, someone needs to pop this woman in the mouth for being a cunt, and Astor, God love him, is too much of a grown-up to do it.

Suddenly, I feel his hand loop around my back, pulling me in so that I'm between his body and the cart, effectively caging me in and preventing me from teaching this woman a lesson.

"Always a pleasure seeing you, Rebekah."

Boo. I knew he wouldn't let the gangster out. "At least spit on her basic white shoes," I mutter, but Astor doesn't listen. Instead, he takes the high road and nudges the cart forward.

I'm forced to walk, so I don't squish Tatum between me and the cart, but that doesn't mean I don't have a parting remark for Ms. Cuntbunny. No one gets away with being mean to my Dr. Potter.

"Agreed," I tell her with a smile, "always a pleasure, Twat."

She gasps and covers the toddler's ears, giving Astor a disappointed look. "Maybe you should spank me," I tell him. "I think she's under the impression you care that she's insulted."

At that, Ms. Thang scurries off with a harumph that Astor and I ignore.

I hear Astor's sigh, and you know what? I don't have time for it. "Do not even act scandalized back there. You are a doctor, I'm sure you've had to give someone a hard diagnosis before."

His front presses closer to my back and I feel his heat everywhere as he leans down, his breath cresting over my neck. "And her diagnosis was that she was a twat?"

I can't tell if I groan at the closeness or the taunting behavior. Either way, my head goes back, resting against his chest. "Stage four, I'm afraid. Someone had to tell her."

"I see."

That's the only warning I get before I feel the pressure of his lips in my hair, placing a kiss to the top of my head. For a moment, we both pause in the middle of the aisle.

"I think it's time you knew the whole story," he finally says.

"Rebekah is my ex-wife."

CHAPTER TWENTY-SIX

Astor

"Whoa. Back up."

I was impressed Keagan made it home without asking any questions. As a matter of fact, she changed Tatum and helped me put the groceries away, before she popped open a bottle of wine, chugging straight from it before passing it to me.

"So you were married, and grocery store twat is none other than the baby shower bitch?" She snorts, wiping her mouth with the back of her hand. "You've gotta be kidding me. It was her baby shower Piper and I went to a couple of years ago?"

I nod, passing the wine back. "I need something stronger to finish this conversation."

"You damn sure do because I want to know why in the fresh red hell you needed a hug at this bitch's baby shower."

I cut her a scathing look. "I didn't need a hug."

Grabbing the bottle of bourbon from the cabinet, I pour two fingers worth and down it in one go as Keagan continues talking. "I'm sorry. You needed support or whatever word Piper used back then."

"I didn't need the support either, but I appreciated Piper coming nonetheless."

Keagan rounds the island and comes to stand in front of me. "If she's your ex-wife, why were you at her baby shower? I know it wasn't because she was the sweetest during your marriage."

At first, I think of lying and giving her the same story I gave my brothers: I was never home. She was lonely, and we parted on mutual terms.

But I promised Keagan the truth. Up until now, only her sister knew the true story.

"Because for months I thought the baby was mine."

Keagan sucks in a breath. "She cheated on you?"

I nod tightly.

"And lied and told you the baby was yours?"

Even thinking about it brings back the embarrassment. "There's more to it than that," I admit, not to protect Rebekah's reputation, but so Keagan knows how her sister became involved.

"I'm listening." Keagan grows quiet, walking into the living room and taking a seat in one of the chairs.

I follow, growing more uncomfortable by the minute. Keagan and I've shared a lot of things, but nothing as personal as this is about to get. "Rebekah and I were married for two years before you and I met at the baby shower."

"You were divorced at the baby shower?" She takes another sip of wine straight from the bottle.

"We were in the process."

"What happened?" Her voice is timid, like she's unsure if she really wants to know why Rebekah and I divorced.

"I couldn't give her what she ultimately wanted." It's a vague answer, but it buys me time before I have to admit the truth.

"Like what? A ten-carat diamond?" She looks proud of that comment. "Or was it twelve?"

I clear my throat fighting the urge to detach—to get up and leave. "It was an heir."

Her breath leaves her in a swoosh of air. "What do you mean you couldn't give her an heir? Did you not want any children?"

A haunting feeling stirs in my chest, icing my insides, reminding me of how I could turn it all off, and I almost let it, until I feel Keagan's hands push my knees apart, kneeling between my legs. "Did you not want kids, Astor?"

She wants me to say yes. She wants to be right about me. To think I went on the Grace of Mercy ship to avoid her sister and the pregnancy. She wants a reason to lump me in with all the other men she knows.

"Quite the opposite." I close my eyes and lean back as I let the words out again. This time to the other McKellan sister. "I've always wanted children. And Rebekah, even more so. We started trying during our engagement. Rebekah didn't want to wait until we were married."

She snorts. "Rebekah just wanted to make sure her divorce settlement would be fatter than her ass."

This woman. "I don't know, but either way, she was disappointed."

I take a breath, calming myself for what I need to say next. "I'm infertile, Keys. I can't have children."

Keagan's eyes narrow, and I know she thinks I'm lying.

"Tatum was a miracle child for me," I explain. "After a year and a half of trying, Rebekah finally became pregnant." I gaze down at Keys, locking eyes. "We were both so excited to be parents that we had remodeled the guest room before the morning sickness kicked in. But then…"

Keagan smooths her palms over my thighs when I hesitate. "You can tell me."

"But then the pain started." I close my eyes so I don't have to look at her. "I had met Piper on the Grace of Mercy a couple of years ago. I knew she was a urologist, so I gave her a call."

"Astor." I feel her lips press against mine, but I don't open up for her. I feel too exposed as it is.

"Piper ran some tests." I open my eyes, so Keagan knows what kind of man I can't be. "I suffer from varicocele, caused from a genetic abnormality that doesn't allow the valves to function properly in my—"

"Balls?" Keagan supplies.

"Basically." I chuckle. "Piper told me that any hope for kids would require a procedure."

"But Rebekah was pregnant, which I'm guessing was the pool boy's child and not yours."

"Another doctor actually." I shrug like her infidelity still doesn't sting. "Rod and I weren't friends or even in the same practice, but he lived two houses down from us."

"Here?" Keagan looks at the door, like she's contemplating finishing what she started in the grocery store.

"No. I moved here after we divorced."

Her shoulders relax a little as she settles back on her heels. "So, this procedure, Piper did it and y'all practiced to see if it worked?" She laughs, but she knows Piper and I better than that. We would have never had some frivolous fling to celebrate.

"I never agreed to the procedure."

"Why?"

This is the hard part. "I don't know. Pride. Anger. Likely pride." I chuckle. "Men are supposed to be able to have children. Especially patriarchs in the family. We aren't supposed to need fertility specialists and doctors extracting sperm so we can create an heir."

"That's a little sexist, don't you think?"

I shrug. "It was how I felt. What kind of man was I if I couldn't procreate?"

"So you told Piper that you didn't want the procedure?"

I nod. "She understood, especially when I told her of Rebekah's pregnancy and upcoming baby."

Keagan falls back on the floor dramatically. "You are such a better person than me. You couldn't have paid me to go to that bitch's baby shower."

Leaning down, I pull her from the floor and into my lap. "I had a reputation to protect. I never told my family about why Rebekah and I were divorcing. All they knew was it was a mutual separation, and that she found someone immediately."

Her eyes narrow. "They could do the math. They knew she was a trifling whore."

I grin. "But unlike you, no one would dare say that to me."

"So, your brothers just minded their own business?" She scoffs. "No way would I have let P-Money get away with that secret."

Neither of us bring up the fact that Piper did, in fact, keep a secret from her.

"My brothers knew I would tell them when I was ready."

"And were you ever ready?"

I lower my head, inhaling her hair as I cradle her against me. "No. But the baby shower changed me. I became angry and detached. All I wanted to do was work. Having my own family became irrelevant. Only my brothers and my job mattered to me."

"But?"

"But the pain in my groin intensified, and I had to see your sister again. But unlike the previous time, there were more tests involved. Tests that made me feel less like a man. I couldn't even walk inside the exam room, much less let her—" I wave my hand between us, "—run some tests. I was embarrassed. Here I was, a prestigious surgeon discussing my sperm count with a colleague."

"Piper has been on worse dates, trust me. That was probably her typical Friday," she says, trying to lighten the mood.

"Your sister knew I was two seconds from bolting. There was no way after the humiliation I felt with Rebekah's betrayal that'd I'd be able to come in a cup again. I couldn't even discuss the pain down—" I can't even finish. Even talking about it now causes me grief. Infertility is hard enough to discuss, but infertility for a man is a blow to everything we are. Men are supposed to be the strong ones, and here I was, barren and without a wife in the prime of my life.

"Hey," Keys loops her arms around my neck, "no judgment here. If it helps, I can tell you about some really bad urinary tract infections, where I literally thought my vag was poisoning me."

I snort. "That's okay. I think I can make it without one of those stories."

"You can always change your mind. I have plenty saved up here." She taps her head, which just makes this whole scene feel like the one I had with her sister.

"You're more like your sister than you think," I tell her.

She turns quiet, waiting for me to tell her more.

"When it was clear I was about to leave Piper's practice and never speak to her again, Piper grabbed my hand and led me to her office. She poured us a glass of whiskey from a bottle she kept in her drawer and we both took a drink. And then another. Then she told me how even fertile women like herself struggled with the reality of never having a child of their own. She never had time to date or even raise a child with the hours she kept, but that didn't mean she didn't want one."

Keagan's face drops. "I'm the reason she never had the time for a child. She was constantly doing things for me."

I tip her chin up with my finger. "She wanted to do those things for you. You were all she had. She talked about you all the time—how proud she was of you."

"But, like you, she wanted a baby."

I pull her into my chest, murmuring into her hair, "We both had barriers in our lives."

"But then you somehow managed to knock her up anyway? Did you both strike some kind of deal and do in vitro?"

"What a story that would have been, huh?" I laugh. "Unfortunately, our story wasn't as interesting. After we had drinks that night, she gave me the cup again. Told me she was going to grab dinner and to leave a sample on her desk." I swallow, the emotion bubbling up. "She knew I wouldn't be able to face her and give her a sample. She said it would be easier if I was tipsy."

"Wouldn't the alcohol mess up the sample?"

I shrug. "She already knew it was low. We had already determined that much the last time. But the last time I was more confident, thinking it was a kidney stone or something. I never thought I was infertile."

Leaning back, I take a breath. "Anyway, I think it was Piper's way of just breaking the ice, getting me used to the idea of running tests on such a sensitive subject matter that clearly wasn't going away anytime soon."

"Did you leave one—a sample, I mean—that night?"

I nod. "Piper called me the next morning, confirming that I had no traces of sperm. She wanted to run more tests."

"Which I'm guessing you didn't do."

"You would be guessing correctly. But you know your sister. She knew I was in pain and knew it would only continue until I addressed it. So she invited me to dinner, where we had a long conversation and a lot of alcohol."

"And sex, I'm guessing."

I bow my head. "We were both lonely and…"

"I get it. You don't have to explain your reasoning to bang my sister. She was hot and had good sense. Not many women would turn down a night with you, Pec-tastic."

"Pec-tastic?" What in the hell is that? "Never mind, it doesn't matter. Your sister and I shared a night in which we didn't use a condom, because why would we? We were clean and I couldn't get her pregnant."

"Oh hell, that was too far. Speed up until the end. Tatum was conceived because there was one soldier left in the tank and he was up for the mission."

Both of us belt out a laugh. "I guess so."

"And you ended up feeling comfortable enough to let my sister touch your penis in the office afterwards and run the needed tests."

I chuckle, noting that none of this news seems to bother Keagan. "Exactly. She wanted to do a procedure and then extract what sperm I had left, just in case it was unsuccessful. But either way, fertility issues aside, she could relieve the pain."

"And you didn't want to do that?"

I take a deep breath. "I needed time to think about it."

"So you decided what better way to create space and time than to go on the six-month Grace of Mercy Mission Ship?"

I grin. "Piper and I set a date for when I returned to do the procedure. But once I was distracted with surgeries, the pain became just something I learned to deal with."

"You were going to change your mind?"

I sigh, feeling exhausted from this conversation. "Yes."

Keagan's face falls. "She knew you wouldn't believe she was pregnant—because of the tests and Twat Face. It's why she made the book and didn't tell you. She wanted you to see the proof."

I nod, shame consuming me from the inside out. "She knew I would need to see results."

Tears swell in her eyes. "She could have told me. I wouldn't have told anyone."

I kiss the tear that falls down her cheek. "Your sister had so much honor. She knew what Tatum meant for the both of us."

"Eighteen years of debt?" She tries laughing off the sting of betrayal.

"A miracle—something we both wanted and thought we never would have." I squeeze Keagan harder. "I think Piper wanted to tell me the news first. I think that's why she was waiting to tell you about her pregnancy. Because Tatum was more than just an oops. She was a miracle."

CHAPTER
TWENTY-SEVEN

Keagan

A week later, and I have almost all of Piper's house boxed up. I kept several—or dozens—of boxes that I thought Tatum would, one day, like to have, like a few of Piper's dresses and her entire jewelry collection. Astor may want to invest in a storage unit.

But I need to get this stuff out of here.

Astor and I are supposed to meet with Piper's attorney for the reading of her will after Thanksgiving (apparently, he's in Maui). I needed to be sure everything was ready to be moved or sold when Piper's wishes are handed down.

Though, if I was smart and knew anything about wills and death, I would have known that I should have called the attorney prior to boxing Piper's things. That way, if she wanted certain items to go to certain people, I wouldn't have to root through the boxes to find it.

But at this point, I don't care. I would say I learned something for any future family deaths, but I don't really need to worry about that now, do I? I never plan on doing this ever again.

My heart won't be able to take it.

It likely won't be able to take leaving Tatum and Astor when I have to return home and back to work, especially since learning about everything that transpired between Astor and Piper. We haven't brought it up again since that night.

But we don't need to.

I loved Astor before I knew everything that happened.

His infertility means nothing. To me, Astor is the same hot DILF as before—when he yelled at Archer for me, who has left me alone for the most part. Instead of calling, he's been sending me project materials and requesting an approximate return-to-work date. I asked him for two more weeks. And as dickish as Archer has been, he granted me the extra time off—which I appreciate, since I know I'm out of bereavement and vacation time.

I know it's only from Astor threatening him, but still. I've been able to get Piper's home situated and spend time with my niece.

And fall in love with her father.

I wonder what Piper would say about this situation now that Astor has told me the truth. Would she give me shit for falling in love with the "asshole" from the baby shower or would she tell me to be careful, that long-distance relationships can be rough—especially for someone like me who already doesn't trust men? Honestly, I don't know. Everything just seems so complicated.

No matter what, to pursue an actual relationship, one of us will have to sacrifice something.

It should be me.

I have no ties to Fairfield other than *Game Tales* and Kenny. I could easily pick up and move, since I don't have a house or a booming medical practice to run.

But then I'd lose my promotion.

And the McKellan women have always put their careers first.

Until Piper chose Tatum.

She would have known her peers would talk when they found out she was carrying the child of her colleague, but she did it anyway. Piper sacrificed her reputation for her little girl.

I used to think nothing was worth sacrificing yourself for, but now, I'm not so sure.

A knock sounds at the front door, thankfully, interrupting my train of thought. I walk over and peer through the window, spotting a familiar set of blue eyes.

"Hi," I say, pulling open the door. "I thought we weren't meeting until tomorrow?" Astor asked if I needed help packing today and I told him no. Tatum had spent most of the night crying and he looked like he needed a day of naps.

"Something came up." He shifts on his feet but doesn't come in. "Can you watch Tatum today?"

"Sure. Where are you going?" I don't even care that I'm being nosy. This man has thawed my heart; therefore, he's forced to suffer the consequences of being with someone who's curious like me.

"I called" is all he says.

"You called who?" Why is he being so secretive?

"Piper's office."

It takes me a second to put it together, to understand what he isn't saying, but then it hits me. "You're having the procedure. You're fulfilling your promise to my sister."

He nods slowly. "And to myself. If anyone has shown me the value of putting pride aside and going after what you want, it's been you."

What? Have I said anything to convince him to go through with the procedure? "I don't understand."

He sets Tatum in her carrier at my feet and presses a kiss to my lips. "You don't need to understand. I'll be back as soon as I can. They had a cancellation and Dr. Teller said they could move up my procedure."

Procedure? "I didn't know you had scheduled it yet."

He swallows, as if this whole thing is uncomfortable for him to talk about. "A couple of days ago, when you watched Tatum."

I narrow my eyes. "You said you were going to the office."

"I did go to the office—just not mine."

Oh, I see how he's going to be. "You could have told me."

A deep line creases his forehead. "I didn't want to disappoint you if I couldn't follow through."

"Why would you disappoint—" I shake my head. "You know what? It doesn't matter. I'm coming with you. We can ask your brothers if they can watch Tatum for us."

He's quick to respond. "No. They can't know about this."

"But don't you need someone to drive you home?"

"I have it handled." He turns to walk away, but I know him now, and know when he's avoiding.

"You're not going alone." I grab his shirt and pull him to a stop. My ass he has it handled… "And you are not driving yourself home after anesthesia." This man thinks he's invincible.

"No."

"Yes." We stand there, eye to eye, him furious and me determined. "You didn't leave me when I needed support, so I'm not leaving you."

He works his jaw and I know he's thinking of all those times I asked him to leave, and yet, he stayed because he knew, deep down, I needed someone.

"Don't get mad at me," I tell him when all he does is glare. "You're the one who made the rules to this thing between us."

"I don't want my brothers to know." His voice sounds like gravel.

"I'm sure they would be more concerned that you were trying to drive home loopy."

"I said I have it covered." He tries injecting a bite to his tone, but he should know he doesn't scare me.

"Cancel whatever ridiculous plans you had and get in the car. I'll text Halle." Grabbing Tatum's carrier, I take a step forward, but Astor doesn't move.

"Or we can stand here while you brood." I shove at his chest. "Unless we're only there for each other when it's at my expense."

I wish I knew all that went through his mind in those minutes that he just stared at me; but I'm thinking it's probably best if I don't, since he looks like he could throw me in the back of his trunk without regret.

"Fine," he finally clips out. "But we don't tell Halle what we're doing."

Goodness. "She won't care."

"No." He seems set on this condition.

"Fine. We won't tell her."

I understand where he's coming from. I wouldn't want to air my medical business out to my family and assistant either, but what if something happens and we need them to keep Tatum longer? It's not like I know anything about this procedure or what it entails. Hell, I don't know all that much about his infertility issues to know what the surgery is trying to fix. All I can hope is that it's an uncomplicated process.

"Let's go." Without another word or even a *go team*, Astor grabs Tatum's carrier and walks to his car. Within fifteen minutes, we're at Vance and Halle's, handing over Tatum.

"You sure you're okay?" I knew Halle wouldn't go for the vague question, *Can you watch Tatum? We need to take care of something.* Vagueness to a woman is a red flag. We like details, and know that when you leave out the details, you're up to something.

I tried to tell Astor, but he insisted that I let him do all the talking. Therefore, leaving Halle suspicious as hell.

"We're fine. I promise I'll be back before dinner."

Halle looks past Astor to me. "We can keep Tatum for the night if you need us to."

I start to nod, but Astor grabs my hand, pulling us toward the car. "Thanks, Hal. I'll be back soon."

Men. I swear.

"What if you feel bad tonight? Don't you think you should have left it open that we might need her to watch Tatum," I say when we're back in the car.

"No, because I'll be fine by tonight."

But he wouldn't be fine because twenty minutes later, when we're parked at the hospital, he wouldn't get out of the car.

"You can change your mind," I tell him. "You're still a man, no matter what that bitch said. Infertility doesn't define you. A good woman would understand."

Astor drags his gaze to mine. "Would you understand? If your husband could never give you a child that shares your DNA?"

I take a moment and really think about how to answer. "Yes, I would understand. I would love him regardless of what he could give me. When I marry a man, it will be unconditional."

It shocks me that I said *when* I marry and not *if*. Seems like Astor has had more of an effect on my life than I thought.

"But if he could try to make it possible, would you want him to try?"

I clasp his cheeks between my hands, so he can't turn away when I say, "I'd ask him how far he was willing to go to get what *he* wanted."

He jerks in my hands.

"What? Was that the wrong thing to say?" Hurrying, I try to fix that strange look on his face. "All I'm saying, Astor, is this isn't about anyone else but you. You love children. It's clear to everyone around you. And if having more children is something that you want, then I would tell you to do it."

"And if it fails?" He swallows thickly. "Would you still love him if he couldn't give you a biological child?"

He must see the confusion on my face because he quickly adds, "Hypothetically, of course." This question doesn't feel all that hypothetical.

"Astor," I whisper in the confines of the car, "do this for you. Not anyone else."

After a moment of searching my eyes, he nods, pulling my hands from his face and kissing the palms. "Thank you."

And then he gets out of the car.

"Wait!" I jump out after him. "I would still love him—my hypothetical husband—even if he couldn't give me biological children. As long as he could be happy with just me."

I don't know how long we stare at each over the hood of the car, but it's long enough that I need to shift my weight to the other foot, and Astor has time to come around to my side and take my hand.

"You're a pain in the ass, you know that?"

I grin, glad he's back to teasing. "I think you like it though."

"That I do, Keys. That I do."

He pulls me into his side, and we walk inside the hospital—together—to finish what he started with my sister.

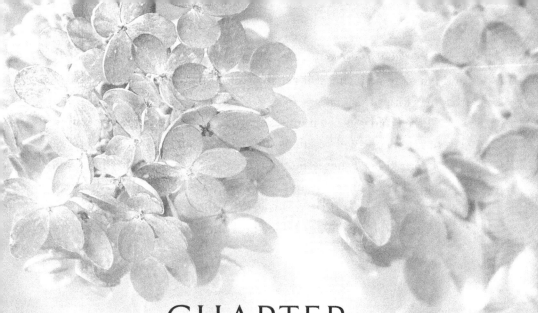

CHAPTER
TWENTY-EIGHT

Keagan

I'm close to a panic attack.

It's been three hours, and no one has been out to tell me how Astor is doing. The doctor said it wouldn't take long at all—less than an hour—and it's been two hours longer than that.

I walk up to the nurses' desk, again, for the third time. "Please. Is there any news?" The woman manning the desk isn't as nice as Carly or Dr. Cox were, when I was here the last time with Tatum and Piper. She doesn't know that my heart started beating out of my chest as soon as we got into the elevator.

But it's not like I can tell this nurse that my sister died here and I can't stand not knowing what is going on with one of the only two people I care about. What if something happened and he coded? What if his heart stopped like Piper's?

Oh, God.

"Please. Please just check with the doctor." I've resorted to pleading and I'm okay with that if it gets her to call the doctor—or anyone—that may know the answers.

"Like I told you two minutes ago, they aren't answering the phone. I'm sure someone will be out as soon as they can."

I don't know if she's lying about them not answering the phone, but I've had all I can take without passing out on the floor. This lady might not know how to get them to answer the phone, but I do.

Astor won't like it, but I hope he'll understand.

"Hey."

Ten minutes later, my knight in scrubs bursts through those doors, looking like someone pissed on his shoes. "Thank you for coming. Like I said on the phone—"

He cuts me off with a look, snagging me by the arm and tugging me down the hall, not bothering to tell the unhelpful woman at the desk what we're doing. "The next time my brother is in the hospital and doesn't call me, I'm holding you personally responsible."

I nod my head, tears already streaking down my cheeks. "He asked me not to say anything." I plead with Vance, who only grunts as he swipes his badge, allowing us through another corridor.

"I'm used to women who don't listen. I thought you were one of them."

I can't tell if it's a compliment or a reprimand. "I'll do better," I promise. "I was just trying to honor Astor's wishes."

"When it comes to his health, he has no fucking wishes unless Duke and I agree to them."

The brotherly love rolling off this man makes my heart hurt. I miss having Piper and her bossy self.

"Do I make myself clear, Keagan?" Vance yanks us to a stop in front of a room that says recovery. "My brother listens to you—he respects you. He'll do what you say."

"Yes, I understand. I'm so sorry. I promise never to obey him again."

With a heavy sigh, Vance pulls me into a hug. "It's okay. I know he's a pain in the ass. You did good calling me."

I shake my head into his scrub top. "He won't think so."

Vance pulls me back and looks me in the eyes. "Yes, he will because he lo—" He stops himself and rakes a hand through his hair. "He'll forgive you; I promise."

And then he opens the door, revealing a pale Astor lying motionless in the bed with tubes in his nose and arms.

I fight off Vance's hold and rush to Astor's side. "Astor." His eyes snap open just as I reach for his hand, hesitating. "Are you okay?" I'm scared to touch him, but don't fight when he grabs my hand and pulls me into the bed, sliding over with a grimace.

Immediately, I start crying, which seems to be my default mode now. "I'm sorry," I apologize for the tears. "I can't stop them. It's the—" I bury my face in his neck, and his arms go around me.

"I'm okay," he promises. "It was just an allergic reaction, but I'm fine."

"Which you wouldn't have had if I knew you were here."

At the sound of Vance's voice, Astor's arms tense around me. "What *are* you doing here?" he all but growls.

"I'm sorry," I mumble, not able to face him. "They wouldn't tell me anything and it had been so long. I thought—"

A sob racks through me and Astor sighs. "It's okay. I'm okay, Keys."

His hold on me relaxes ever so slightly, but his tone doesn't when he addresses his brother. "It was a simple procedure."

I hear a chair scrape the floor and I imagine Vance is settling in for an explanation. "A simple procedure you decided to keep from everyone?"

"Don't talk to me like I'm a toddler, Vance. I had it handled."

"And you thought what? That when I found out my brother was in the hospital without my knowledge, that I wouldn't be upset?"

Astor sighs, his voice a teasing whisper as he mumbles in my ear, "You're so getting punished for this when we get home."

"The doctor said you had to abstain for two weeks after," I remind him based on our earlier conversation with the doctor. Apparently, this procedure has a fast recovery time, but Astor will still need to take it easy for a few days and not have sex for a couple weeks.

"We'll get creative," he returns, his voice leaving no room for negotiation—not that he would get any from me.

"Look, Vance," he says, addressing his brother louder than he did me. "I know you're still anxious about surgery, but I'm fine."

Finally, I poke my head out of Astor's shoulder, and see Vance's elbows on his knees, his jaw ticking as he stares angrily at Astor. "Were you fine when you reacted to the sedation?"

"Tsk, tsk, brother. You know better than to violate patient confidentiality."

"Astor! You scared the hell out of her!"

And apparently, he scared Vance too. I never thought when I called him that he would act this way.

Astor flashes me an annoyed look and I bury my face again, mumbling that I'm sorry. "I'd never reacted to a medicine before, you know that. There's no way either of us could have known. Besides," he holds up his hand with the IV, "it's nothing a little antihistamine can't fix."

"Never again, Astor. Promise me."

I don't quite know why Vance is so worried about this, but I don't blame him. You can't help getting defensive when it comes to the lives of your siblings.

"I promise," he finally says after a moment of tense silence. "Now, can you please go find Dr. Teller and make him discharge me."

I hear something like a grumble then a "fuck you" before the door closes, leaving Astor and me alone.

"Are you mad?"

I feel him lean over and place a kiss to my head. "I'm not mad. Vance would have eventually found out."

"I shouldn't have called him."

He grunts out his agreement. "I shouldn't have let you come. I should have known it was too soon for you to be here."

I don't want him feeling guilty when I basically forced myself into being here. "I was fine with the kids on Halloween," I argue.

"It was the Children's Hospital, not the same hospital as—"

I cut him off, turning over, so I can look at him. "I was triggered because I was scared something happened to you."

His tired eyes stare right down into my soul. "Is that your way of admitting you like me?"

For the first time in hours, I chuckle. "Yeah, Grandpa. That's my way of admitting I don't want to kill you anymore."

"You're supposed to be taking it easy."

At least Astor has the decency to look away when he lies. "I am."

"Just because you have on your sweats and are home, doesn't mean you're resting." I snatch the diaper out of his hands, noticing a fine sheen of sweat dotting his forehead. "When was the last time you took something for the pain?"

The constant ache in my chest flairs when he breathes through his nose while his eyes pinch shut. "I don't need anything."

"Oh, good. For a minute there I thought you had some sense. Good to know I was wrong." I nod to the sofa. "Go sit down. I'll deal with your lies in a minute. I assume Tater Bug is wet."

He nods tightly.

The fact that he's not arguing shows that this stubborn man is in a lot of pain. The doctor said he'd be sore, but staying on top of the pain with pain relievers would keep it under control. I should have known Astor would be a hard ass about it.

Grabbing the wipes, I walk backward toward Tatum's room and point with the diaper. "Sofa. Now. Don't make me push you."

I don't wait and see if he follows directions. My guess is he doesn't, but I'll deal with that later. A little girl needs a diaper change, and like her auntie, she's not known for her stellar patience.

I make quick work of Tatum's bottom, getting her settled and in the swing, so she can have a little fun while I argue with her daddy, who

I find miraculously on the sofa, folded over his knees, pulling in laborious breaths.

Walking over, I sit down gently, careful not to jostle him. He doesn't even lift his head. "Did you take something?"

His only response is a slight shake of his head.

I let out a deep breath and take that as my cue to be the adult in this relationship, but when I move to get up, he reaches out and stops me with a hand on my knee. "It'll pass in a few hours."

"Ha." I pat his hand. "The doctor said the soreness would be better in twenty-four hours, not that it would pass."

His hand still covers most of his face. "I don't want to take anything with Tatum here."

Tingles dance in my stomach, and it takes me a second to compose myself enough to answer. "While I can appreciate you putting Tatum first, I'm sure if she could talk, she wouldn't want to see you writhe in pain for an entire day. Besides, it's not like you're taking a narcotic."

It's just over the counter pain meds. He'll function just fine.

But he doesn't want them.

Because his manhood took a hit today, and somewhere in his brain, I'm guessing enduring pain makes him feel better about it.

"I'll be fine."

I don't bother babying him anymore. "You're taking the medicine." I can't stand seeing him like this. As a matter of fact, I hope Twat Face invites us to her next baby shower. I would love to tit punch her for even contributing to this man's demons. It's bad enough that he's right: society doesn't think of men being the ones unable to have children. We expect them not to cry or be weak. Astor might not have an Archer yelling at him every day, but he has scars all the same. His ex-wife made him feel worthless, like he wasn't a man if he couldn't produce heirs, and rather than assure him that wasn't the case, she lied and let another man impregnate her. Like her marriage meant nothing since he couldn't have a child.

And now, here he is, years later, trying to let go of the stereotypes in his head to get what he wants.

Standing, I ignore his mumbled words of protest and make my way into his fancy kitchen, locating the pain meds—still in the bag—on the counter. "Good job, doc. Way to be a hypocrite. I bet your patients would love to know you treat post-op instructions like a wish list."

I catch a hint of a smile peek through the uncovered side of his face. "Perks of being a doctor," he says.

"Perks of being an idiot."

I don't care how macho he thinks he is; the man was put to sleep and underwent a procedure. He may think his superhero body can handle it, but the slight tremble in his arms and sweat on his face say otherwise.

I grab a pack of crackers from his pantry with a water and the meds, and walk to the sofa where Mr. Stubborn sits. "Here. Eat a couple crackers first. Piper was a hard ass about not taking meds on an empty stomach."

Opening the package, I hand over a cracker and wait while Astor just... stares at me.

"Please don't make me look like the asshole by yelling at a man in pain."

That damn grin appears again and it's unsettling how my chest reacts to it. "Eat, Astor. You haven't since you were discharged."

"I don't think I can," he finally mumbles.

I look at him confused. "Why not?"

He looks away and swallows hard.

"Are you going to make me guess?"

For a moment, I think he intends on ignoring me, but he finally gets out that he feels nauseated from the anesthesia.

"Could you try something like a Saltine cracker? Just a bite?"

He looks at me like he'd rather chew on the sole of a tennis shoe.

"We gotta do something. You can't endure the pain on your own. It'll just make you feel worse."

He shakes his head. "I'll be fine."

"Yeah, yeah. You've said that already. Excuse me if I don't believe you."

With a gentle smile, Astor eases to his feet, purposefully looking away so I can't see his discomfort. "I'll go lie down for a little while and see if that helps. Will you watch Tatum for me?"

Didn't I already tell him this earlier? "Yeah."

Do I know he's trying to get away from me? Yes, I do.

But it's too late.

He's stuck with me now.

CHAPTER TWENTY-NINE

Keagan

"Hey," I open the door, "thanks for coming."

Before anyone asks, Vance called checking on his brother. I simply reported his symptoms, and he said he would bring some medicine over.

This. Was. Not. My. Fault.

Vance nods, pushing inside and closing the door behind him. "Is he up?"

I shake my head. "He's still lying down. I didn't want to disturb him."

Vance looks around the house for a moment and then sighs, setting the paper bag on the counter. "There's antiemetics for the nausea in the bag. Have him take one and if he feels better in half an hour, have him take the pain medication with food."

Vance sounds so clinical. "You're talking like we're dealing with someone with sense. Not someone who'd rather suffer for days than follow his discharge instructions."

Vance's lip twitches. "Then I suggest you get creative."

"Creative? I'm trying to make him comfortable, not putting on an art show."

Vance apparently isn't staying as he takes a step backward toward the door. "Get some food and meds in him, and make sure he ices the area every couple of hours, and he'll be back to his charming self tomorrow."

"Where are you going?" I whisper-shout as Vance reaches for the door handle. "Can't you go in there and tell him all those things?"

He chuckles like I've said the most absurd thing in the world. "I could, but he'd likely only pull a muscle when he threw me out. Trust me, if anyone can convince Astor to do something, it's you."

"Why do you keep saying that? The man doesn't listen to me at all."

Vance flashes me a grin, and then shuts the door in my face.

What am I supposed to do now? Walk in there and say please? Is that the creativity Vance suggested? Heaven knows I don't use that word often. In my life, saying the word please is a last resort.

But I need to try something. Anything. Tatum needs her father in tip-top shape, so Auntie Keys won't feel bad about teasing him. It's the natural order of our relationship and Astor is throwing it off by making my heart hurt worse.

And I'm tired of pain.

Therefore, I need to eliminate all pain from my life.

Starting with the big guy in the ridiculously sized master bedroom.

Grabbing the largest mixing bowl I can find, I toss in a bottled water, Astor's meds, the kitchen hand towel, and an ice pack. Dr. Potter better be prepared to compromise on at least two of these items. Otherwise, we will argue, and I hate to do that to someone who doesn't feel well. But when they can't save themselves, someone has to step in.

I check on Tatum as I pass her room, noting her sweet coos and suckling as she snoozes away with a dry bottom and a full belly. Her father, on the other hand, isn't as peaceful when I push open his bedroom door.

There on the bed, the blankets pushed to one side sits a man in deep denial.

"I brought you some goodies."

Astor pulls up to a seated position without moaning, which is impressive, considering he's drenched in sweat. "How's Tatum?"

He completely ignores the bowl of meds, choosing to focus just past me as if Tatum will appear behind me and let him know she's good.

"Your brother dropped by," I tell him, ignoring his question like he ignores me. "He wants you to take this medicine for the nausea." I hold up the pill as proof. "I even brought you water, so there are no excuses."

He at least has the nerve to look exasperated. "You called my brother?"

I don't see any reason in answering this question, even though I'm innocent this time. "Would you like me to hand you a pill?"

When I was being a pain in Piper's ass, she would just stop asking me if I wanted to do something. Instead, she acted like I already agreed and then gave me choices on how I wanted to get it done.

The strategy, while complete trickery, always worked with me, so I'm hoping it works for Astor.

"I said, I'm—"

"—thirsty. I gotcha covered." I hand over the water and open the pill bottle, plucking out one white pill. "Do you need anything else to get this down?"

See? Easy peasy. Just don't act like he has any other choice but to take the medicine.

Slowly, Astor reaches out and takes the pill. "What did you tell Vance?"

I eye his mouth, a subtle suggestion that if he wants to know what I said then he better swallow something.

With a deep and likely pained sigh, Astor places the pill in his mouth and takes a sip of the water, swallowing. I don't know what causes my muscles to relax, or the breath I was holding to release, but I'm appreciative. At least he's one step closer to feeling better.

"What did you tell Vance?"

I turn back to the bowl and pull out the towel and ice pack. "That you were an enormous pain in the ass and for him to please bring me something to knock you out. I can't take any more of this together time."

He snorts. "I see. I'm sure he was happy to oblige."

I shrug, concerned about the dark circles framing his eyes. "He said you need to ice."

The barely-there smile he had drops as his sharp gaze goes to the items clutched in my hands. "Get those away from me."

I expected pushback.

"Don't be ridiculous. You know swelling can cause more pain." I mean, he is a doctor after all. He knows by not bringing the swelling down, it will take longer to heal.

Astor caps the water bottle and pushes back farther onto the bed. "I don't care. Get it away from me."

Alrighty then.

That's totally not happening.

"Are you telling me that you want your junk swelling up to the size of a beachball, all because your pride can't take the hit of icing your crotch?"

I may not be Piper, but I know a thing or two about pride, so I can understand Astor's reluctance. But again, someone has to save him from himself.

"Fine, since you're gonna be weird about it…" I storm out of his room and into the kitchen where I grab another towel and ice pack before barging back into his room. "I don't understand why you're being so ridiculous about this. First, you argued about the wheelchair at the hospital."

He eyes me cautiously as I plop down on the other side of the bed. "I didn't need a wheelchair."

"Just like you don't need pain meds and ice." I slip off my clothes, leaving on only my bra and underwear, feeling the cool air mix with the heat of his stare on my almost-naked body. "I'm beginning to see a trend here. Don't you, Dr. Potter?"

Astor's eyes widen. "What are you doing, Keys? Remember two weeks," he warns.

Like I could forget.

I lie back on his pillows, grabbing the remote and turning on the TV, finding a romcom that I know will annoy him. "I'm getting comfortable."

"Why?"

He swallows carefully, tracking my methodical movements as I let my legs fall open. "Hand me the ice pack."

When all he can do is stare, I reach out and grab it myself, along with the towel, and place it over my hoo-ha—which doesn't appreciate the freezing temperature.

But I'm making a point here.

"What are you doing?" Astor's hand reaches out, like he's going to snatch off the ice pack, but then he sees the warning in my eyes if he even so much as touches it.

"You need to put your pants back on," he says instead.

I ignore him, staring at the TV, spotting a nineties romcom. "What's it worth to you?"

Astor looks at my exposed skin and back at the ice pack I dropped for him to use.

"All you need to do is ice for ten to fifteen minutes. Basically, the introduction of this movie."

He doesn't move. Instead, he keeps his gaze trained on the ice pack. "You shouldn't be icing yourself there."

"Trust me, before you, my vagina was colder than Elsa's castle. This is nothing." I shrug. "But if you're feeling chivalrous, you can join me, so I'm not the only one with her legs spread in this bedroom."

I can tell when he finally surrenders. His head drops to his chest and his shoulders relax. "I'm only doing it this one time," he warns.

"Well, things are gonna get weird because I'm going to ice mine several times a day."

He groans and stands.

"Go ahead and take one of those pain pills while you're over there. Seems like the nausea is passing, since you're arguing more."

He flashes me a bored look and grabs the pill bottle. "I need to know you will wake me if Tatum needs me."

I won't because he needs the rest, but I know he's looking for security here. "I'll wake you if I can't help her."

I'm not waking him just because she cries.

Astor nods tersely and takes out the medicine, swallowing it down quickly. He tosses the ice pack on the bed with a huff. It makes me smile.

"Do you want me to close my eyes?"

I wave my hand at his sweatpants. I haven't seen *everything* since the procedure. His cock could be seriously swollen and he may not want me to look.

"No. You insisted on making this awkward. Who am I to change the pace now that it's my turn?"

Just in case, I keep my eyes focused on the TV.

"Just so you know, I won't forget this." He says the words more like a threat and less like a thank you. But I still treat it as a thank you.

"You're welcome. Anything for Tatum's Papa." And anything to make sure he's okay and not in pain. It's funny how love works.

Astor grunts and climbs into bed, lying next to me with his back against the headboard. I try not to look when he opens his legs and places the ice gently over his underwear, squeezing his eyes shut and taking a few deep breaths.

"Are you in pain?" I finally ask when he opens his eyes.

"No, just uncomfortable."

It's better than a lie.

"What movie is this?" He tries acting like this is a normal night for us, which I can appreciate. It's not often Dr. Potter is vulnerable, but he's allowing me to see him in this state—something he didn't allow his brothers to do.

I'm taking that as a good sign.

"It's a movie you won't like, so you might as well doze off while I

218

watch it." The man was sedated, had an allergic reaction, and then had more drugs pumped into him, all to go home swollen and in pain. He needs to rest like yesterday, which I feel like he's going to fight me on, but then his hand slides across the bed, finding mine, and intertwining our fingers.

His eyes are closed, and I think he's dozing off until he turns his head toward me, opening his tired eyes and locking them onto mine. "Stay."

I don't know if he's talking about staying in the bed with him or in a forever sense, which would be crazy. Just because I think I'm in love with Astor, doesn't mean he feels the same—at least he hasn't said anything to indicate otherwise. Neither have I, if we're getting technical here, but still. Astor and I have been through something traumatic. It's probably best if we take things slow. Staying forever would be rash. Astor's career and family are here, my career is in Fairfield, three hours away. Not that we couldn't pull off a long-distance thing, but knowing me and my suspicious nature and hatred of men, we'd only end up fighting every day until we called it quits.

Neither of us deserves that sort of ending. We've been through too much together to let it end badly and cause things to be awkward for Tatum. We have to think about her and her future with both of us in her life. A relationship could cause problems.

And besides, now is not the time to talk about it with an exhausted Astor. So I offer him a sweet smile, and pull his hand to my lips and kiss it. "I'll stay… until it's time to go."

For a moment, Astor just stares at me. I feel like he wants to argue or say more, but exhaustion takes over and he closes his eyes instead, his breathing finally leveling out.

Or at least I thought.

"Keys," Astor adds groggily, his eyes still closed, "the next time you ice your pussy in my bed, it'll be for an entirely different reason."

CHAPTER THIRTY

Astor

Three weeks later…

Keagan is reading Tatum a bedtime story when I read the text again.

I didn't mean to pry when I picked up her phone to take it to her.

But it was from *him*.

That bastard had sent her two texts back-to-back.

One said, **I knew you weren't that stupid,** and the other said, **Don't forget my coffee.**

I'm surprised he didn't add *bitch* to the end.

I couldn't control my fury—it was the only reason I unlocked her phone and read the rest of his messages. And the more I read, the more pissed off I became.

Archer: I've been patient with you. I'm giving the account to

McGee. He at least comes to work and doesn't make excuses that he's grieving, when really he's just fucking his sister's widow.

She never answered him. But then the next day he texted again.

Archer: If you're not back to work on Monday, you're fired.

And that's when she answered.

Keagan: The reading of the will is on Monday. As soon as it's finished, I'll be there.

That was Friday. Today is Sunday.

"When were you going to tell me, huh?" I snap, just as Keagan closes the nursery door.

Her eyes go wide. "What are you talking about?"

I hold up the phone like it's some kind of proof. "I'm talking about you telling Archer you're returning to work tomorrow."

"Oh." She swallows harshly. "I was going to tell you tonight."

I scoff. "Really? While you were packing your bags?"

I don't know what I'm more angry about, the fact that she kept this from me or didn't tell Archer to go fuck himself.

Keagan takes a step forward, putting a hand on my chest. "I was going to tell you when the time was right. You've been recovering and doing so well that I didn't want to damper your progress."

"I've been fine!"

The procedure only slowed me down a day. After that night of icing with Keys, I was fine. I didn't need any pain relievers or ice, which Keagan felt was a mistake. The point is, my health was fine.

And so were me and Keagan.

We spent the last three weeks binge watching movies together, making dinner, and cooing over the adorable faces Tatum made. We were happy. We were content.

Taking a settling breath, I lower my voice so as not to wake Tatum. "Why are you going back to that asshole?"

"Why wouldn't I?" Keagan scoffs. "I can't just take a six-month mission trip like you did, Astor. I don't make that kind of money."

"I could help you," I offer. "You don't have to go back. You can stay here with me and Tatum for as long as you need."

She blinks back tears. "As long as I need to do what, Astor? We can't just keep living in our own little bubble. Eventually, you'll have to return to work and so will I. The world just doesn't stop because we've had a shitty couple of months."

I understand what she's saying, but I'm not ready to let this go yet. "Things have changed."

She nods. "They have, but there are other things that haven't." Her hand comes up and cups my cheek. "My career is in Fairfield. I know Archer is a volatile piece of shit, but I earned that promotion. I worked hard for it. I can't just give that up, Astor. I can't lose everything."

"But you haven't lost everything. You have us."

Her hand slides to the back of my neck as she moves in closer, molding herself to me. "It's because I do have both of you that I'm doing this."

I pull her away, so I can look her in the eyes. "I don't understand."

Keagan's cheek twitches as her lip quivers. "You and Tatum are all I have left in this world."

"Then why leave?"

"Because I can't keep hiding. I can't avoid my reality. I need to work, Astor, and you need to take care of Tatum on your own."

I understand her need to have a career, and I support that choice, but this doesn't seem that simple.

"You're scared."

She laughs, but it lacks humor.

"Don't act like I'm being ridiculous. We've been through too much to start lying to each other now."

"You're right," she admits, sliding to the floor. "I am scared. I'm scared people will think I'm a floozy who stole my sister's love—"

"I wasn't—"

She holds her hand up, stopping me. "People won't know that you both weren't in love. They'll only know she died having your baby. They will always talk, Astor."

"I don't care. I've dealt with rumors before."

But that's not all she's worried about, I can see it in her eyes.

"Love can't be born from grief," she admits softly, "and Tatum deserves the two most important people in her life to be a constant."

"And you don't think we can?"

She shakes her head. "I'm saying I need time to decide."

Suddenly, my decision of taking six months on the Grace of Mercy to figure things out comes back to bite me in the ass.

"I'm asking for time, Astor. Can you give me that?"

A stranger would think we were a family.

They'd see Keagan's bracelets scattered about on end tables and countertops in my house—even her bra hanging to dry in the laundry room.

They'd see an unmade bed and leftovers in the fridge.

But most of all, they'd see that we started a grocery list that's hanging on the refrigerator next to the picture of us, smiling down at a little girl.

From all the pain and heartache, Keagan and I managed to build our own family. It isn't perfect. It isn't typical, but it's ours.

At least it was until last night.

"All that's left is for you to sign here, Ms. McKellan."

Tears well in Keagan's eyes as she looks at me. There's something she wants to say, something we both do, but we haven't.

Because I promised her time.

Time that I don't want to give her, but time that she deserves.

I think what scares me the most is that she'll be like me. She'll know what she needs, but she'll let fear stand in the way of the life she wants.

Because time doesn't always heal all wounds.

Sometimes, time is simply a reminder of what you lost and what you will never gain.

Keagan and I were forced together by tragic circumstances. Our love story began and, will ultimately end, with tears.

It's not the relationship we imagined—it's not the life we dreamed of.

But through the pain and the grief, we did find happiness.

We found it in each other.

We found it in Tatum.

Keagan is wrong. Love can be born from grief; she just needs to realize it.

So I'm giving her the space her sister once gave to me.

I'm giving her time to come back to us.

With one last look, Keagan turns away and signs her name on the line, handing the pen to me.

Piper's will has been executed.

Her estate is finalized.

And Keagan will leave.

"We're all set." The attorney stands, extending his hand, not reading the tension in the room. "Again, I'm sorry for your loss. Piper was a wonderful woman."

I nod, agreeing, and shake his hand.

Piper was truly an angel.

And in her usual fashion, she left most everything she had to Tatum, setting up a trust for when she's older. The rest of her money and assets, she gave to Keagan, who never even looked at the check or the deed. She just slid it over to me and said, "Give it to Tatum."

And that was it—an anticlimactic ending.

"We appreciate your time, Arthur," I say, putting an end to our meeting.

Taking Keagan's hand in mine, I grab Tatum's carrier with the other and we walk out to the parking lot, where Keagan's car awaits her with her suitcase and boxes from Piper's house.

"You don't have to go today," I tell her. Now that our time is ending, I'm growing more desperate.

Keagan turns, her face splotchy from crying. "Yeah, I do."

Because if she stays, she might not leave.

Fuck it.

I'm not that same man I was before. My life has changed, and like Keagan, I don't want any regrets. If Keagan never finds her way back to us at least I will have said what I needed to say. I won't live with any more secrets between us.

"When I divorced Rebekah, I swore I would never get married again." Keagan freezes, listening carefully. "I didn't need a relationship to give me fulfillment. I could get that from my career. I could get it by focusing on making everyone else's dreams come true. But I was wrong, Keys."

I take her hand. "I was wrong because no matter how many goals I achieved, I had no one to share them with."

Tears streak down her face. "Please," she begs, "please don't make this harder than it already is."

"I don't mean to," I admit, "but I need you to know this before I give you time. I love you—and it's not because you're Piper's sister or Tatum's aunt."

A sob wracks through her and she pulls away, putting space between us.

But it doesn't matter, I'm going to get this out. "I love you because you always call me out on my shit. You're beautiful and funny. And while you might think you're mean, I don't. Even in your darkest moments of pain, you pushed it aside for Piper, for Tatum, and even for me. The reason Piper loved you so much was not because you were related. It was because you brightened her entire life. I know because you did the same to mine. You keep saying I have a 'hero mode,' but it's you who built the game. I am only a hero because you made me rise to even be worthy of your presence."

Her body is shaking so hard. I want to go to her, but I know she'll stop me.

"People might say one day that you stole me from Piper, but when they see us together, they'll know it was me who stole you from the world. I've never loved anyone like I love you. So take your time. Find your answers. And whatever you decide, we'll support you."

Burying her face in her hands, Keys takes a few breaths, reining in the tears, before she looks at me. "And if I decide I can only be your friend?"

Nausea churns in my stomach. "Then we'll be friends." The words taste like acid, but I owe her this. I owe her time to decide on her own. It doesn't matter if I'm certain Keys belongs by my side; it only matters if she wants to be.

"And if I just want to be Aunt Keys to Tatum?"

I grin. "Then you'll be the best sucky Aunt Keys there ever was," I confirm, throwing back the words she once said to me in the hospital.

"And if I want to come home to you and Tatum?"

Now, there's an option I can fully support. "Then I'll keep the ice packs stocked." Because she will suffer for the agony she's putting us through. When—not *if*—she comes back, I will make sure the only thing swollen is her pussy.

Keagan chokes on a laugh, finally smiling. "Don't go falling in love with someone else, Dr. Potter. I might need time, but not time in a prison cell."

Taking a step forward, I wrap my arms around the woman who's brought out more emotions from me than I ever knew existed. "Goodbye, Keagan."

And then I kiss her one last time.

CHAPTER
THIRTY-ONE

Keagan
One month later…

"I hate it here."

Kenny pushes a margarita in front of me. "Well, fuck you too."

"I didn't say I hated you, Cry-Kenny. I very much still love you. I just miss them."

Kenny cocks a brow. "Have you told him that?"

I shake my head, swirling the crushed ice. I asked Astor for time. I couldn't very well turn around eight miles down the road after leaving him and tell him I missed him. That still wouldn't have given me the answer I needed, which I still don't have.

There's no question I love the man, but how long will that last? Forever? Until the grief wears off? No one knows but time.

"He sent me a video the other day," I tell Kenny instead. "Tater-bug was smiling and making this weird gargling noise." The memory brings a smile to my face. "He said she was trying to say daddy." I chuckle. "She was likely pooping." But Dr. Dreamy felt sure she was trying to talk to him. It was so dang precious and made my heart ache in my chest.

"Has he gone back to work yet?"

My stomach clenches. "No. Not until after the first of the year. He's started interviewing nannies though." Halle said she was unimpressed so far, but feels certain they will find the right person eventually.

"Are you about to cry?" Kenny sounds horrified at the thought.

"What? No." I absolutely was. "I'm just feeling left out."

"With nanny interviews?" I can tell Kenny is exasperated with me. It's understandable. I've been nothing but a giant ball of emotion since I returned home, if I can even call it home anymore.

"I mean, I just thought I would be the one helping select a nanny, not Halle. I've been there nearly every day of Tatum's life, and his assistant is helping him choose." I shrug. "I know it's irrational, but I just thought I would be included in making sure we weren't leaving some crazy person in charge of our kid."

I realize a minute too late that I said 'our kid,' when Kenny's gasp is louder than the bar's music. "Oh, girl. Do you hear yourself? You have claimed this man and this child. What are you still doing here?"

"It was a slip of the tongue," I lie. "You made the margarita too strong."

That perfectly tweezed brow lifts. "The margarita you've yet to drink."

I sigh. "Okay, fine. The kid and her daddy are mine. Are you happy now?" I realize what a mess this situation has become. "But they shouldn't be. They need a woman who will put them first always. They deserve someone who doesn't need to prove herself with a career title."

"And that's not you?"

I stare down at the lime-flavored drink. "I'm sitting here, aren't I? I'm the one who left them for my job." And time. But they both go hand in hand. I needed the time to decide if this truly was love, and if it was, could we do a long-distance thing while I worked at *Game Tales?*

Kenny reaches behind the bar and slides me a bottled water instead.

"News flash, Keys, darling. Millions of people have families and work day jobs. You don't have to just choose one anymore."

"I do, though. *GameTales* won't accept me working three hours away, and I can't expect Astor to leave his practice. He's saving lives for goodness' sakes."

"Have you asked him if he'd be willing to, though? His answer might surprise you."

I feel my eyes narrowing. "No, I haven't asked him because I do know what he'd say. The man spends his life sacrificing for others. He would have no problem sacrificing for me. Hell, he spent half a year doing charity work! He would move for me." I'm sure of it.

The line that I'm sure Kenny tries reducing with numerous face creams, forms on his forehead. "And why is this a problem?"

He just doesn't get it. "Because, Kenny, you didn't see those kids at the Children's Hospital when Astor was around. He comes alive when he's giving of himself. He matters to Bloomfield. He matters to his brothers and patients. I can't take him away from them just because I want to prove to Archer that I can pitch a story better than Ass Face."

Kenny nods, but I can tell he still doesn't get it.

"I can't ask him to do that, Kenny. I can't take away Tatum's family. His brothers are so involved in her life. I can't take that from them."

"Don't you think he should have an opinion on the matter, though?"

"No, Kenny. I don't. Astor is exactly where he should be."

"So then it's you."

Has Kenny always been this exhausting? "What are you talking about?"

Kenny hops up on the bar like the terrible employee he is. "You said Astor was exactly where he's supposed to be. But you hate it here. I think it's reasonable to think that you're the one in the wrong place." He tucks a wayward lock of hair behind my ear. "As much as I'd miss you, I'd rather know you were happy. And you are happy with them, boo. Don't let Archer take away the best thing to have ever happened to you."

"Archer isn't. I want to be here. I want to work at *GameTales* and prove myself."

Kenny flashes me a sad smile. "Prove yourself to who? Archer, the man who thinks you're better suited scrubbing toilets. The man who likely hired you to avoid a lawsuit. Haven't you noticed you're the only woman working at *GameTales*? The rest are men. Do you think Archer gave you a chance because he believed in you? Men like Archer don't believe in anyone but themselves. Stop being loyal to someone who is not loyal to you."

I could punch Kenny in the face.

"How can you say that to me?" I shove him away from me and stand. "You're supposed to be my friend!"

Kenny jumps down and rounds the bar, gripping my shoulders in his hands. "I am your friend, and as your friend, I would be doing you a disservice by not telling you that staying here and working for Archer proves nothing. You claim that you don't need a man's approval, but that's exactly what you're doing. You're giving up a man who loves you, and a little girl who adores you, because Archer has made you believe that you can't have it all."

He shakes me. "But you can have it all, Keys! Do you think Archer gives up his Friday afternoon golf days or his summers in Venice with his wife and kids? No! He doesn't. He has it all."

"But he's a man. Men have it easier than women."

"The reason he has it so easy, Keys, is because of you! He knows you'll work holidays and weekends. He knows you'll put in as many hours as it takes to get the job done. You create the time he has for his family, and why?" Kenny clenches his jaw, his anger exploding out of him in a violent burst of words. "Because he's so good to you?" He shakes his head and scoffs. "Wake up, Keys. This isn't about proving to the world that you're equal to men. Trust me, they already know. But what's more important to you… proving a point to people who already know or being happy? I don't know about you, but I'd rather go home to a husband and my precious daughter than go home, hoping my hard work was noticed."

Tears streak down my face as his words sink in. "Tatum isn't my daughter."

"Of course she is, Keagan! Fuck! Stop doing this to yourself! Was Piper your mom or sister?"

I think about all the times Piper played both roles, taking pictures at my graduation and then tossing back drinks at the after-party with me. "She was both," I admit tearfully.

Like Kenny knows I can't take any more, he pulls me in for a hug. "And you can be too. Be Tatum's mom and her crazy Aunt Keys. You don't have to be one or the other—just be happy, sweetheart. You aren't happy here. You've never been happy at *GameTales*. Don't be a martyr. You know all too well that life is short. Take yours by the balls. Screw society norms, create your own way. Find your happiness and don't let anyone take it from you. You've given so much to this world, darling. It's time to reap what you've sown."

My hands fist Kenny's shirt as I hold him close. "What if Astor doesn't want a life with me now? I asked him for time because I wasn't sure."

"Trust me, he wants a life with you, and newsflash, Keys... Relationships don't come with guarantees. If you're waiting on assurances that you'll never get hurt, you'll die alone."

Is that what I'm doing? Protecting myself? Leaving Astor before he crushes the last piece of my heart?

"Look, Keys," Kenny pushes me back, so he can look me in the eyes. "Do you love the man?"

It's a simple question. One I haven't wanted to admit. "Yes, I love him."

"Then stop making excuses. Stop trying to prove yourself to all the wrong people. The only opinions that matter are the two people waiting on your call tonight."

I can't get Kenny's words out of my head. Have I really been working hard for all the wrong people?

What am I asking? Of course, I have. I've fought so hard to prove myself to someone who already knows what I'm capable of and takes advantage of my determination. Maybe Kenny is right—okay, he's right. Archer is never going to consider me an equal because narrow-minded people like him will never change. And while promoting change is admirable, giving up your life and happiness in the process isn't.

I dial the number that now comes first on my favorites' list. It only rings once before the screen reveals a familiar face of scruff. "Gramps," I tease, "you have to hold the phone away from your face when we're doing video calls."

It takes a second before Astor rights the camera, replacing the scruff with an annoyed smirk. "I know how this works, but I was trying to keep one hand on Tatum while she's on the changing table."

"Uh, oh. You didn't barf on her, did you?"

He must lean the phone against the wall because I can now see a wiggly girl and her smoking hot daddy in the screen. "See for yourself. She's barf and poop free." He seems very proud of himself.

I clap my hands and cheer, watching as Tatum's legs start kicking with the excitement. "I'm so proud of you, Dr. Potter. You're getting better at this whole poopy diaper thing!"

Astor rolls his eyes but grins. "I had to move her up in diaper size today. I guess I'll take the twelve boxes of the smaller size to the hospital."

My heart pauses. I've missed another milestone—a silly one, but a milestone, nonetheless. "Learn to keep size comments to yourself, Dr. Potter. Girls don't appreciate it."

Astor laughs and catches a baby foot, shoving it into footy pajamas. "Are you driving up in the morning? I thought we could stay up late playing Santa and Mrs. Claus on Christmas Eve."

The smile he wears should be enough to convince me to get in the car and drive the three hours to Bloomfield, but... "I can't. Archer is making us work."

His face falls, and I feel like a royal jackass. "But I'm taking my bag, so as soon as I get off, I'm heading your way."

He slips Tatum's other foot in the pajamas and zips her up. "We'll wait up for you then." I don't have the heart to tell him that Tatum will remember nothing of her first Christmas, nor will she care if she has a plethora of toys around a tree that Santa supposedly brought. She's only a few months old, she can't even play with anything.

But I think Astor knows that. And I think he doesn't care. It's his daughter's first Christmas, he won't let it be anything less than perfect.

"You ready for Auntie Keys to read you a story?" He scoops Tatum up in his bulky arms and grabs the phone, heading for the rocker Piper bought when she was pregnant, and sits.

Grabbing the new book I picked up at the bookstore yesterday, I turn to the first page, and do what I look forward to all day. I read to my loves.

CHAPTER
THIRTY-TWO

Astor

H alle opens the door, dressed in an apron. "You made it!"

"Of course. We wouldn't miss Christmas Eve lunch." I considered it, though. Tatum decided it would be fun to stay awake most of the night.

Ever since Keagan went back home, I've only seen her through video chats when she reads to Tatum.

We haven't talked about her decision or how much time she still might need to come to an answer. All I know is neither Tatum nor I have been able to sleep since she's been gone. I find myself making excuses just to talk to her.

Me: Which bow is she supposed to wear with this outfit?

Keagan: Where are you going?

Me: The park.

Keagan: Are you meeting anyone?

I almost lied, just to see if she would get jealous. But I don't want to play games with Keagan. If she wants to be with me, then I want her to come to me without any influence. She has enough doubt to deal with; she needs to be sure when she decides.

But I'm growing impatient.

"Come on in before your brothers burn down the kitchen," Halle says, seeming like she's actually worried.

"You let them cook?" I don't think I've ever seen either of my brothers make a meal.

"Ha! That would be better than what's actually going on."

I look at Tatum finally asleep in her carrier. Traitor. Could she have not done this at two a.m.?

"Should I leave Tatum in the living room?" If there's a shitshow in the kitchen, then I'd like to keep my daughter from being collateral damage.

Halle turns, thinking about it. "How 'bout I take Tatum and you go handle your brothers?"

The way she offers makes it sound like I'm getting the shittier deal, but after doing nothing but waiting and worrying over Keys, dealing with someone else's drama might be a refreshing change.

"Okay, but don't blame me if the fine China gets broken in the process." Vance is not known for his calm demeanor.

Halle takes the baby and waves me off. "It wouldn't be the first time."

With that comment, I walk into the kitchen and see boiler pots on the stove and Remington on the island with a lit cigarette between his lips. "I got fifty bucks on Duke," he says, pointing to the table where Duke is standing on one side and Vance the other.

"Why Duke?" I ask absently, trying to figure out what's going on.

Remington blows out a ring of smoke and laughs. "Check out his hand."

I expect to see scratch marks or swelling like Duke had already landed a few blows, but that's not what I find.

"Holy shit," I mutter.

"Yep. Looks like baby brother beat both y'all bitches to the altar."

At the mention of altar, Vance's gaze snaps to me. "He fucking married her!"

Duke doesn't bother confirming it, but he doesn't really have to, the wedding band on his left hand is proof enough.

Remington laughs. "I don't know who this woman is, but I support her marriage to Dr. Dumbass, if it produces this kind of reaction from Vance-hole."

Vance's jaw ticks as he stares at me in fury. "You know what this means?"

Unfortunately, I do. "We're fucked."

Duke managed to stay alive throughout lunch.

Now that I've left, though, I can't promise how long he'll remain that way. Him marrying Ramsey, his childhood friend, is… problematic, but it's done—at least for now.

Pulling into the driveway with Tatum still asleep in the back seat, I spot something on my front door. With it being Christmas, I could have missed a package, but then again, the postal service wouldn't have left dozens of notes. They would have left one.

There's only one person who's ever plastered notes to my door, and that's exactly the person I've been missing.

Glancing into the back seat, I check on Tatum before I pull out my phone, finding I missed a text from Keagan.

Keagan: Got your letter, but it was too late. I already made my decision.

My heart sputters. I knew I shouldn't have held onto the envelope as long as I did, but I didn't want to sway Keagan's decision with outside influences.

But it had been a month—one long-ass month—and she still hadn't made her decision.

The envelope was the last card I had to play.

Unlocking my phone, I respond to her text.

Me: *Are you going to make me guess?*

I use the same question she would ask me when I didn't want to answer.

Three dots appear, indicating that she's typing.

Keagan: *Don't get smart with me. I was just waiting on you.*

I'm confused.

Me: *Why would you be waiting on me?*

She's quick to respond.

Keagan: *You told me if I ever ran, you would chase me. I'm disappointed in your follow through, Dr. Potter.*

I grin.

Me: *I was merely giving you a head start.*

Honestly, she only had until tonight. I had no intentions of not spending Christmas with her.

Keagan: *Just know you only have yourself to blame.*

I don't know what it says about me that I'm excited to see what she's done. It feels like it's been so long since I've truly smiled.

Getting out of the car, I approach the door, anticipation growing as I pluck the first note from the door.

You're the only one I want to ice my vagina with.

Of course, that's the first one I read. I shake my head, a big, stupid grin on my face as I scan the neighborhood street, looking for her car. I don't see it anywhere, but I can feel her. She isn't far. I know it. She's just being dramatic Keys, making me wait a little longer for the answer I desperately need.

I miss the smell of your formaldehyde.

I can't hold back the burst of laughter. "I'm not that old, Keys," I shout out into the open, grabbing another note.

Piper once asked me how far I was willing to go to get what I wanted.

Funny, Piper asked me the same thing.

I didn't know then, but I know now.

I can't grab the notes fast enough. I don't even know if I'm reading them in the right order. All I know is I have to read every single one as fast as I can. I need her answer.

I'm willing to go all the way.

I need you. I need you so much that I'm scared—scared that I'll end up in jail when other women look at you. But I'm going to work hard to control my crazy.

Because I love you, Dr. Potter.

I love your bossiness.

I love your cock.

But most of all, I love your baby—okay, fine. I love you most of all too. Let's call it a tie between you both.

Trauma might have brought us together, but love kept us together. I see that now.

Let me love you, old man. I promise I can.

I drop the notes to the ground and pull out my phone, dialing her number. She answers on the first ring.

"Dr. Potter."

There's something playful in her voice—a stark difference to mine. "One."

There's a pause. "Why are you counting?" At least she has enough self-preservation to seem concerned that I'm no longer in a playful mood.

"I'm counting because if you don't show yourself by the time I get to five, Tatum won't be the only one I take over my knee."

She chokes out a laugh, but it's the garage door opening that grabs my attention.

"Someone isn't being all that merry and bright this holiday season." The garage door lifts slowly.

First revealing her legs. Second her hips. And lastly the smirk on her face.

I'm on her in seconds, yanking her body into mine and threading my fingers through her hair. A breath escapes her like she can finally relax.

"Your notes," I start, needing her to confirm what the notes implied.

Her hands go to my face, cupping my cheeks as she holds my gaze. "I want to come home, Astor. Will you let me, even though I needed time to realize my stupidity?"

Pressing my forehead against hers, I breathe her in for the first time in a month. "It's not stupid to give yourself time."

"No," she corrects, "it was stupid not to realize that even a day without you and Tatum is too long."

At least we agree there.

I press my lips to hers. "What about *GameTales*? Are we buying a helicopter?"

She chuckles. "Not unless you just want to impress Tatum's friends with your wealth."

"Does that mean—"

She nods, her eyes narrowing. "—that, like you, Piper had a hero mode too?"

I smile, remembering the day the attorney handed Keys a stack of papers. Keagan had pushed the documents to me and told me to give whatever was in the stack to Tatum; but in true Piper fashion, there was a note—her last piece of advice to her little sister, along with a sizable check that Keagan didn't know about.

Dear Keys,

Mom used to say we go through refining seasons. I used to think she was spouting poetry that sounded good but had no value.

But I was wrong.

One thing I learned through Mom and Dad's death was that refining seasons prepare us for who we're destined to become.

Pain is meant to teach us to enjoy the times of happiness. It serves as a reminder that we had the privilege of loving a person so much that their absence is crippling.

But most of all, the pain reminds us that we made it through the refining season.

A season that reminded you that you were strong, that you could heal, and that you could still love through the loss.

Storms will always come when you least expect them.

Use the thunder. Let it be louder than your fear.

Embrace the lightning. Let it light your way through the darkness.

Because you, my darling, are braver than anyone I've ever known.

You are meant for so much more. You are meant to change the world.

The question is, how far are you willing to go to prove it?

Don't be afraid to get out of the boat, Key-Money. Ignore the noise of the wind and the waves.

Get out and swim—because I taught you how.

Make me proud.

All my love,

Your big sister.

"Piper invented hero mode," I tell her.

"And, apparently, she had one hell of a financial advisor." Her eyes water. "I could have bought a yacht with the check she left me."

I cock my head to the side, grinning. "But you didn't buy a yacht."

She shakes her head. "No, I didn't." Her smile couldn't get any bigger as she elaborates. "Instead, I made two thousand copies of Ass Face's dick pic and plastered them all over the walls with the words: *Eat a dick. I quit.*"

I've never been prouder. "So, what's your plan now?"

She shrugs. "I don't have a non-compete clause in my contract. All my clients are coming with me to the new company I'm opening right here in Bloomfield. I won't be satisfied until I'm *GameTales'* biggest competition in the gaming industry."

That's my girl. There's that fire.

"I think that's the best business plan I've ever heard," I agree.

She loops her arms around my neck. "I don't appreciate you making me fall in love with you, Dr. Potter."

Without giving me a warning, she jumps, wrapping her legs around my waist. "But I'll let you make it up to me with forever—and good dick during nap time."

I chuckle. "I think I can handle that."

"Good," she praises, "because you no longer have a choice in the matter."

CHAPTER THIRTY-THREE

Astor

Four years later...

"Me! I can do it!"

There's a bow in Tatum's hair the size of an airport. I've gotten used to bows lying around the house, tucked in between the sofa cushions and in the sheets. They are no match to the amount of tweed bracelets I find on the counters, in the fridge, and in my underwear drawer. All I know is women (and little girls) shed accessories like they shed hair. And I don't hate it one bit.

Holding the plastic crown out of her reach, I narrow my eyes at the cute, demanding little girl. "The crown and the bow won't both fit on your head. You need to pick one."

It was the wrong thing to say.

I should know that by now.

You don't come between a woman and her prerogatives.

Her little hand goes to her hip, her eyes narrowing back at me. If

Piper could see this kid, she'd laugh until she cried. Tatum Potter is an exact replica of Keagan. If I didn't know she was mine, I would swear Keys had her created in a lab. "Mama says where d'ere is a will, d'ere's a way."

Mama is a pain in my ass.

"Yes." I sigh. "Mama could probably make this work, but not Daddy."

She jumps for the crown. "I can do it!"

Fine. Fuck it.

I hand her the crown and watch as the four-year-old shoves the toy crown in front of the UFO-sized hair bow. "D'ere, see? I told you."

She did tell me.

However, she also looks like if the wind picks up, she'll topple over, but I'm done arguing with her. If she wants the bow and the crown for this occasion, then she can have it. I've already spent an insane amount of time fussing over it.

"You look like a beautiful boho princess," I tell her with a smile. I learned very early on that it wasn't enough to be an ordinary princess; she and Mama had to be Boho Princesses. Because, clearly, those princesses are elite, even in the royal families.

"D'ank you. Now can we go in and see Mama?" Again, totally Keagan. She should be ashamed of the influence she has on this child.

"Of course." I hold out my hand for her to take, but instead, she slips the gift bag off my wrist. "I hold dis."

"What am I going to hold then?"

Tatum points to the cake box in my other hand, the bag from the candy store hanging off my other wrist. I've grown accustomed to carrying everything in one hand, so I can always have one hand holding a smaller hand that inevitably wiggles away at some point.

"Will you stay by my side?" I give her a look that says, *I'm no fool, little girl. I will not have a repeat of the mall incident.* "You're not going to have an impromptu game of hide and seek, are you?" I nearly had a heart attack when she disappeared from my side and hid in the racks of clothes. I told Keys I didn't care what themed-day the preschool was having, I refused to take this kid back to the mall by myself.

Those long dark eyelashes flutter up and down. "I'll be good. Cross my heart." If she wasn't lying, the crossing her heart motion would be precious, but I know this game all too well. The McKellan women make you gullible with those lashes.

"You'd better. I'm counting on you to make this special for Mommy." And I don't mean by giving her a heart attack because I lost our daughter in an office building with twenty-five floors.

"I said, I promise." She acts like I'm being the most ridiculous person in the city.

"Okay then, let's go."

A huge grin takes over her face as I push open the door, waving at Francesca, Keagan's secretary. "She's expecting you both," she tells us.

"Thanks."

I look down at Tatum, radiating with excitement. "You ready?"

She nods excitedly, and I push open Keagan's office door.

"Happy Birfday!"

Abandoning the gift bag on the floor, Tatum rushes Keagan, who scoops her up and swings her around. "Look at you!" She adjusts the crown on her head. "My pretty little Boho Princess."

"Daddy said I couldn't wear bofe the crown and bow."

Keagan winks over the top of her head. "Well, Daddy is still learning the ways of royalty. He'll get there."

See? Ridiculous.

"Haha," I tell them, setting the cake on Keagan's desk before leaning in for a kiss. "Happy birthday."

"Thank you." Her whispered words flutter over my lips, warm and inviting.

I pull back and tuck a wayward lock of hair behind her ear. "We know you're under a deadline and not feeling very inspired."

She groans into my neck. "Is it too late to take you up on the stay-at-home mom thing?"

Opening a new company comprised of only women is hard, managing multiple accounts at a time is even harder, but if anyone can do this, Keagan can.

"Maybe later. For now, you need to be a boss." I was teasing about the stay-at-home mom arrangement. Keagan needed to spread her wings and prove to herself that she could do it on her own.

"We brought your crown!"

Tatum is tired of being squished between us and pushes against my chest, which makes Keagan laugh. "You did? I so need my crown today!"

She puts Tatum down and we watch as she roots around in the bag, pulling out the crown and candy necklaces. "Here it is!" Running back, Keagan lowers down, so Tatum can place the crown on her head, which is sitting more to the left than the middle. But Keagan doesn't care, she simply kisses Tatum's chubby cheek and then slips on the necklace. "Thank you, sweet girl. This is the best birthday ever."

Tatum grins as she takes in their candy jewelry and crowns, but then she seems to remember she forgot the most important accessory. "Where's the rings?"

"They're in the gift bag," I say. "See if you can spot the one with your name on it."

Like her mom, Tatum always enjoys a challenge. She's just starting to read (recognize letters) and Keys loves spending the evenings reading to her. They've been starting with all the birthday cards (the clean ones) between Piper and Keys. It was something Keys demanded when Tatum first called her Mama. The term is so simple and the one milestone parents look forward to, but not us.

When Tatum said her first word, 'Mama,' Keagan absolutely fell apart. Sure, we clapped for Tatum and got her to say it again for the camera, but afterwards, when Tatum went to bed, I followed the sobs into our closet, where Keagan was sitting, clutching the quilt her sister made for Tatum out of all their restaurant shirts. *"I'm not her mama,"* she had said as she stared up at me, her lips quivering violently. *"We need to correct her."*

I lowered down to the floor and took her into my arms. "If the situation were reversed and Piper raised your daughter, would you want that child to grow up loving her like a mother?"

"Yes, but she can call me Auntie Keys, not Mama."

"But why? Why should she call you an aunt when you're a mom to her?"

She shook her head and pushed me away. "Don't try to turn this around."

"I'm not. I'm simply asking you to see yourself like Tatum does. Many people have many parents. Stepfathers are dads, foster mothers are moms, and sisters become moms. The moniker doesn't specify DNA. Anyone can become a mother; all it takes is unconditional love." I tipped her chin up. "Do you love Tatum like your daughter?"

"Of course."

"Then why can't she know two mothers? I think Piper would want her to be able to celebrate the mother who brought her into this world and the mother who raises her in it." I kissed her lips and pulled her closer, my words filling the space. "That little girl in there loves you like her mother. Don't take that away from her. Give her the honor of knowing both women in her life."

That night, Keys pulled out all the memories we had packed up from Piper's house. She pulled out each card Piper kept. Each letter. Each note. She pulled them all out and she read them and cried. And the next morning, she asked Tatum to smile for Mama.

"Found it!"

Tatum's shout clears the memory as I adjust my hold on Keagan and step back. "Let me see if you're right." I hold my hand out for the box, taking it and flipping it over in my hand. "Yep, good job, kiddo. You picked the right one."

Tatum squeals as I kneel, opening the box and pulling out the cherry-flavored Ring Pop. "Give me your hand, Boho Princess." I took over doing this for Keagan's birthday after Piper died. Keagan said it was a tradition between her and Piper to celebrate their birthdays with crowns, candy necklaces, and Ring Pops. But since I wasn't part of that tribe of birthday princesses, the least I could do was act like a prince and place the crown and ring. Though, when Tatum became big enough, she stole my glory, but not today. Today is a special birthday.

I slide the oversized ring onto Tatum's little hand. "Now, you're officially the Boho Princess." It always amazes me what a little make-believe and love can do for these women in my life. If you treat them like princesses, they will treat you like a king. And that feeling of being loved and respected will never grow old. I always want to be their provider, their security, their comfort in good times and in bad.

I kiss Tatum's forehead. "Now, hand me Mama's ring." Tatum eagerly dashes back to the bag and returns with a black box just like hers. This moment has been in the works for years. I started this tradition of black boxes with Ring Pops inside a couple of years ago. My reasoning was two-fold. Black boxes brought forth a memory of pain for me just like Ring Pops did for Keagan. We needed to remember that within pain dwells joy. We simply needed to learn to look deep enough. So we changed those memories into something more.

We made them a tradition—a reminder of a time that nearly broke us, and a time that brought us together. Ring Pops and black boxes no longer hold our happiness captive.

"Go, Mama." Tatum nudges Keagan. "Let Daddy make you a Boho Queen."

Keagan chuckles, but does what she's told and steps in front of me. I take my time with Keagan, drawing out her coronation just a little longer. No matter what she told me on the phone, we weren't skipping this birthday because she was busy. And I'm definitely not allowing her to work all night. Whether she finishes her project or not, she's coming home to a house full of people for a surprise party. Keagan will never celebrate her birthday alone and not in the company of the people who love her. So, I let her think I agreed to her ridiculous offer of just doing a cake at lunch for her big day. It's the only compromise I'll make today.

"I think Daddy forgot how to open mine," she says to Tatum, since I've yet to open her box.

"I didn't forget." I glance down at the black box in my hand. "I just wanted to remember what it looked like."

The girls look at each other with confusion.

"Since I'll never hold a ring like this again."

Keagan sucks in a breath and takes a step back. "Astor, what are you doing?"

Lifting my gaze to hers, I admit, "I lied. I said we could raise Tatum together, but we can't."

A crunch goes through the room. Tatum decided this ring ceremony was taking far too long, and she needed to munch on her candy necklace to pass the time.

"That's not enough for me anymore, Keys."

Tears well in Keagan's eyes when I crack open the box, revealing not a Ring Pop, but a two-karat yellow diamond. "You were wrong. You said this relationship could never work—that it wasn't possible for love to be born from grief."

I pull the ring from the box, pinching it between two fingers. "But it did. Our friendship might have started through grief, but our relationship was born from love and respect." I lean forward and take her hand, pulling her closer. "Let us prove ourselves wrong again."

I slip the ring on her finger. "Be my wife and prove our love can last a lifetime."

Keagan's hand shakes in mine, and I know what she's thinking.

"I won't leave you."

She scoffs. "You don't know that."

Every day that has gone by, we've found love, purpose, and faith in each other. We don't need to be afraid anymore.

"True." I kiss the top of her hand. "But I'm willing to take the chance and spend every minute I can loving you."

"She says yes!" Tatum finally swallowed the mouthful of candy and joined the conversation. "Say yes, Mommy, so we can have cake."

I give Keagan a one-shoulder shrug. "You're holding up the celebration."

Slowly, a smile inches up her face. "I can't believe you bought me a blood diamond."

"They were fresh out of friendship rings, so I settled for a conflict-free diamond—yellow for your sunny disposition and boho attire."

She pushes at my shoulder. "Smartass."

"Marry me, Keys. Guarantee me that you're mine for the rest of our lives."

I don't do things halfway. I want all of her, even the parts she's scared to give.

She blinks back her tears before pulling in a breath and firming up her voice. "I guarantee you my forever."

"Is that a yes?" Thank goodness for little girls who need just a little more clarification.

"Yes," Keagan laughs, pulling the candy necklace from Tatum's mouth—she's eaten far more than we realized, "I'll marry your Daddy."

"Forever?"

She presses her lips to mine. "Not even death will part us."

EPILOGUE

Astor

"Oh, Astor!" She moans, and immediately I'm annoyed.

"Stop. I know what you're doing."

She wiggles, her eyes rolling back into her head. "I'm serious, you need to take notes because this…" she moans again, and I ignore the snickering behind the sheet, "…is so much better than sex. I don't know why you kept this a secret for so long."

My eyes narrow to slits. "This isn't funny, Keys."

"Oh, no, it definitely isn't. This is ah-mazing." She points to the doctor shielded behind a drape over her legs. "Tell him what you're doing, Dr. Katner. He's a doctor. He should be able to replicate this at home, right?"

The nurse at her side smothers a laugh, but the only person brave enough to keep taunting me is my wife, laid out on a table getting artificially inseminated because I haven't been able to get her pregnant on my own; something I thought I would handle a lot better than I am. I had the procedure; I should have been able to knock up my wife, but after a year of trying, we ended up back at the fertility specialist.

It was Keagan's idea.

We wanted another child, and between the two of us, she had the winning argument. *"Are you going to be a quitter in this marathon or are we going to do what we've always done and fight for what we want?"*

I couldn't allow her to be the responsible one.

So I went through all the tests again. Endured the shame of feeling like a failure that I couldn't do something as simple as procreate.

I went into that room to jack-off into a cup in order for the doctor to run some tests when someone shoved me from behind, locking us in the room. "What are you doing?"

Keagan sways toward me, her hips inviting me closer with the movement. "I decided I didn't want you to look at other women to get off." She's referring to the magazines they keep in the room to help you—you know—get there.

She pulls off my shirt and then hers. "If you're going to get off, it's going to be to me."

I grin, loving this aggressive side of her, and yank her to me. "Really?" I skim my nose up the side of her neck. "Perhaps I need privacy?"

She snorts and unbuttons my pants, easing them to the floor. "Perhaps you should just fuck my tits and hush."

Her foul mouth has me rock hard in a matter of seconds—something that I never thought would happen in a clinic.

"See," she taunts, noting the bulge inside my boxers, "he needed me."

She lowers to her knees, taking my boxers with her. My head falls back with a groan. "You're gonna get us thrown out of here."

Her warm hands come together around my cock. "Grab the lube, Dr. Potter. Let me show you how this is done."

I'm so horny I can't even argue with her. Reaching behind me to one of the many bottles of lubricant, I squirt some on my cock and her hands.

"*Now my tits, don't be shy, Husband. This isn't the first time you've lubed me up.*"

I'm going to come before she even applies friction. "*Keys…*" Her name comes out of my mouth more like a garble than a plea.

"*I'm gonna have another baby with you, Dr. Potter. But this time, it's gonna be way more fun.*"

If I wasn't seconds from fucking her against the wall, I would bask in the revelation that she already considers Tatum a child we had together. Because we did. And now, we want another one. This one with mine and her DNA—a sibling for Tatum to carry on the traditions that Keagan and Piper started.

Keagan's hands tighten around me as she pulls me closer by my cock and eases it between her tits. "*Add the lube, Astor, or this won't be nearly as pleasurable as it can be.*"

I squeeze out nearly half the bottle and toss it across the room. We won't be needing it anymore since my wife's dirty mouth is inevitably going to shorten this event.

"*Mmm…*" She lets me go, so she can push her tits together, creating a small opening. "*Go ahead, Astor, fuck me.*"

If I didn't need this clean sample, I would shove my cock so far down her throat that those filthy words would be replaced by moans and gags.

Grabbing on to her shoulders, I thrust into her tits, both of us throwing our heads back with the motion. This is destined for disaster.

I shove the sample cup into her hands. There's no room for pride in this room. Not with my wife on her knees, my cock shoved between her tits. "*The minute you get the sample, I'm gonna fuck you senseless.*"

She has the nerve to look smug, like this was her intent all along. Distract me and turn this event into something a lot more pleasurable for me. "*I'm looking forward to it.*"

That's it; I can't take any more. I thrust into her softness, relishing her intake of breath as I use her body for what we need—a baby.

"*Get ready.*" My eyes pinch shut. If I look at Keagan on the floor, her stunning blue eyes staring up at me with no embarrassment, no fear, I'll come all over her chest.

"Just let go. I got you."

And I do, filling the sample cup before snatching it out of her hand and setting it on the counter. I'm frantic, sweating and more pent-up than one should be in a doctor's office. "Your pants, Keagan. Now."

I will chew a hole in them if I have to. I refuse to waste one more second not being inside her. "Okay." She laughs when I take matters into my own hands and unbutton her pants, shoving them down to her ankles. "Step out." She does and I only free the one leg. I just need her hot center wrapped around me.

"Oh my gosh." I spin her in my arms and slam her back against the wall. "Astor! Someone is going to hear us."

Didn't I tell her we were going to be thrown out of here? She shouldn't start things she can't finish. "Should have thought about that," I hoist her up and her legs wrap around my waist immediately, "when you were spouting out all those dirty words."

I shove my cock inside her in one thrust. "Oh fuck." We both groan. She feels so good wrapped around me. Her muscles contracting and stretching to accommodate me.

"I love you." She holds my face in her hands. "Baby or no baby, I am yours forever."

Yeah, I make her scream inside that exam room for the next half hour until she comes on my cock, and we walk out of there with a smile.

Keagan's moan has me snapping back to the present. "Dr. Katner says he's going to give us one of these little things to take home."

I step up to the exam table and take her hand. "I need no tool to please you."

Last night I asked Keagan if she was disappointed that we ended up going the IVF route. Sometimes it's important for women to live out their dreams in a particular way, but I should have known my wife would laugh in my face, come straddle me, and say, "Our dreams weren't accomplished by taking the path well-traveled. We like to climb mountains barefooted."

"Alright, here we go." The doctor's voice has me squeezing Keagan's hand.

She was right.
Our family isn't normal.
Our relationship isn't normal.
And we're okay with that.

Did you love Astor and Keagan's story? They have bonus epi-
logue you can find here.
https://dl.bookfunnel.com/w5yih2j2yj

Can't wait for the next Potter brother? Pre-order Duke's book,
The Sculptor, now!

If you love the broody Potter brothers, try my Commander in
Briefs Series! It's even in a box set for 9.99! That's six surly Marines
and one arrogant baseball player in one set!

OTHER BOOKS BY
KRISTY MARIE

21 Rumors
A Romantic Comedy Series- All novels are standalone and feature different couples with crossover characters

IOU
The Pretender
The Closer
21 Rumors Box Set

The Commander Legacies
A Second-Generation Contemporary Series- All novels are standalone and feature different couples with crossover characters

Rebellious

Commander in Briefs
A Contemporary Series- All novels are standalone and feature different couples with crossover characters

Pitcher

Gorgeous
Drifter
Interpreter
Commander in Briefs Box Set

In the Hands of the Potters

A Contemporary Series- All novels are standalone and feature different couples with crossover characters

The Potter
The Refiner
#3 Coming Soon
#4 Coming Soon

For more information visit www.authorkristymarie.com

ACKNOWLEDGEMENTS

I heard once that we go through refining seasons in our life. The statement resonated with me so much that I wanted to write a story about finding hope and love during a tumultuous time in one's life. I've been through several refining seasons, and it was during those times when I thought there was nothing left of me to break that I found the real me—that I found profound love.

I hope you enjoyed this book as much as I enjoyed writing it. Leaving reviews is one of the best ways you can support independent authors. So, if you loved or hated *the Refiner*, please consider leaving an honest review.

A million thank yous to my crew, who endure a whirlwind of insanity when I sit down to write a book.

My daily writing crew, Rebecca, Catherine, and Amy. We all know I wouldn't finish books without the sweet peer pressure. I love you, ladies!

Sarah P., I couldn't have done this without you. Thank you for reading this book a million times and still finding the energy to cheer me on. You, my friend, are magical.

Aundi, Melody, Keri, and Ri, you guys just blow my mind daily. Thank you for your patience, support, and hate messages. LOL. I live for each one.

Becky, you keep being amazing every day. Eventually, you'll get tired one day and come back down and join us ordinary people.

Jaime, I dropped the ball here, but I'm fortunate you love me despite my annoying time management skills. Also, I'm coming for that hug!

Jessica, thank you for literally holding down the fort and responding sweetly when you likely wanted to curse when I dropped last-minute tasks in your lap. Too bad you can't back out now.

Autumn, we should probably consider *Fuck It* dolls for Christmas gifts, don't you? I think it would make our lives a little more entertaining. Thank you for always enduring my seasons of crazy.

Sarah S., I think it's safe to say you cannot escape me. I *really* could not have done this without you keeping it all together and knowing what I needed to stay beautiful. SUPERSTAR is what you are. Choo! Choo!

Stacey and Letitia, who were tasked to make this book shine, you guys knocked it out of the park as usual!

And to you, the reader, stories only exist when they're read. Thank you for reading. Thank you for supporting independent authors who are everyday women just trying to support their families. WE APPRECIATE YOU!

Last but not least, and on a *very* personal note, I could have never written this book or this series without the real Potter and Refiner in my life, my Heavenly Father, Jesus Christ. I am forever yours to mold

Made in the USA
Monee, IL
27 November 2023

47510964R00149